13 Nightmares

Dennis McDonald

13 NIGHTMARES

This is a work of fiction. All of the characters, names, incidents, organizations, and dialogue in this novel either are the product of the author's imagination or are used fictitiously.

dennismcdonaldauthor.com

ISBN-13: 978-1495909283

ISBN-10: 149590928X

DEDICATION

To Angie,
who wrote these words to me in 1978:

May your writing touch everyone's heart
and cause amazement in their minds
as you have in mine.

Thanks, Angie.
Your words have always been
an inspiration to me.

You are dearly missed.

CONTENTS

INTRODUCTION

The monsters came in the dead of the night.

While everyone else slept, they rose up from under the house on Adams Street and roamed the dark. Thirteen-year-old Danny Corbin was the only one who knew what horrors hid in the shadows of his bedroom. With his eyes closed, he pretended to be asleep for fear he would see them by his bed. Then they would have him. That was rule number one. Never look upon the monsters. The horrid nightmares would snatch you away if you even took one peek. Danny imagined they waited for him just beyond his closed eyelids. *Don't open your eyes,* he told himself. *Breathe in and out real slow. Sleep. Sleep.*

No one else in his family was aware of the horrors shambling through the dark house. They slept in their beds in blissful ignorance while his imagination conjured the terrible creatures wandering the quiet rooms. He alone understood the special procedures needed to keep them at bay. One important defense was to never see the light go out when going to bed. Always close your eyes when shutting off the switch. Failure to do so gave the monsters free rein to enter your bedroom.

Tonight, the lights out rule had been broken. Danny had been too absorbed in a new comic book to see his mother reach in and shut off the light. The shock of the room going to sudden darkness caused his body to shake in panic. Now he would have no choice but to depend on the First Rule to help him survive the night.

Don't look at the monsters. Not even a peek.

He pretended to be asleep while his heart pounded and threatened to burst. In his mind's eye, he envisioned the horrors populating the shadows of his bedroom. The Wolfman, Frankenstein, and the Mummy stood leering over his bedside. These were all bad, but there were worse things he imagined. An even darker terror resided deeper in his imagination. He had seen it once, three years earlier, after his family first moved into the house. Then, he had heard something coming down the hall and opened his eyes for a mere second. A large, hunched form stood in the open door to his room. The thing stared back at him with eyes darker than the shadows around it.

The sight turned his skin to ice and caused him to throw the blanket over his head.

That night he learned the First Rule. *Don't look at the monsters. Not even a peek.*

Danny was older now and wanted to put away his childish fears like the old toys he never played with anymore. He suspected what he feared was just products of an over active imagination. *Real monsters weren't standing over my bed. It's so stupid,* he told himself. *To think monsters hide in my bedroom at night. I need to grow up. I'm thirteen years old. Start being a man and not a wuss. Come on. Take a peek and see for myself.*

He shifted his body under the blankets and still pretended sleep. He heard nothing but the blood pumping in his ears. He attempted to lift his eyelids, but couldn't. The weight of fear kept them closed. The memory of the thing he had seen three years earlier robbed him of all courage. If he saw the horror again, he would scream and wake his mother and younger sister in the next room. He didn't want to explain why he had cried out like a little girl. Instead, he calmed his breathing and pushed the thought of monsters from his mind. Minutes passed as he lay perfectly still. He concentrated on his hearing and sensed nothing.

Now, take a look.

He attempted to move his eyelids, but they remained closed tight.

Prove there is nothing to fear in the dark. One look is all it would take. The monsters live only in the shadows of my imagination. What would my best friends Tod and Rodney think if they saw me lying in the bed like a scared baby? What would the cute girl across the street say if she knew how big a coward I am? Take a peek!

His eyelids refused.

TAKE A PEEK!

His eyes popped open. A mosaic of shadows, created by the streetlight coming in through the bedroom curtains, stretched across the ceiling. He turned his head to the right. Nothing stood by his bed. He looked to the left. No nightmare horror waited there to snatch him away. Danny let out a sigh of relief.

There were no monsters after all. Tears of joy misted his eyes at this new realization. *There was nothing to fear.*

Danny raised his head to look toward the bedroom door and gasped. A deformed shadow with misshapen eyes, blacker then any bottomless void, towered over the end of the bed. Hands resembling living spiders reached out to where he lay frozen in fear. He couldn't scream for it was trapped in his paralyzed lungs. He now knew the truth. Nightmares were real and monsters do exist in the dark. The revelation shattered his mind like the time he hit a baseball through the neighbor's window.

"No peeking, Danny," the horror croaked in an inhuman voice as it clutched him with spindly fingers of inky black.

SEESAW

Sarah was locked in the closet again.

It always happened when Auntie Marge drank. The chain of events was the same: first the drinking, then the beating, and finally the dark closet.

Sarah wrapped her arms around her folded legs and rocked in a cramped dirty corner. The whipping from the belt her aunt had used on her tiny body still stung and burned. One welt across the back of her thighs felt like fire. She hated when the belt hit her thighs. Those hurt the worst. She rocked back and forth, thankful her aunt had locked the door and left her in the dark. Though she hated the closet more than anything in the world, at least in here, the whipping and the cursing stopped. She only hoped her aunt would remember to let her out soon because she had to go pee. She didn't want to pee in her pants because that would bring another spanking. Sometimes she had no choice, especially when her aunt passed out and slept for hours before unlocking the closet door again.

Sarah cried. She tried to be a big girl and hold back the flood of tears filling her blue eyes. Alone in the dark, she lacked any will to do so. The tears came like rain. Though only seven years old, she had lived a lifetime of pain and neglect. In here, the memories of her parents returned to her. Not pleasant memories like most little girls have. No, her parents had been drug addicts. *Meth heads* is what her auntie called them. *Stupid meth heads! Cranksters! And you're going to be just like them, Sarah! Just like them!* Sarah closed her wet eyes more tightly and put her hands over her ears. She tried to block out her aunt's voice but the words were coming from inside.

The really bad images began to seep into her young mind. She wanted to hold them back, but they floated to her when she was in the dark closet. Scenes from the night when she'd awoken with the first shotgun blast coming

from the front room of the trailer home. She could still see herself, five years old, dragging her only toy, Mr. Fuzzy, behind her. She walked barefoot down the filth-littered hall and stared into the living room. Mommy was in a chair, a gaping hole blown through her chest. With her head leaning back and mouth hanging wide open, she looked surprised her life had ended in this way.

Daddy sat in the recliner with the barrel of the shotgun up under his chin. He smiled at her, showing rotted teeth.

"Life's a bitch, Sarah," he said with eyes wide from the effects of the meth. "Life is a full-blown bitch."

Boom! The shot was deafening in the confined quarters of the trailer. The sound nearly knocked her down as his head disintegrated in a shower of blood and bone. Lifeless hands dropped the smoking shotgun to the floor and then she was alone with the corpses of her parents. She didn't know how long she had stayed in the sweltering trailer but she still remembered the flies and the stink.

The police were first to arrive, then the nice lady from social services who spoke in a soft voice. She got clean clothes and stayed in a foster home while they ran her from one court session to the next. Finally, she ended up with her Auntie Marge. The first few months, the nice lady would pay a visit to her aunt's house. Auntie Marge hid the whiskey bottles and combed Sarah's hair to make her look pretty. They all sat in the living room and she would lie and tell the nice lady how much she liked being with her auntie. She dared not tell the truth because a very severe beating would be waiting for her after the nice lady left. Time passed, and then the nice lady didn't drop by anymore. It was just her and Auntie Marge now.

Sarah wrapped her arms around her scabby knees. She missed Mr. Fuzzy. Even though she tried to be a big girl now, she still wished to hug the old brown teddy bear when she was in the closet. The policeman who had taken Mr. Fuzzy away had said something about it being contaminated by the crime scene. Auntie Marge didn't allow her to have toys. Sarah swiped away tears and felt around with her left hand until she found an old tennis shoe. She hugged the shoe to her chest and imagined it was Mr. Fuzzy. Sobbing, she rocked back and forth in preparation for a long night.

"Sarah."

She froze and listened. *Did someone say my name?*

"Sarah," a raspy voice whispered.

Looking down, she focused her tear strained vision on the sliver of dim glow coming from under the closet door. A shadow blocked the light. *Someone is standing on the other side!* It wasn't her auntie. Sarah could always tell when Auntie Marge came to the closet to let her out. She was a big woman and made a lot of noise when she moved through the house. *No, this is someone else.*

"Sarah." The voice came through the keyhole in the closet door.

She didn't make a sound. *Who else would be in the house besides her auntie? No one,* she decided. *Whoever the stranger is, maybe he will let me out.* She didn't want to spend another minute in the dark. She had to go pee real bad. *Whoever is on the other side of the door can't be worse than spending another night in the closet.*

"Let me out ... please," she whispered back.

"Only if you will come and play with me."

"I will ... just let me ... out. Please."

"Promise you will meet me in the park."

"I will. I promise."

The lock clicked, causing Sarah's heart to jump. Leaning forward, she opened the door to peer out. No one waited in the room beyond. She stood and exited the closet, shutting the door quietly, so Auntie Marge wouldn't hear her escape. Happy to be out, she wondered who had let her free. Fearful, Sarah searched her bedroom to see if anyone was hiding from sight. No one waited in the shadowed corners or under the bed. Moonlight filtered in through dingy curtains she moved aside to see the window closed tight. She looked out into the backyard, expecting someone to be standing there, staring back at her, but she saw nothing but moonlight and shadows.

"Meet me in the park," the creepy voice had said to her.

She'd made a promise to do so, but now, faced with leaving the house in the dead of night to meet a stranger, Sarah had second thoughts. Since Auntie Marge didn't allow her to leave the house, she had sneaked out many times. Normally, Sarah would just wait until her aunt had fallen into a drunken stupor before slipping out her bedroom window. It was always during the day, though; she was too scared to go out after dark. Mikey, a boy with a runny nose, once told her a story about the police finding a missing little girl in the woods. Found dead with her panties around her ankles and her throat cut from ear to ear, was what Mikey had said. He'd even made the motion with his finger of the knife cutting a throat while he uttered an ugly, strangling noise. Sarah didn't want to be that little girl. No way. She had been through a lot in her young life, but dying in the dark after some strange man pulled down her panties would be too horrible to imagine. She didn't know why a man would want to take down her panties, but knew it would be a terrible way to die. She was too scared to go into the park after dark.

But you promised, Sarah. Breaking a promise is a bad thing.

Sitting on the grimy toilet in the bathroom, she made a decision. Slip out just long enough to see if there was someone waiting for her in the park. That is what she would do. She had to know who had come into Auntie Marge's house and let her out of the closet.

She found her jeans and tennis shoes, put them on, and then grabbed a pink hoodie jacket. The weather was turning to autumn and the nights were getting colder. Now dressed for sneaking out, Sarah went to check on her auntie Marge. Sprawled in the recliner in the front room, Auntie Marge snored with her mouth open and her face pointed toward the ceiling. An empty whiskey bottle rested in her lap. The sight reminded Sarah of what her mother had looked like in death. She forced the terrible image from her memory. She didn't need to remember any bad thoughts when she was free from the closet. Those memories were kept in there like her old tennis shoes.

Sarah returned to her bedroom and crossed to the window. It made a grinding noise as she forced it up. Pushing away one corner of the screen, she slipped her small body through the gap and dropped to the ground. A soft thud sounded as her tennis shoes landed in the muddy dirt beside the house. She squatted in the dark and looked into the back yard. Shadows from overhead trees swayed in the slight breeze, creating a shifting tapestry of light and dark patches. No one was there. She waited to see if any lights came on inside the house, on the chance her aunt had discovered her escape. The house remained quiet. The only sounds were those of a neighborhood late at night: the passing of a car on another street, the far-off wailing of a train engine, a dog barking, and the steady drone of crickets.

Sarah's heart raced in fear. She almost decided to climb back into the window and return to her safe bedroom, but her curiosity to see who had unlocked the closet door was too strong. She stood and walked along the side of the house and hid in the shadow of a large tree in the front yard. Across the street was the park. The slide, swing set, and merry-go-round were illuminated by the glow of a single streetlight. The rest of the park was dark and shadowed. Sarah bit her lip, something she did when concentrating.

Meet me in the park, the creepy voice said.

She waited as a car passed with loud-bass rap music thumping from inside. Once the vehicle turned a corner, she darted across the street and slid under a large bush she'd used many times to hide from Auntie Marge. From her new position, she searched the rest of the darkened playground. No one waited in the shadows where the streetlight did not reach. Sarah lay under the bush and tried to catch her breath as dead leaves clung to the back of her pink hoodie. She decided the park was too scary after dark and good little girls were safer in bed at this time of night. She started to crawl out from under the bush and return home.

"Hello, Sarah," the raspy voice spoke over her shoulder.

Sarah's heart jumped as she leaped to her feet and lunged forward to run away. She tried to scream but a long hand of bony fingers was across her mouth. Another hand held the hood of her jacket. Her feet left the ground as she was dragged back under the big bush. In her mind flashed an image of Mikey drawing his finger across his throat. The thought flooded her senses with panic. She wrestled harder against the hands holding her.

Let me go! Her mind screamed. *Let me go! Please!*

"I'm not going to hurt you, Sarah," the voice whispered, harsh and rough in her ear. "I want to be your new friend."

Sarah stopped struggling. She wasn't going to be able to escape from the stranger. His hands were just too strong. She resigned herself to her fate and lay still in the dark. Like a beacon to safety, the street lamp shone through the mosaic shadows of the bush. Tears began to form in her soft blue eyes. *They will find me tomorrow with my throat cut open and my panties around my ankles. Maybe it will be Mikey who will find me.*

"Sarah, don't be afraid," the voice rasped. "I'll let you go now."

The hand across her mouth released its grip, allowing her to breathe. Sarah took a big gulp of air and pushed herself away from her captor. Scrambling out from under the big bush, she ran to the streetlight pole before turning around to see who had grabbed her. On the edge of the lamp light stood the dark form of a tall figure wearing a hat. He was hunched over and leaning on a cane.

"Who … who are you?" she asked, wiping tears from her eyes with a sleeve.

The figure stepped forward into the light. His face was gaunt and long with skin like thin leather stretched over bone. Eyes were dark and sunken deep within his skull. He smiled, showing long yellow teeth framed by thin bloodless lips. A shabby black stovepipe hat perched upon his head, with wispy long white hair growing out from underneath. The stranger wore a long black coat with a dark fur collar to match. Gnarled and aged hands, with thin fingers and long, broken, yellow nails, gripped the head of a walking cane. *He looks like Mr. Scrooge or a chimney sweep from Mary Poppins,* Sarah told herself. *Something from merry old England.*

"Mr. Beasley." The man removed his hat showing sparse strands of snow white hair. "At your service."

"Are you going to hurt me?"

He put the hat back on his head and tapped the top with his cane to pop it down in place on his skull.

"My sweet Sarah," he smiled, "Mr. Beasley doesn't hurt little girls."

"You came into my house and unlocked the closet?" Sarah asked as she leaned against the streetlight pole. She was ready to run away if he tried to grab her again.

"Let me see ... ah, yes, that was me." His sunken dark eyes blinked a couple of times. "Nasty bit of business, that. Locking a sweet young Sarah in a closet. Nasty bit of business."

He showed a thick pink tongue which he licked over his yellow teeth.

"How did you know I was in the closet?"

"Mr. Beasley knows things like that." He leaned closer to Sarah on his cane. "What you should ask, little girl, is why old Mr. Beasley let you out of the terrible closet."

Sarah stepped back ready to run. "Why did you?"

"To play, of course." Mr. Beasley rose to his full height and opened his arms like a showman. "Look around, Sarah. No one comes to play in the park after dark. All the children are home in bed. After dark is the only time Mr. Beasley can come out to play, but alas, no one is here. The playground is silent and waiting for the dawn and the return of the children. No one is here during the night to play with Mr. Beasley. Will you stay and play, Sarah?"

He stepped back into the dark beyond the streetlight and crossed over to stand next to the seesaw. He placed one long fingered hand upon the upright half.

"Come ride with me on the seesaw."

Sarah hesitated. Mr. Beasley seemed to be both an old man and a child, scary and nice at the same time. *Like a clown,* she thought. *What's the harm in riding a seesaw with him?* Putting her hands in the pocket of her hoodie, she crossed the distance.

Mr. Beasley smiled. "That's a good girl, Sarah Andrews."

"How do you know my name?"

Mr. Beasley shrugged his shoulders. "I just know." The strange man showed another smile. "For this one magical night your name is going to be Lady Andrews. Like the actress Julie Andrews. You know who she is, don't you, Sarah?"

"Mary Poppins."

"That's right," Mr. Beasley lowered the end of the seesaw down to where she could climb on. "What a smart little girl you are, Lady Andrews."

Sarah smiled and sat on her end of the seesaw. The hardness of the wood caused the welt on her thigh to burn again. Her hands gripped the iron bar tightly as Mr. Beasley went to the other end and lowered it. Sarah felt her end of the seesaw rise up as her feet left the ground. In one swift motion, Mr. Beasley leaped on the other end. The seesaw creaked as it raised Sarah up to its full height. She looked down the long length of wooden plank to where Mr. Beasley sat at the bottom, smiling up at her with yellow teeth and sunken eyes.

"Mr. Beasley is going to tell you something, Lady Andrews." The strange man kicked off on his end, sending Sarah back to the ground. "It may be confusing to you at first, but you will know the meaning of it through time." He looked down at her from his new height, a strange gaunt shadow against the night sky. "Do you understand?"

"I think so." Sarah pushed off the ground once again and the seesaw creaked as Mr. Beasley returned to the earth. "What is it?"

"Life is like riding this seesaw." The old man kicked off once again. Sarah felt her stomach flip as she dropped toward the ground. "You know why, Lady Andrews?"

"No." Sarah laughed. She was having fun riding a teeter-totter in the dark with this strange old man. She kicked off and up she went again.

"Life is like a seesaw because it goes up and down, high and low, and people ride on it but never really get anywhere." Mr. Beasley smiled at Sarah. "Their destination is always the same, no matter how long they ride. You know what that destination is?"

Sarah thought about the question for a second. "They die?"

"Precisely." Mr. Beasley rose once again to block out the stars. "Death is their destination. You're no stranger to death, are you?"

"My mommy and my daddy."

Mr. Beasley nodded. "A nasty bit of business that was, eh?"

Sarah didn't say anything else. She wanted to forget all the bad memories in her young life and just have fun on the seesaw with this very odd-looking man. Mr. Beasley remained quiet, too. The only noise between them was the creak of the teeter-totter as it went up and down. Through the night they rode the plank of wood, laughing at each other. They continued as the moon passed overhead. Sarah had no idea how long she'd been riding the seesaw by the time Mr. Beasley stopped and deftly slid off his end.

"The ride is over, Lady Andrews," he announced as he lowered the plank for her to get off. "You'd better go home before your aunt finds out you're gone."

"Do I have to? I'd rather be here with you than home with Auntie Marge."

"Dawn is coming soon. Mr. Beasley can't be out in the park after sunrise."

"Do you live here in the park?"

"For now." He reached out and patted Sarah on the head with a bony hand. For a second, Sarah thought she smelled the stench of blood and death. It was an odor she remembered coming from the corpses of her parents in the stifling trailer. "Be a good little Sarah and return home now."

"Will I see you again?"

He smiled again showing yellow teeth. "Yes, but I'll find you."

Sarah turned and ran across the street to her bedroom window. She lifted the screen and slid back into the house where she shucked off her tennis shoes, jacket, and jeans before sliding under the covers of the bed. In minutes, she was fast asleep.

* * * *

"How did you get out of the closet last night?" Auntie Marge asked her across the breakfast table, a cigarette hanging from her thick lips. She studied Sarah with bloodshot eyes.

"The door was open, so I let myself out." Sarah dipped a spoon into her corn flakes and tried to eat as fast as she could before the school bus arrived. She had only a couple of hours of sleep before Auntie Marge, coughing and hacking, shook her awake.

"I don't remember unlocking it." Auntie Marge took a long puff of her cigarette. "I don't like locking you in there, Sarah, but you shouldn't make your auntie upset when she is in one of her moods. If you were a good girl, I wouldn't lock you in there. Only bad girls get locked in the closet." She coughed loudly. "Just remember what I tell you about going to school. You don't tell anyone about being in the closet or getting a spanking, do you understand? Only a bad girl would tell on her auntie. You know what happens to bad girls, don't you?"

"Yes, Auntie Marge."

Sarah got up from the breakfast table and grabbed her school bag. The horn of the school bus sounded on the street outside.

"Do what I say, Sarah. If you tell on Auntie Marge they will come and take you away to a terrible prison, where they stick bad little girls. It's far worse than the closet. Just remember that."

Sarah shut the door to the house and ran out into the morning sun toward the school bus. Once inside, she sat in her seat and ignored the shouts and noise of the other students. She stared out the window toward the park and the seesaw. In her mind, she replayed the good memories from the night she had spent with Mr. Beasley. Good memories were something she had very few of lately. She thought of Mr. Beasley and a small smile crossed her lips as the bus lurched on to school.

*   *   *   *

"Tell me you didn't just do that!" Auntie Marge shouted so loudly that Sarah dropped the pile of laundry she was carrying from her room. The reek of alcohol bombarded her with every word the woman yelled. "You little tramp, I told you not to let the dirty clothes build up in your room! We have a dirty clothes hamper! Are you stupid or something?"

"Sorry," Sarah replied while trying to pick up the clothes. "I forgot."

"Forgot! Forgot!" Spittle flew from Auntie Marge's mouth. "You're stupid! A stupid little white trailer-trash girl whose parents took drugs and killed themselves! You're just as stupid as they were!"

Sarah knew what was coming next and braced for the pain.

Grabbing her by the collar of her shirt, the large woman yanked her off her feet and dragged her back to her bedroom.

"Cheap trailer trash too stupid to know the dirty clothes go in the hamper!" Auntie Marge threw Sarah on the bed. "What am I going to do with you, Sarah? What do I have to do to teach you to be good and do what I ask?" She yanked a leather belt off a nail on the wall.

"Please … don't hurt me," Sarah pleaded as she covered her head in her hands and waited for the first blow.

"Stupid bad girl!"

The belt struck her in the lower back. The second blow smacked her on the back of her calf. The third struck Sarah on one shoulder with a loud slap of leather against flesh.

"Don't hit me anymore," Sarah sobbed.

"No! I won't hit you anymore!" Auntie Marge flung the belt across the room shattering a glass knick-knack of a ballerina that had been on Sarah's dresser. "What should I do with you then? You're a bad girl, Sarah! A stupid bad girl!"

Sarah flinched when Auntie Marge grabbed her roughly by the collar of her t- shirt and yanked her from the bed.

"No … don't … please," She cried for she knew what came next.

"Bad girls belong in the closet, Sarah!" Auntie Marge dragged Sarah, kicking in protest, along the carpet to the closet door. "That is where you're going to stay until you realize just how bad a girl you've been!" She swung the door open and shoved Sarah inside.

"No … no … I'm afraid … don't, Auntie Marge. Don't!"

The door slammed shut in Sarah's face. She heard the click of the lock.

"I'm sorry, Sarah," Auntie Marge's breathless voice spoke loudly on the other side. "Until you can be a good girl, I have no choice but to leave you in there and this time I know I locked the door."

"No!" Sarah screamed with all the power of her lungs. "Let me out!"

There was only silence. Auntie Marge had left the bedroom and returned to her bottle by the chair in the living room.

"Let me out!" Sarah repeated her desperate cry as she pounded her fists against the locked closet door. "Please."

There was no answer.

Sarah fell back and huddled in the corner as the darkness closed in around her. She hugged her knees to her chest and fought the tears welling in her eyes. The raised welt on her shoulder burned and she knew it had left a nasty mark on her skin. She tried to focus her watery eyes on the sliver of dim light coming from under the closet door.

Will Mr. Beasley come? Will he save me? She asked herself in the silent dark. *If he lets me out, I'll run away. Run away from Auntie Marge and never look back!*

Minutes passed like hours. Sarah sobbed and rocked herself in the dark corner, fighting off the terrible memories that haunted her when she was locked in the closet. The memories came anyway. Bad images began to replay in her mind. She could hear the deafening boom of the shotgun as her father's head disintegrated with the shot. Once again, she held the teddy bear, Mr. Fuzzy, in her hand. She looked down to see its button eyes and fluffy face covered with blood and gore.

No-o-o-o-! Sarah's mind screamed with terror.

"Lady Andrews," A raspy voice whispered through the closet door.

Sarah forced back the memories and returned her focus to the closet. A shadow blocked the light from under the door.

"Mr. Beasley?" she whispered back.

"Nasty bit of business this. Locking poor Sarah in a closet. Nasty indeed."

"Let me out … please."

"Come play with me in the park, Lady Andrews. The seesaw is waiting."

The closet door unlocked with a dull click. Sarah eased the door open to look around her room. No one was there. She quickly left the closet and shut the door quietly behind her.

I'll run away for good, Sarah decided as she found her tennis shoes and grabbed her pink hoodie. *Life anywhere would be better than living here with mean old Auntie Marge. I'll run away with Mr. Beasley.*

After lacing up her tennis shoes, Sarah stood and crossed to the bedroom window; the room was illuminated by moonlight from outside. She raised the window sill and forced aside the corner of the screen to slide out and drop to the yard.

"No you don't, you little bitch!" Auntie Marge bellowed from behind Sarah in the bedroom. Sarah felt strong hands grab her by the hoodie and the seat of her pants. Next, she was yanked back into the house.

"What did I tell you about sneaking out of this house?" Auntie Marge shouted as she dragged her back toward the closet. "I don't know how you got out but you're going back in there for a very long time!"

"No!" Sarah struggled against the hold her aunt had on her. Being dragged across the carpet, she felt herself slipping out of the pink hoodie. She wiggled until the jacket slid off her. Jumping to her feet, she shoved the surprised woman aside. Auntie Marge fell against a bedroom mirror, which shattered against her weight. Broken shards of mirrored glass cascaded down as she slid along the wall and landed on the floor with a loud thump.

"You little piece of white trash!" Auntie Marge shouted with a look of rage and hate in her eyes. "I'm going to kill you for that!"

"Leave me alone!" Sarah bolted out the bedroom. Crossing the living room, she heard Auntie Marge cussing and shouting behind her. Sarah swung open the front door to the dark of the night outside. Auntie Marge's footsteps shook the whole frame of the house as Sarah ran out into the front yard.

"I'm going to knock the snot out of you!" Auntie Marge hissed.

Across the street, the park waited in the light of a single streetlamp. She saw no sign of Mr. Beasley. She ran and slid underneath the big bush, hoping the shadow of the leaves would camouflage her. Trying to be quiet and catch her breath, Sarah looked back toward her house. Auntie Marge crossed the street, her face twisted into a mask of violent hate. Along the way, she had picked up a thick piece of wood, which she swung from side to side.

"Come out, Sarah," she hissed. "Time to get a real spanking."

Auntie Marge's shadow fell across the bush where Sarah hid.

"I'm bleeding." Her aunt held up an arm dripping with blood in the streetlight. "That mirror cut me good, Sarah! But it is nothing compared to what I'm going to do to you!" The wood she held made a swishing noise as she whipped it from side to side. "Why don't you come out and take your spanking now!"

Auntie Marge's wooden club struck the bush where Sarah hid. The blow shook the leaves and caused Sarah to jump and cry out.

"I know you're hiding in there, Sarah!" Auntie Marge thrust the piece of wood into the bush repeatedly. "Get your spoiled ass out of there and let me give you a proper spanking!"

Sarah leapt up and ran toward the darkened seesaw.

"Go away!" she yelled. "Help!"

"There you are!" Auntie Marge threw the piece of wood with all her might. It hit Sarah in the back of the leg and sent her sprawling into the gravel underneath the upraised end of the seesaw. Stones bit into her palms and knees. She turned over on her back. Above her, the raised half of the seesaw pointed up toward the streetlight and the night sky. In the next heartbeat, Auntie Marge's angry form blocked the light. She reached down to grab Sarah by the leg and yank her out from under the seesaw.

"You're going to pay for cutting me!" Auntie Marge screamed. "You little piece of white …"

The raised end of the seesaw came down hard on her aunt's skull with a loud thunk. The large woman collapsed face first into the gravel as Sarah scooted away from Auntie Marge's hand, which was still gripping her pant cuff. She looked up to see Mr. Beasley holding the other end of the seesaw.

"Nasty bit of business is this one, eh, Sarah?" he said as he lifted the seesaw off her aunt's head. A wild stare shone in the sunken shadows of his eye sockets. "Very nasty indeed."

Auntie Marge let out a muffled sound as her hand struggled to touch the wound on the side of her skull. "Sarah, I'm hurt …" She sounded distant and weak. "Go call 911 …"

Mr. Beasley came around the seesaw and knelt beside the prone form of her aunt.

"Do you remember what I told you about riding a seesaw?" Mr. Beasley's smile showed his long yellow teeth. "No matter how long you ride in life, your destination is always the same."

"You die."

"Yes." His smile grew bigger. "This one has reached her destination. Turn your head if you're squeamish, Sarah." His long thin face seemed to stretch even thinner. In the streetlight, his teeth grew longer and sharper.

"I'm not."

Mr. Beasley grabbed and rolled her aunt over so that she looked up at him. Even though she was still dazed, Auntie Marge's eyes filled with shock as Mr. Beasley bent over her with a mouth of long sharp inhuman teeth. She gasped loudly as her eyes widened in absolute terror. With a hissing noise escaping from the huge maw, Mr. Beasley bent down and bit into the face of Auntie Marge. His monstrous teeth sank deep into the flesh.

"Oh God … help me … aooooo!" Auntie Marge's voice gurgled and died off.

With a violent motion, Mr. Beasley ripped upward with his head. Sharp teeth pulled up flesh and bloody sinew from the woman's face. He swallowed down the bloody mess with one quick bite. He bent down again and this time he sank his teeth into Auntie Marge's flabby throat. Blood erupted as her body quaked in the final throes of death. Mr. Beasley tore another huge bite of flesh and swallowed it whole

"Sweet," he croaked with glee as his pink tongue licked over blood on his teeth.

"She was a bad lady," Sarah said.

"That she was." Mr. Beasley took a handkerchief from the pocket of his black jacket and wiped the gore from his lips and face. His mouth shifted back to its normal shape.

"What will become of me now?" Sarah asked as she stood and brushed the dirt from her jeans.

"You will go back to your house and go to sleep," Mr. Beasley answered as he put away the handkerchief. "In the morning the police will come and ask you questions. Tell them you don't know what your aunt was doing in the park after dark. They will know what to do with you."

"Can't I just come with you?"

"No." Mr. Beasley reached out and touched Sarah on the top of her head. "Being with Mr. Beasley is no life for a little girl."

"Where are you going?"

"Dear Sarah, there are other little girls locked in other closets." He showed his toothy smile. "Now run along and get to bed. You will have a new life starting tomorrow."

Sarah nodded and left the park. She took one last look over her shoulder before crossing the street. Mr. Beasley stood in the dark, his gaunt shadowy form a silhouette against the playground equipment. As she watched, the dark form faded away, leaving only the park nestled in shadows. She turned and ran to her house.

Once home, she changed into her pajamas and washed her face and hands in the sink. Sarah looked in the bathroom mirror as she brushed her blonde hair. *I want to look pretty for the police in the morning,* she told herself. *Maybe the nice lady from social services will come to see me as well.*

She rehearsed her sweetest smile in the mirror.

DEAD LINE

The girl's blood dripped from his knife.

Max Camron looked in frustration at the line of text mocking him from the glow of the computer screen. The sentence marked the end of his progress in the next great horror novel. The last words he'd typed before the horrendous accident. Since the tragedy, he wondered if those words would be the last he would ever write in his life.

Every night, he followed the same pathetic routine. He would turn the computer on and let the unfinished line glare back at him from the ethereal glow of the monitor as hours passed in painfully slow procession. With sleep-starved eyes, he willed himself to write the next sentence in the story. No words came. When morning finally brightened the windows of his study, he turned the computer off and shuffled to bed with a prayer he wouldn't dream about the accident. Sometimes, he caught his reflection in the bedroom mirror. His appearance reminded him of a mindless zombie from one his horror shorts—face gaunt and pale, curly hair a matted mess, eyes glazed and emotionless. He now lived as a lifeless husk with no purpose except to sit and stare at the monitor in the middle of the night. A modern day gargoyle, dressed in a t-shirt and faded jeans, perched before the same dead line in his unfinished manuscript. *There is a stage below grief and sadness,* Max thought. *There is numbness.*

The girl's blood dripped from his knife.

The words tormented him. *You can't write anymore Max. Not since Mary's gruesome death. You've lost the ability.*

The manuscript was long overdue. He'd fallen behind the deadline even before the accident. The novel was titled *Ripper in New York,* a tale of a resurrected Jack the Ripper, murdering through the streets of Manhattan. Not the most original plot, but his talent was to take tired ideas and transform them into best sellers. He wasn't another King or a Koontz yet, but his last three novels were successful enough to garner him a nice advance for this story. After the tragedy, the publishing house had been gracious enough to extend his deadline, but time was running out. He could only rely on the goodness of a publisher for so long. There was a contract involved. He had to get this novel done.

Why the hell can't I write anymore? Taking off his glasses, he leaned back in the desk chair and rubbed his tired eyes. *Damn, I hate writer's block. This shit has been going on for three months.* He glanced down at the time reading on one corner of the computer screen. *One thirty-eight in the fucking morning!* Since Mary's death, he was awake only at night and slept through the day like a vampire from a Hammer horror movie. The dead of the night became the only time he felt any semblance of life. He kept every room in his condo dark. The one light on was the glow of the computer monitor in his study. *Horror is best written in the dark,* he always told others.

Max put his glasses back on and looked at the screen. Again, no words came to him.

God, I hate fucking writer's block.

In the last three months, he tried everything to break the block and start writing again. Booze didn't help. Pot did nothing. Cocaine was a waste of money.

The writing died with Mary.

Max glanced up at her 8 x 10 picture sitting on his writing desk. Her beautiful brown eyes and lovely face smiled back at him through the glass of the frame. *Mary was so full of life and laughter. She supported me completely in the long years I struggled to be a published writer.* In his mind's eye, another image of her face replaced the framed one on his desk. He now remembered the way she looked after the large truck skidded through a red light and turned over onto the new suburban he had bought with the advance. The rending of metal and the shattering of glass was deafening. Mary died instantly, crushed by the collapsing ceiling of the SUV. Belted next to her in the driver's seat, he found himself holding her lifeless hand. In shock, he looked over to see Mary's once beautiful face crushed as if by a vice between the twisted metal of the roof and the dash. Blood and brains oozed out onto the dashboard and dripped onto the floor. In a heartbeat, Mary was gone.

Max looked away from the framed picture as he forced the horrible image of her crushed face from his mind. Nausea threatened his stomach. Pushing away from the desk, he walked over to the one window in the room. He slid aside the curtain and gazed at the dark world outside. The condo was on the second floor and looked out over the swimming pool, now lit by one golden-hued halogen streetlamp. *Mary used to love the swimming pool. She swam all day. Sometimes, I would wave down to her from this window.*

He ran his fingers through his curly hair. He wasn't going to cry. He had no emotion to draw upon for tears. There was only a deep emptiness inside. *Mary was gone.* To be a published novelist was as much her dream as his. Mary believed in him more than he believed in himself. When he faltered with doubt, she pushed him even harder. When he suffered from writer's block, she could always think of a way to snap him out of it.

"I'll be your muse," she would say. Then she would lean her body over his shoulder and type the next sentence or paragraph to get him kick-started. *It always did the trick.*

The girl's blood dripped from his knife.

Max let out a sigh and leaned his forehead against the cool of the window. He placed both palms against the glass and half-closed his eyes in weary sadness.

What's the next line, Mary? I can't do this without you.

From his position, he looked down and gazed at the lit computer screen reflected in the window glass. Through his half-closed eyes, he caught sight in the reflection of a misshapen shadow standing in front of the computer. Max's eyes blinked twice as his heart jumped.

What the hell?

Reflexive action took over and he spun around to face the dimly-lit room. He heard the click-clack of typing on the keyboard. The shape of something dark retreated into the shadows where the glow of the monitor did not reach. Max froze in fear.

Am I going crazy? What the hell did I just see? Is there someone else in the room?

His eyes darted toward the corner. Someone or something else watched him from the indistinct darkness. The hair stood up on his neck and arms.

Crossing the room, he switched on the overhead light and found no one waited amidst the bookshelves and furniture. Nothing dark and horrid stood in the corners.

He let out a long sigh of relief. *You're a horror writer, Max. You have an overactive imagination. What you witnessed was just a trick of your tired eyes. Quit scaring yourself.*

Still, he decided it would be best to leave the light on as he returned to the computer. He sat in his office chair and gazed at the screen once more.

The girl's blood dripped from his knife. Turning, the killer fled

Max's heart turned to ice. Someone or something had written additional words to the story. A chill ran through his body and caused goose bumps to appear on his skin. He wasn't going crazy. The new words were proof he wasn't alone in the room! He leapt out of the chair and raced into the hall. From the doorway, he looked back at the computer desk, half expecting to see shadowy hands typing on his keyboard or a deformed figure in black sitting in his writing chair. No one was there. The room was empty.

Max took his cell phone out of his pocket.

I have to call someone and tell them what is happening. Police? What would I say? Some phantom was in my room writing on my computer? They will think I'm crazy. I'll call Shelley instead.

Shelley Boatwright was both Max's literary agent and his closest friend since the accident. He punched the number on the cell while still watching the interior of his study. It rang four times.

"Hello," a weak voice said on the other end.

"Shelley, this is Max," he said in a low voice. "Sorry to call this late but you have to listen to me. Something strange is happening here. Someone or something is writing on my computer."

"Is it a prowler? Did somebody break in, Max?" Shelley's voice was stronger and more awake now. "Did you call the police?'

"No." He took a nervous breath and continued. "I saw a shadow of something at my desk and it typed words I did not write."

"Max, are you drunk?"

"No, Shelley, the words are here on the screen."

"Is this your way of telling me you aren't going to have the book done by the deadline, Max? I've got to have the finished manuscript to show the publisher by eleven in the morning, or the deal is off. No more extensions. You understand that?"

"Yes, Shell, but someone is here with me. I can feel it."

Shelley chuckled. "Maybe you have a ghost writer, Max."

A ghost writer? A realization hit him in the core of his being. *It was Mary.*

"Max, honey, are you still there?" Shelley's voice buzzed in his ear.

"Shell, I'll call you back, okay?"

"You're going to get the manuscript done tonight?"

"Yes. I'll make the deadline." He shut the phone and put it back in his pocket. *How could I be so stupid! It's Mary trying to help me start writing again.* He couldn't believe it but somehow, deep inside, he knew it was true.

His heart pounded when he re-entered the room and shut off the light. He stood by the door as his eyes readjusted to the new dark and the dim light cast by the monitor. Taking a deep breath to steady his nerves, he crossed again to the computer desk and sat down to face the screen. The words glared back at him.

The girl's blood dripped from his knife. Turning, the killer fled

"Mary, are you here?" he said aloud. His voice trembled with fear.

"I'm here, Max." The reply came from the shadows behind him. Mary's voice sounded as if her mouth was filled with something wet and soppy. "I came back to help you."

Pent up grief swept through his heart and Max felt tears running down his face. He started to turn in the chair to look at her once again.

"Keep facing the computer, Max," she said in her distorted fleshy voice. "I don't want you to see me like this."

He felt the nearness of her behind him. Something touched his shoulder. He caught sight of it from the corner of his eye. It was a hand of blackish-gray flesh bloated from death. Lifeless fingernails were extended and broken.

"Mary, I've always loved you," Max said through his tears. "You believed in me when no one else did. You made me the writer I am today."

"Max," her voice, soggy and wet, whispered, "that's why I came back. You have a deadline to make."

"I can't do it, Mary." He swiped away the tears from his face. "Since you died, I haven't been able to write anything."

"I'll help you." The bloated lifeless hand left his shoulder. She continued, her voice ragged and barely discernable. "The girl's blood dripped from his knife. Try this for the next line: Turning, the killer fled through the rain washed streets of New York, where neon reflected on the wet pavement like runny watercolors."

Max typed the words. He thought of the next line and typed it is as well. More sentences came to him and he felt his writer's block collapse like a dam busted open by a raging flood. Words poured from his fingertips and onto the screen. The entire night passed with the clicking of the keyboard and the presence of Mary, impossibly, behind him. He finished one chapter, then a second. Finally, when the sunlight touched the window to his room he wrote the last lines of the manuscript. Without hesitation he picked up his cell phone and punched Shelley's number.

"Hello."

"It's me, Shel."

"Max, tell me you're calling to say you have the manuscript done."

"It's done. All of it."

"In one night? How did you do it?"

"Shelley, let's just say …" Max paused and looked at the framed picture on the desk. In the reflection of the glass, Mary stood behind him, her face grotesquely misshapen like a Picasso drawn in dead meat; her once beautiful eyes bulged out of a face of crushed flesh and bone. "… I found my muse again."

THE RED CHURCH

Hell found me in the last place one would expect—a church.

As I scribble these words into this journal, I hear the bloodcurdling screams of my wife from the depths below. I know I do not have much time before it'll be my turn to scream. I'll tell my story as fast as I can.

My name is Michael North, a freelance photographer with a passion for shooting rustic old buildings in rural Oklahoma. With the centennial of statehood fast approaching, my publishing agent came up with the idea of producing a coffee-table book filled with pictures of old abandoned farm houses, rusted windmills, churches, and ghost towns dotting the countryside throughout the state. I jumped at the project and spent most of my weekends over the last six months driving along back country roads searching out interesting structures to shoot for the picture book. My new wife, Jackie, traveled with me and we became a working duo. She would write poems to accompany my pictures while I shot the sites we discovered with my Nikon digital camera. It is in her poetry notepad I am writing this account in the hope someone else will read these words. Of course, if you do find this account, it means you've come to the church as well and may suffer the same fate as I have.

Earlier today, August 27, we ended up in a rural country store in Cripple Creek. If I knew then what I know now, I would drive past that store and straight back home and never look back. I would have had a life with Jackie, a nice home and maybe children someday. I wouldn't be scrawling these words as fast as I can while the moon eclipses and my wife screams from the basement below for me to save her, for God to save her, for anyone to save her.

Where was I? Oh yes, the corner store in Cripple Creek located at the only traffic light in the small town. A normal-looking country store with gas pumps, ATM, DVD rentals, home-fried chicken, and plenty of beer posters pasted across the windows. I've been to a hundred just like it. If you are reading this, you probably went there, too.

The old guy running the place saw the camera around my neck when I entered. He wore a blue work shirt with the name Lenny monogrammed on the front. You wouldn't suspect him of anything but being a nice old man. Unless you looked into his eyes; they were as dark as pools of ink. Eyes really are the mirror of the soul—now I know it's true.

"Are you a news reporter?" he asked while ringing up the two cans of coke I purchased.

"I'm a freelance photographer," I replied. The only other occupant in the store, a brawny teenager with a dumbfounded look, stared slack jawed at me as Lenny sacked the cans of pop. I decided the kid must be mentally handicapped.

"What do you photograph?" Lenny asked.

"Old farmhouses and scenic structures representing the changing face of America's rural history." I replied, and asked like a fool, "Do you know of any interesting places in the area that I can photograph?"

Lenny smiled. "Well, there's the red church."

I borrowed Jackie's notepad to write the directions on how to find the place and spent the next hour crisscrossing a network of dirty country roads like a madman obsessed; a blind fool racing headlong toward the nightmare of his end. I want to say now to anyone who is reading this journal that I'm the one to blame for my fate. My wife protested and wanted me to turn back because it was late in the afternoon and we were getting lost. I didn't listen. Now, she is paying the price for my stupidity with her blood and flesh.

I had just decided to give up my search and turn around when I spotted my objective: an abandoned one-story clapboard church sitting on a hill with the late afternoon sun shining behind it. From a distance, the building appeared to be the picture of a normal country chapel. I imagined it once filled with the families of farmers, crammed into the wooden pews, fanning themselves against the summer heat as they sang hymns on Sunday morning. After services, the preacher would be waiting at the door, shaking the hands of each of the congregation before they returned to their rural farm life. I imagined a scene like a movie, the sun shining through an opening in the clouds onto the little church like a blessing from heaven. I envisioned the setting like something out of a postcard or a great American novel. As I drove nearer, an ugly reality replaced the fantasy.

Somewhere through the years, the church had fallen out of grace with God.

I soon saw things that didn't fit my mental picture of an idyllic country church. The most noticeable was the fact the desolate little chapel had been painted blood red. The clapboard siding, the double front doors, the steeple—all looked as if someone had dipped the paint brush in fresh blood. The stained-glass arched windows running along the side of the building were shattered and broken, with pieces of jagged glass jutting down from the frames like sharp fangs. The steeple had wood slats missing, exposing the beams of the tower like ribs showing through the carcass of a dead animal. Entire sections of shingles were missing from the roof, leaving rotted holes. Dozens of crows, the only congregation now attending the church, perched upon the gable of the roof. They watched with knowing black eyes as I pulled the SUV into the weed-covered front yard.

"Why would anyone repaint the church in red?" I asked my wife as I exited the SUV and slung my Nikon around my neck. "These churches are always painted white. Who'd come do that? What would be the purpose of it?"

"I don't know, but I don't like this place," Jackie replied as she closed the car door behind her. Several crows took to the air, cawing and flapping in the blue sky above the church. "It gives me the creeps. Can't we just leave? It's getting late."

"Let me snap a few pictures first," I answered.

I was intrigued. The building looked out of place, a dark and bloody stain surrounded by the summery wheat fields of Oklahoma; it was unlike anything else I had encountered in my back road travels. I raised my camera and shot a few quick photos of the exterior as I walked closer to the broken windows. I peered through the shattered glass into its interior where beams of sunlight shone through the holes in the roof to provide a hazy illumination to the shadows inside. I saw no pews, which had probably been removed from the congregation hall years ago; instead I noticed two large mesh cages in the center of the unfurnished main room. Each was the kind of cage hunters used as a kennel for their bird dogs. Several raw bones littered the floor around the kennels.

"What do you see?" Jackie asked nervously.

"I think someone's been using this place to house their hunting dogs. There's a couple of makeshift kennels inside." I began walking toward the front doors of the church.

"You're not thinking about going in there, are you?" Jackie asked as she followed behind me.

"Just to take a few shots of the interior, then we're out of here, babe."

I walked up the steps to the painted red double doors and noticed strange symbols carved into the wood of the frame.

"Jackie, what do you make of these?" I asked.

She peered closer at the door. "Some of the words are in Latin. I took a semester in Latin a few years back and nearly flunked the course. I can't tell you what they mean but it looks like Ecclesiastical Latin."

"Latin?" I pondered aloud as I placed my hands on the brass knob of the door. "This doesn't appear to be a Catholic church. Most of these rural chapels were built by Baptists."

"The symbols look satanic to me. I think someone has been using the church for devil worshipping."

"Satanists right here in the heart of Oklahoma? I guess it's possible. This church is way out in the middle of nowhere so no one would interrupt their ceremonies."

I opened the door with a rusty creak and stuck my head inside. No dogs barked or charged the door. The place seemed quiet except for the cawing of crows circling overhead like a gathering cloud.

"I'm not going in there," Jackie whispered, her voice tinged with fear.

"Stay here and wait for me," I said and slipped inside the chapel. The air inside was much cooler than the outside heat. An oppressive stillness weighed down upon me as I crossed the floor through the sporadic beams of sunlight coming from the holes in the ceiling. The walls on the inside of the church were not covered in the usual graffiti I had grown accustomed to finding in other abandoned rural buildings. Apparently, teenagers hadn't found this place and turned it into a party house yet. Or they stayed away from the church in fear. I now know it was the latter.

The floor was littered with crow droppings and in the rafters overhead many of the birds huddled like spectators watching me with their eyes of pitch black. I reached the mesh wire kennel cages and bent down to examine the bones. They appeared to be canine.

"Are those human bones?" Jackie hissed from the open front door of the church.

"I don't think so. I think they're dog bones, perhaps from coyotes."

"You mean there are coyotes around here?" She looked around fearfully and then stepped inside. "I'm coming in with you."

With her heels clopping across the hard wood floor, Jackie joined my side.

"Do they keep dogs in that cage?" she whispered.

"I don't know."

"Who'd do that?"

"Probably a local hunter or a dog hoarder."

I pulled up the camera and shot several photos of the church interior; my Nikon flashed like silent lightning in the confines of the chapel.

"Oh my God, Michael," Jackie gasped. "Look at the pulpit!"

I stopped shooting and followed her over to the church pulpit. On the floor was spread a black cloth with silver symbols similar to what decorated the front door frame. In the center of the black cloth, a freshly decapitated head of a coyote stared up at us with lifeless eyes. Flies buzzed and crawled across its face.

"Let's get out of here, honey," Jackie whispered. "Someone is doing weird rituals with dogs here. I want to be far away when they return."

"I'm going to take some more pictures and turn them over to the SPCA when we get back. They have to know what's going on out here." I flashed the Nikon and caught a couple of good shots of the dog head. Through a flash of light, I noticed the door in the wall at the back of the pulpit. A satanic looking symbol was scrawled across its front in black spray paint. I began walking toward it.

"Where are you going?" Jackie asked.

"There might be more evidence beyond that door."

"Skip it," Jackie pleaded. "Let the county sheriff deal with it."

"I'm just going to take a peek." I turned the knob and slowly opened the door. A set of stone steps led down to a dismal looking basement. I looked back to Jackie. "There's a basement. I'm going to see what's below. You stay up here."

"You want to leave me in a satanic place of worship with a bloody coyote head? Not very likely. I'm going back to the car."

"That's a better idea."

She turned and hurried out of the chapel. Seconds later, I heard the beep of the SUV unlocking and the slamming of a door.

Letting out a nervous breath, I descended into the basement of the church. Fading sunlight from small windows set in the walls at ground level lit the dank room. My heart pounded. I felt like a little boy about to see something obscene and forbidden.

At the bottom of the steps, I took in the spectacle of the basement with a combination of horror and fascination. My eyes could not look away and my breath froze at what I saw. A painted mural stretched across one wall showing a satanic figure sitting upon a grand throne. Unlike any other rendition of Satan I have seen, this Lucifer had the head of a dog. Two large curling horns protruded from the dog head and clawed hands gripped the throne. Around the canine-like legs of the devilish figure, the forms of dogs stood with red hungry eyes. In the background of the painting, the artist had rendered a total eclipse in the sky. The image of the dark moon ringed by the corona of the sun reminded me of something I had forgotten.

The newspaper today had announced that a total lunar eclipse was to take place in the early hours of August 28, the next morning.

I stepped back to take a picture of the wall mural when my foot knocked over something on the floor. I turned to look at what my heel had struck. A long, black unlit candle mounted in a brass holder lay tipped on its side in the dim light. I studied the rest of the floor and saw an upside-down pentagram chalked off across the stone tiles; at each point of the drawn star stood a black unlit candle in a brass holder. I swallowed in fear. Some evil ritual was going to be performed in this place tonight, something correlated to the upcoming total eclipse.

It was time to leave, I realized too late.

At that moment came the sound of something walking through the grass outside the basement windows. At first, I thought a coyote might be prowling about, but then a face pressed against the basement window glass. I saw the large retarded boy from the Cripple Creek country store peering into the basement. My heart jumped as I ducked into the shadows praying he hadn't seen me. His face disappeared and the sound of his steps crunching through the grass faded. I let out a sigh of relief, but only for a second. The horn of my SUV began sounding from the front of the church.

Jackie! A sudden fear shot through my brain. *Oh God, what have I gotten us into?*

I ran back up the steps and into the main hall of the church. The frantic sounds of the SUV horn had grown silent. Instead, I heard the noise of men shouting, the breaking of glass, and my wife screaming in terror. I felt no fear for myself. I only wanted to save my wife. I charged across the church floor and kicked the front doors open. Outside, in the setting Oklahoma sun, six men surrounded my SUV. Through the shattered side window, two of the men dragged my wife, kicking and screaming, out of the vehicle. Directly behind the SUV was a rusty tow truck with the words Lenny's Towing Service scrawled on the side.

Yelling, I ran down the steps. Someone tackled me from behind and threw me into the high weedy grass. A heavy weight on my back forced me against the ground. I spat grass out of my mouth and turned my head to see the retarded boy holding me down. I struggled to escape, but he was too heavy and too strong. He reached and grabbed the camera strap around my neck and twisted it tight. I fought for air and felt my head go faint.

"Don't kill him yet, Cleavus," said a voice I recognized from somewhere beyond my fading perception.

"Are we goin' to spill blood now, Pa?" the large boy sitting on my back asked.

"Soon. When the moon darkens."

The camera strap loosened enough for me to catch a gasping breath. The weight lifted and I shifted to look toward Jackie. She was stretched out with one man holding her arms and another pinning her legs. The men looked the part of typical homegrown country boys, the kind you see in any small town. Some still wore their work shirts as if they had just gotten off the clock at their jobs. Jackie's eyes were closed and she appeared to be sleeping peacefully. I said a silent prayer she wasn't dead, but, in hindsight, I should have prayed she was.

"Don't worry, the little missus is fine," the familiar voice said. In the next second the face of Lenny entered my field of vision. "I've just put her to sleep for a spell."

"What'd you do to her?" I asked as I caught my breath.

"I used a little chloroform," Lenny said and smiled slightly as he produced a brown bottle and white piece of cloth. "Puts you right out."

"Why are you doing this?"

"You don't get to ask the questions." Lenny's face grew closer and more menacing. "I do. I'm going to ask you one question and you're going to answer me."

From out of my vision, I heard Cleavus make a hissing laugh like escaping steam.

"What question?" I looked back at Lenny's face, into his eyes of dark evil.

"Tell me, what does the name of God spell backwards?"

"Why are you doing this?" I pleaded.

"Answer the question or I'll have my boys rape your wife right now. What word does the name of God spell backwards?"

"Dog," I answered weakly.

Lenny smiled. The chloroform soaked cloth slammed down tightly against my mouth and nostrils and everything went black.

* * * *

When I opened my eyes I was crammed in one of the wire-mesh kennel cages. The chloroform had left me feeling sick and nauseated. My knees and back ached terribly from the steel mesh digging into them. I turned my head to see my wife, Jackie, still asleep and curled in the other dog cage. We were both back in the main hall of the abandoned chapel. A camping oil lantern burned a dim yellow in one corner near the pulpit, putting out just enough light for me to see the crows perched in the shadows of the rafters. From somewhere in the darkness came voices and the loud baying barks of dogs. The front doors opened and three men entered the chapel. Each wore black-hooded robes and carried large machetes. Behind, a fourth man followed, dragging three large hounds on chains. The dogs barked and whined as they were forced across the floor of the church and down into the basement below.

Finally, Lenny entered with the hulking form of Cleavus at his side.

"Let me and my wife out of here!" I screamed.

"Oh, the photographer is awake," Lenny said. From the folds of his robe he produced the Nikon. "Didn't I promise you'd get some great pictures at the red church? I looked through them. Great shots."

The terrible sounds of dogs yelping in pain and men laughing arose from the depths below the church. I knew instantly what was happening. The dogs were being butchered.

"What kind of sick psychos are you people?" I asked. "You're killing innocent dogs to perform some stupid religious ceremony!"

Lenny kicked the side of my cage while Cleavus laughed. "Do you think we're going to stop with just killing dogs tonight? It's the time of the darkening of the moon. Only human sacrifices can appease the true lord of this world. The blood of the hounds is just setting the stage for what is to come."

They left me. I turned my attention to the lock and chain holding my cage door shut. There was no way out.

"Mike," Jackie's weak voice called out from her cage.

"I'm here, my love," I said.

"What are they going to do to us?"

My heart broke for I knew in the depths of my soul exactly what they were going to do. "Jackie, remember when we first fell in love? The day of our wedding and our honeymoon?"

"Yes."

"You must remember those good times and know that I love you no matter what happens tonight. Do you understand?"

The voices of the men grew louder as they walked up from the basement and into the chapel. There were six of them, all dressed in black robes that made them look like the crows watching from the rafters.

Lenny stepped from the crowd.

"It is so decreed that the Lord of Lies should be paid in blood at the time when darkness steals the light of the moon. The sacrifice cannot be paid in dog's blood. The demand is for human blood." Lenny pointed up toward a rotted hole in the ceiling of the church. "Look, the moon is disappearing. The time is now. Who will be our first sacrifice?"

"Take me!" I screamed.

Lenny smiled his evil grin. "Where are your manners? Don't you know it's ladies first?"

Laughing, the men pounced upon Jackie's cage and hefted it up off the ground. She screamed in fear and looked toward me, her eyes wide with terror. The men carried her off into the darkness of the steps leading down to the basement as I shouted every obscenity I could think of behind them. I fought frantically to get out of the cage and bloodied my hands in the process. Turning my weeping eyes toward the eclipsing moon still visible through the gaps in the roof, I prayed for God to protect my wife and take her soul. Then I remembered Jackie's poetry notepad I'd stuffed in my back pocket earlier. I removed it with bloody fingers and flipped the pad open to a blank page. I always keep a pen in my shirt pocket and was thankful to find it still there. I began writing like a madman as the pen scratched the paper and the crows looked down on me from above.

I scribbled this account in the hopes someone will find this notepad on my body, if it is found at all. My time is running short. The moon in the sky above is nearly dark and the screams of horror from my wife have died. God has taken her soul. I now know why the church is painted red—because it is coated in the blood of those who have fallen victim to its evil. A sound is coming from outside the church. It is the howling of coyotes in the distance, their mournful cries directed toward the total eclipse of the moon. The men are returning from the basement. I see them now entering the chapel with cloaks drenched in blood. I have no more time and I must hide this journal.

There is no hope left because Hell has found me.

Dennis McDonald

THE GIRL NEXT DOOR

Wrapped in plain brown paper, the package arrived at the rambling two-story boarding house on the corner of Ninth and Harbor. The landlady, Miss Rosenberg, caught sight of the parcel while having her morning tea on the porch. Leaning her three hundred pounds forward in the straining wicker chair, she called out to the short black man trimming the shrubs at the edge of the lawn.

"Calvin?"

"Yes, Miss?" Calvin replied as he lowered the sheers and wiped sweat from his brow with the sleeve of his stained work shirt.

"Go get me the package in the mailbox."

"Yes, Miss."

Miss Rosenberg settled back in her chair to finish her cup of tea. She watched Calvin amble over to the mailbox. The only black man she would ever let stay at the boarding house, Calvin followed her orders and worked hard for his rent. She made sure there was plenty of work to be done, too. He was always weeding, painting, fixing, mowing the lawn and tending to her needs. The other tenants referred to Calvin as the "house-nigga." Miss Rosenberg smiled to herself because she liked the term. Calvin was too much of a simpleton to know it was a derogatory title.

Showing white teeth in a smile, Calvin returned with the parcel.

"Who is the package for?" she asked. Certainly the mysterious package was not for her. It couldn't be. She didn't have family or friends.

"It's addressed to Mr. Henner. It's not heavy."

"Don't just stand there grinning like a fool; give it to me and get back to trimming those bushes. I want the whole front yard done."

"Yes, Miss."

She wiped her hands on her faded print dress, and accepted the package. *Calvin was right,* she thought, *the parcel was addressed to Mr. Henner and very light.* She turned the box over and examined it. There was no other writing except the address. *Who would send Mr. Henner a package?* She frowned. The old drunk rented the room next to her apartment and had no family. His only friends were other drunkards who lived in the building. *So who sent him the package?*

No one, she decided. *He must have ordered it himself. That would explain why the old man has been stalling with this month's rent. He spent the money on what's in this package.* Therefore, she had every right to find out what was inside.

Examining the seams at the end of the paper wrapping, she decided a little steam might just loosen the glue enough to give without tearing the paper. Mr. Henner would never know she'd peeked, if she was careful and glued the paper back when done.

"Calvin?"

"Yes, Miss?" Calvin looked up from the hedge.

"I'm going inside. You finish the hedges and then mow the backyard, you hear?"

"Yes, Miss."

Rising out of the wicker chair, she tucked the package under one flabby arm and entered the boarding house. Her second floor apartment, the best of the seven in the tenement home, was reached by climbing a flight of worn wooden steps. She stopped at the bottom and looked up. The steps seemed harder to climb each day. Sighing, she eased onto the staircase as the wood creaked beneath her weight. Stopping twice to catch her breath, she made it to the top. Wheezing for air, she entered her apartment and locked the door behind her.

*   *   *   *

Minutes later, she stood in her small kitchen holding the package over the steam whistling from her tea kettle. The steady stream of vapor did its trick and loosened the tape holding one end of the paper on the package. She peeled the brown paper apart and slipped the wrapping from the cardboard box. The box, painted sky blue, had bright pink letters printed across the lid saying:

CHRISSIE

Miss Rosenberg felt her heart flutter with fascination. There were only two strips of scotch tape keeping her from finding what was inside. She grabbed a butter knife from a kitchen drawer and cut the scotch tape carefully. *Now I'll know what the old drunk had spent my rent money on.* To her, violating someone else's mail was one of the most exhilarating pleasures she had ever known in her life. *It's dirty and crude,* she told herself. *I imagine this must be what sex feels like.*

With her heart pounding, she lifted off the lid.

The first thing she noticed was a printed paper with a picture of a naked young blonde girl with her hands on her hips. Picking it up, she read the letters next to the image:

> Hi. I am Chrissie, your own personal love slave. My only purpose is to satisfy your every need and pleasure. I am yours to dominate and hold. I am supplied with three orifices you may use anytime you please. To bring me to life, just inflate my body with the valve stem in my left heel. We are going to have so much fun together. I am Chrissie. Love me.

A sex doll!

Miss Rosenberg's mind reeled from the realization. She looked down at the box as a single painted blue eye stared back at her from the folds of flesh-colored plastic. *A perverted sex doll! Of all the filthy things to bring into my boarding house!* She dropped the cardboard box onto the kitchen table in disgust. *My rent money has been spent on this dirty toy!* She began to contemplate what she should do about this outrage. Evict Mr. Henner immediately. *Oh yes, that is what I'll do. Throw the old pervert and his sick toys out into the street!*

But wait … I can't. I'm the one who opened the package illegally. If I throw him out because of the doll, Mr. Henner will know I opened his mail. He will go to the police. I don't want to explain why I opened the package. I don't want them snooping around and finding out about the social security checks I still receive that are addressed to the last handyman. The one buried under the floor of the tool shed. What if the police start asking around? What if they ask Calvin why he was digging in the tool shed after midnight? No, that will not do.

Miss Rosenberg replaced everything back into the box, re-glued the paper wrapping, and contemplated what to do. Finally, she had a plan. She would just ask Mr. Henner for the rent money and, if he couldn't pay, she would evict him out into the street. She double checked the package to see if there were any signs of her intrusion.

There was none.

* * * *

Miss Rosenberg snapped awake from a troubled nap filled with dreams of shadowy figures and whispering voices. Confused and disorientated, she looked about her small three-room apartment. Something had woken her. Late afternoon sunlight lit the room, the last rays catching the specs of dust floating in the air. She saw someone standing in one corner. Her heart jumped. It was Gonzales, the dead tenant buried under the tool shed. He stood in the shadows, his head bowed, holding his stained hat in his ghostly hands just as he had in life. His head rose to look at her with dark eyes full of hate. He stared at her … stared into her. She gasped and shut her eyes in fear. *Oh God, no,* her mind screamed. *He's come for me!*

Rap! Rap! Rap!

Her eyes reopened with a start. Someone knocked at the door. She glanced into the dark corner of the apartment. Ghostly Gonzales no longer stood there. He had returned to the shadowy corners of her nightmares. *Nothing but a dream,* she told herself.

Rap! Rap! Rap!

This time the knocking was louder. She eased up out of the worn padding of the recliner and adjusted her print dress before crossing the room. *Please, God,* her inner voice whispered, *don't let it be the police.*

She opened the door. Mr. Henner stood there dressed in a threadbare gray jacket and baggy green pants supplied by the Salvation Army down the street. He was thin from a diet of too little food and too much alcohol; his cleft chin sat upon a scrawny neck bristling with gray whiskers. He smelled of cigarettes, alcohol, and greasy burgers from the diner where he washed dishes during the day. A bottle of whiskey in a brown paper sack stuck out of one pocket of his jacket.

"What do you want?" Miss Rosenberg asked.

"Calvin said a package came for me today." His watery blue eyes stared evenly at her.

"I have it, but you aren't going to get it until you pay this month's rent."

"Isn't holding someone's mail against the law?"

"So is not paying your rent on time."

For a second they stood silent. *This is the part I like best,* she told herself. *Next will be the pleas for more time to pay the rent. I love it when I have one of my renters by the balls.*

"All right." Henner let out a long sigh. Gnarled fingers, yellowed by nicotine, reached into a jacket pocket and produced a worn leather wallet. He began counting out bills.

Miss Rosenberg was shocked. She hadn't expected him to have the money and now didn't know what to do. If she took the payment it meant having to put up with the perverted old bastard living next door to her for another month. She couldn't say anything about the sex doll or he would know she had opened his mail. She was trapped. Disappointment welled inside her as she watched him count out the bills. *He must have gotten a raise at the diner,* she realized. *I'll have to increase his rent next month.*

"Two hundred dollars." He handed the money toward her. "I've paid up. Now where is my package?"

"Fine." Miss Rosenberg pocketed the cash. Frustrated by how her plans had fallen through, she took the box from the kitchen table and handed it to him. "Here it is. I hope you enjoy it."

Mr. Henner's eyes came alive with a youthful glow as his trembling hands took the box from her.

"You didn't open it, did you?" He studied her for a second.

"Why should I?" she lied. "I don't care what junk you get in the mail as long as you pay your rent."

He left without another word, walking to his door down the hall more quickly than she had ever seen the old man move before. Miss Rosenberg slammed the door to her room shut. *Damn! What luck!* She had hoped to evict the old man but now had to let him live there for another month. She imagined what Mr. Henner would do now that he had the sex doll within the private confines of his room. The sick perversions taking place next door would be beyond her reach.

Almost.

On the counter by the sink, she found her favorite drinking glass with the best acoustics. She crossed her apartment and placed it against the living room wall at the spot where the wallpaper had long been worn away from her listening. If she couldn't stop what happened next door, she could eavesdrop in on the filthy actions. Maybe overhear something to help her throw Mr. Henner out of the house.

"I've waited so long for you, my love." Mr. Henner's voice resonated in the amplification provided by the glass. Indiscernible muffled sounds came through the wall. She strained to hear and imagined the old man eagerly tearing through the paper she had so carefully glued back together. A few more seconds of silence passed then the sound of wheezing and puffing. The old bastard was blowing up the doll, Miss Rosenberg realized. *He is going to give himself a stroke trying to inflate that plastic whore!* A vision came to her of old man Henner, red-faced cheeks puffed out, blowing into the valve stem in the left heel of the doll.

"Look at you," Mr. Henner's breathless voice echoed in the confines of the listening glass. "You're even more beautiful than I dreamed. Your hair is so lovely."

More muffled noises. Low whispering came through the wall. She strained with all of her might to hear what was being spoken. *Is it Mr. Henner's voice?* she wondered. *Is he whispering to the doll?*

The next sound caused Miss Rosenberg to wrinkle her face in disgust. The rusty springs of the old man's bed creaked in a steady pattern. In disbelief, she removed the glass. Her ear ached and legs were numb from lack of circulation. She wouldn't have believed the old man could get an erection, but there he was, making love to that aberration of nature. She couldn't allow such sick perversions next door.

Somehow, she would have to stop it.

* * * *

The next afternoon Miss Rosenberg stood in the hallway outside her apartment, watching Calvin as he swept the floor with a broom. She turned to the sound of someone's shoes pounding up the wooden steps from the foyer. Mr. Henner, arms filled with various shopping bags, bounded up the stairs with the energy of a man twenty years younger. Clean-shaven and with his hair combed and washed, he looked better than she had ever seen him. *One night with that plastic toy and he thinks he is a new man,* Miss Rosenberg thought. She read the logos on the shopping bags he carried. Most came from a women's clothing store down the street.

"Good day, Calvin," Mr. Henner said as he passed them in the hall. He ignored her presence.

"It is a fine day at that, Mr. Henner," Calvin replied between sweeps of his broom.

"Yes, it is." Mr. Henner adjusted his bags so he could put the key in the lock to his room.

"I have an announcement, Mr. Henner." She crossed her arms across her girth. "Since you have so much money to buy so many things, I'm going to raise your rent twenty dollars starting next month."

"Fine." Mr. Henner opened the door to his room. His blue eyes flashed a glance at Calvin sweeping in the hall. "Did you know, Miss Rosenberg, slavery was abolished over 130 years ago? I bet you never told Calvin."

"Mind your own business," she snapped back.

"You first." Mr. Henner entered his room and shut the door behind him.

"What did Mr. Henner mean about slavery being abolished?" Calvin asked.

"Nothing," she answered, feeling the flush of anger through her cheeks. "Nothing at all. After you finish sweeping, Calvin, I want you to scrub down the foyer floor."

"Yes, Miss."

Flustered, she entered her apartment. Rage welled up inside her, causing her temples to ache. *How dare he tell me to mind my own business? I own the boarding house. I'm the landlady. I have rules to follow. I could find half a dozen other homeless drunks to rent his room. I have dealt with other problem tenants before, but none as disgusting and rude as this old pervert. How am I going to throw him out?*

Her eyes darted to the listening glass sitting on the end table. Like a beacon, it drew her across the room. *Everything I have planned has gone wrong. He didn't even complain about my raising the rent. Must listen in again on the chance I'll overhear something I can use to get rid of the old letch.*

She picked up the glass and placed it against the wall. The bottom felt cool against her ear.

Mr. Henner's muffled voice spoke, "It looks lovely on you, my dear. Here, try on this black bra."

Miss Rosenberg frowned. *The old kook is talking to that sick doll as if it is a living woman. Maybe I can have him committed and put away.*

"Oh yes, you're so sexy in that one," Henner spoke again. "Come kiss me. I like it when you kiss me like that—"

Feeling disgust at the thought of the old man kissing and sucking on the plastic doll, she strained to hear more. Long seconds of silence followed. Someone's whispering filtered through the thickness of the wall. Not Mr. Henner's voice. The whispering sounded soft and feminine, though she couldn't make out what was being said. Only odd muffled movement and low inaudible voices followed. She listened intently for another half hour until her ear ached and her legs were numb. Disappointed, she put the glass back on the end table and settled into the recliner. Using the remote to switch on the television, she eased back to watch a night of sitcoms and news; anything to take her mind off the perversions next door.

* * * *

Miss Rosenberg awoke again with a start. Before her, the television cast the only light in the room with the flickering images of an infomercial. She had fallen asleep during Leno again but something had awakened her. Her eyes darted toward the corner of her apartment but there was no Ghostly Gonzalez standing the in the shadows. Something else had interrupted her sleep. She used the remote to turn down the volume on the set. Soft music and loud thumps came from the apartment next door.

What was that old man doing up at this time of night?

With difficulty, she eased her large body out of the recliner and grabbed the listening glass off the end table.

"Goddammit! I said to come over here and dance with me!" Mr. Henner's voice boomed through the wall into her apartment, so loud and unexpected that Miss Rosenberg dropped the listening glass. It shattered on the floor, spraying glass shards across her house slippers. "Shut up! You will do what I say! Don't make me hit you again!

The old man is yelling at the doll! Miss Rosenberg realized in disbelief. Next he laughed like a mad man. *He has gone completely mad. I'll have him committed.* A crash came from the room followed by more cursing and yelling. That was it. She had had enough of Mr. Henner. Storming out of her apartment, she crossed to the next door down the hall and knocked so hard it shook in its frame.

"Open the door this instant!" Miss Rosenberg shouted above the noise coming from the room.

"Oh, crap ..." Mr. Henner replied. The music went quiet.

"Open this door now!" Miss Rosenberg felt anger rising again within her.

"Just a second." The door latch slid aside. Mr. Henner stood, dressed in a pair of dirty boxer shorts. One hand gripped a half-empty bottle of whiskey; the other held the sex doll around the waist. Chrissie was life-sized when inflated, Miss Rosenberg realized. The doll's plastic arms were out-stretched toward her as if she wanted a hug. Red painted lips surrounded a mouth fully open in a wide O. The doll's blonde hair was a matted mess. A black spaghetti-strapped negligee covered the pink plastic of her body. A spaghetti strap had slid down, exposing one fake breast.

"Miss Rosenberg. What a pleasant surprise. Is there a problem?" Mr. Henner asked in drunkenly slurred words.

"What is going on in there?" Miss Rosenberg's gaze looked past the doll into the room beyond. The place was a wreck. Toppled furniture, empty bottles, and clothes were strewn about the floor. On the couch rested a black lace bra.

Mr. Henner staggered as he spoke. "We were just having a little party."

"It's three in the morning! You're making enough noise to wake the whole building!"

"I'm sorry. It's my honeymoon. Have you met my wife? Her name is Chrissie." He pushed one plastic hand toward her to shake. Miss Rosenberg stepped back in revulsion. The thought of touching the vile piece of plastic sickened her, especially after Mr. Henner had sex with the thing.

A voice deep inside her asked: *Why not me instead?*

"Keep that plastic whore away from me! This kind of behavior is unacceptable in my house. You can expect an eviction notice in the morning."

"We will try to be quieter. Why don't you come inside and join us for a drink?"

"Absolutely not!" she snapped back.

"I promise to …"

"No promises. I'm throwing you out tomorrow!"

"Fine!" Old Man Henner replied. He stepped back into his room to close the door. Miss Rosenberg caught a glimpse of the face of the sex doll. For a second, she thought she saw the doll's mouth twist into a wicked plastic smile. Then the door slammed shut.

Stunned Miss Rosenberg stood in the hall for a second. *Did that horrid thing smile at me? Or was it my imagination?*

Her headache throbbed again as she returned to her apartment. At least now she had a reason to throw the old bastard to the curb. Retrieving a dust pan and broom from a closet, she bent down to sweep up the remnants of the broken glass she'd dropped earlier. When she swept the last pieces into the dustpan, she heard a sound come from the other side of the wall. She pressed her ear to the wallpaper and heard the low whispering of a woman's voice.

* * * *

Because she'd been up late the night before, Miss Rosenberg slept late and missed evicting Mr. Henner before he left for work. Instead, she filled out the eviction papers and waited for him at the top of the stairs when he returned home. As he ascended the steps, he looked at her like a puppy dog about to get a spanking for making a mess.

"I'm throwing you out today," she announced and handed him the eviction papers when he reached the top step.

"You know you can't do this." Mr. Henner's face turned stern as he took the eviction notice from her. "I have thirty days to find a new place."

"I want you out now!"

"Why, because I have a girl in my apartment?"

"It's not a girl, you sick pervert. It is a blowup plastic sex toy. I won't allow that filth in my house."

"Her name is Chrissie."

"I'm ordering you to leave this property." Anger rose from deep within, increasing in its fury.

"I won't. You have no legal authority to remove me. I've paid my rent and that is that. As for Chrissie, I love her and she is staying with me."

"Listen to you. Do you even hear what you're saying? You think that blowup toy is a real woman."

"She is real to me. Sometimes providence, God, or some higher force grants you something in your life you wanted so badly. Chrissie is that something. I love her. Of course, you wouldn't know about that."

"Meaning?" Miss Rosenberg asked, knowing exactly what he meant.

"Have you ever been in love? I doubt it very seriously."

"You wouldn't know!" She fought back more rage. She didn't have to put up with this kind of treatment. She was the landlady.

"Oh, I know, all right. I've been living here for ten years. The whole time you've shut yourself up in the walls of this building while ruling over the tenants with your rent payments and your cheap rooms. Poor Calvin, you treat him worse than a dog. Always telling him to do this and fix that. If there is love in you, it dried up a long time ago."

"You think you're so great, slobbering all over that plastic slut?"

"She helps relieve the pain of loneliness!" Mr. Henner's face turned red with anger and spittle flew from his mouth. "Of course you wouldn't understand. When was the last time someone wanted to touch you? Never? You know why? Because no one wants to make it with a vicious fat cow …"

"Shut up!" Her rage exploded. She shoved all of her two hundred pounds against old man Henner's chest. His eyes widened in horror as he lost his footing on the top step and went over backwards. A strangled cry of shock became the last sound he made before his spindly body hit the steps. Bones breaking, he bounced down the wooden staircase and ended up in a heap at the bottom with his thin neck twisted at an odd angle. Dentures jutted out from his bloody mouth as his body went through its last spasms and died.

Oh, God, I've killed the poor bastard! Miss Rosenberg realized. She descended the steps toward the dead man.

A side door to the foyer opened and Calvin came out of his small living quarters. Fear and disbelief shone in his eyes at the sight of Mr. Henner, dead and broken, at the bottom of the steps.

"What … what happened?" Calvin asked as she reached the bottom of the stairs.

"Mr. Henner lost his footing on the steps, Calvin. He took a nasty fall."

"But I heard you shouting. I heard fighting," Calvin sputtered.

She grabbed him by the arm, hard. "You didn't hear anything, Calvin! You understand? "

"Yes, Miss."

She stared at the body and pondered the idea of burying him next to Gonzalez under the floor of the tool shed. One more social security check a month would help her pay the bills. She had to cancel the idea when Mr. Cranshaw came out of his room to investigate the commotion in the foyer below.

"What happened?" He called from the second floor railing.

"It's Mr. Henner." Miss Rosenberg announced. "He fell down the stairs. Call 911."

Mr. Cranshaw darted back to his room to make the call. She turned to Calvin and shoved him against a wall.

"When the police arrive, you didn't hear a thing before Mr. Henner fell, you got that Calvin?"

"Calvin didn't hear anything."

"Right and you better stick with that story," she snarled in a hissing voice. "You don't want me to tell the police what you buried underneath the tool shed, do you? They will take you away, Calvin; a poor nigger like you won't have a chance. They will lock you away forever. Do you understand?"

"Yes, Miss," Calvin responded, his voice quaking in fear.

She released him and waited for the police to arrive.

* * * *

The police, ambulance, and EMTs invaded the boarding house in a flurry of sirens and activity. Miss Rosenberg watched calmly as the emergency workers loaded the body of Mr. Henner into a black bag and then onto a stretcher before rolling him out of the foyer. Many of the other tenants, huddled in the hallway, talked about poor Mr. Henner and how dangerous those old wooden steps were to climb. She knew it wouldn't be long before they would return to their rooms and drink themselves into a stupor. Mr. Henner would be nothing more than another unfortunate who had passed away at the old boarding house like so many before him.

A handsome detective named Branson climbed up the stairs to ask Miss Rosenberg some questions. *He smells vaguely of Old Spice and Italian cooking*, Miss Rosenberg decided. He proceeded to take notes on what she knew about the death of Mr. Henner. How long has Mr. Henner been a tenant? Ten years. Did she hear or see anything when the accident happened? She was in her apartment when she heard Mr. Henner's footsteps on the stairs. He always came home from work at this time of the evening. She heard him cry out and the sound of someone falling down the stairs. She came out of her apartment and found him dead at the bottom. He must have tripped or had a heart attack. Did Mr. Henner have any next of kin? No. At least she didn't think so. Would she come down to the station to fill out some forms? Why, yes.

Miss Rosenberg spent the next two hours signing death certificates and arranging a pauper's funeral for Mr. Henner. When the detective brought her back to the boarding house, it was well after dark. Exhausted, she climbed the steps to the second floor. Removing the key to her apartment from her purse, she noticed the door to Mr. Henner's room.

When I clear out his belongings and donate them to the Salvation Army, that will be the last trace of dirty Mr. Henner, she reminded herself. *But not tonight, I'm too tired.*

She entered her home and switched on the lights. She glanced over to the listening spot on the wall.

There is one piece of business I can do tonight and it will make me sleep a lot better, she told herself. *I'll take care of the perverted sex toy next door, once and for all.*

She crossed over to the kitchen drawers, rambled about the utensils inside, and found an ice pick with a wooden handle. For a moment, she imagined stabbing the point, over and over, into the painted blue eye of the plastic sex doll.

I'll be done with you, Chrissie, and throw you out with the rest of the garbage.

Taking the pass key to Mr. Henner's room, she proceeded to his door. While putting the key in the lock, she noticed the lights were on in the apartment.

I don't remember them on when I came up the stairs, Miss Rosenberg thought. She turned the key and opened the door; the ice pick ready to stab any intruder.

A single lamp was lit on an end table. She didn't see or hear anybody in the living area. Not comfortable with shutting the door while exploring the dead man's apartment, she left it open. Entering, she surveyed the room. The place was a mess. Littered about the floor were whiskey bottles, clothing, and assorted pornographic magazines. She recognized the empty women's-clothing sacks Mr. Henner had carried up the steps the day before and remembered why she was in the apartment.

I'm going to kill a sex doll, she told herself as she gripped the ice pick. *Where are you, Chrissie?*

She turned her attention to the door to the adjoining bedroom. With heart pounding, she slowly turned the knob. Expecting to find the doll on the bed, she opened the door and clicked on the light. Chrissie wasn't there. She entered the room and looked about. The place was a pervert's haven, with naked centerfolds on the walls and a dresser top filled with dildos and other sex toys she couldn't even begin to identify. Stained and dirty sheets covered the bed which she searched under, finding more toys and magazines, but no sex doll.

You really were a sick bastard, Mr. Henner, that's why you had to die. You won't be committing any more of your perverted acts now. I just have one more thing to take care of and that's the plastic slut.

Out of the corner of her eye, a shadow passed across the doorway to the bedroom. Miss Rosenberg turned, expecting to see someone standing in the entrance, but there was no one.

Get a hold of yourself. You're letting your imagination play tricks on you.

The door she'd left open to the hallway closed with a loud bang.

Miss Rosenberg's heart jumped and she nearly dropped the ice pick.

"Is someone there?" she shouted. "Calvin, is that you?"

No answer.

She stepped back into the living room, the ice pick feeling greasy in her sweaty hands. She saw no one. Checking all the closets and every place where the sex doll could be stashed, she found no Chrissie, either. One of the other tenants could have sneaked in and stolen her for his own perverted pleasure, but she had the only pass key. *Where did Chrissie go?* She slid the ice pick into the pocket of her print dress, went out into the hallway, and locked Mr. Henner's door behind her.

At the railing overlooking the foyer, she called, "Calvin, I need to talk to you."

Calvin stepped out of his room.

"Yes, Miss?"

"Did you go into Mr. Henner's room tonight and take something from there?"

"No, Miss. It wouldn't be proper, being that Mr. Henner is not even cold and buried yet. That wouldn't be proper at all."

"All right, then. First thing in the morning I want you to come and get me. We're going to clear Mr. Henner's room out so I can get it ready to rent again. Do you understand, Calvin?"

"Yes, Miss."

"Go to bed and I'll see you in the morning."

"Yes, Miss."

Calvin disappeared into his room, leaving Miss Rosenberg alone in the hall. She sighed to herself. She had never known such fatigue as was now weighing down her body. The search for the sex doll would have to continue in the morning during daylight. Once back into her apartment, she settled with a tired groan into her recliner. She didn't even bother to turn on the TV.

No Leno tonight. I'm just too tired.

Exhausted from the day's events, Miss Rosenberg fell into a deep, troubled sleep.

* * * *

Haunting dreams.

The nightmare returned, more vivid and intense than ever before. Under a full moon, she stood outside the tool shed. Inside, Calvin dug into the dirt floor with a shovel. Thunk. Scrape. Thunk. Scrape. Thunk. Scrape. Sweating from the exertion, he dug out Gonzalez's final resting place. The nightmare shifted to her helping Calvin drag the dead body of the Mexican handyman, wrapped in a black tarp. Together, they rolled the corpse into the hole, where it landed with a sickening thud. She threw Gonzalez's sweat-stained straw hat into the makeshift grave. Calvin began covering the black plastic tarp with dirt.

The nightmare changed.

She still stood in the tool shed but something made her turn to look at one window. Chrissie's lifeless plastic face was pressed flat against the glass, her mouth forming a large O.

Miss Rosenberg screamed and ran out into the night toward the boarding house. The dream allowed her large body to move faster then it ever could in reality. She swung open the door to the entrance foyer. Mr. Henner, twisted and broken, was at the bottom of the steps leading up to her floor. She stepped over his body which began to twitch and flop like a dying fish.

"Fat cow. Fat cow," the dead Mr. Henner croaked around the dentures sticking out of his bloody mouth.

She ran up the steps, a feat she would never have been able to do in the waking world. At the top of the staircase, she looked back. Mr. Henner's body was gone, replaced by Gonzalez standing at the bottom of the stairs. With his straw hat in his hands, he began to climb the steps. Hate shone in his eyes like black pools.

Oh, God, he's coming for me! Miss Rosenberg's mind screamed in the dream.

She turned to open the door to her apartment. Gonzalez's footsteps sounded on the wooden staircase behind her. For agonizing seconds, the door wouldn't budge as each footfall grew closer. Without warning, it swung open and she fell into her living room. She rushed to shut the door on the specter of the man she suffocated with a pillow while he lay in a drunken stupor. Gonzalez had refused her sexual advances and the rejection cost him his life. A debt he continues to pay each month with his social security checks.

In the dream, she slammed shut the door and locked it. She turned only to find Gonzalez now standing in her living room. His face twisted in death just as it had when she'd removed the pillow after he stopped breathing. He lunged at her with ghostly hands.

* * * *

With a stifled scream caught in her throat, Miss Rosenberg awoke with a jolt from the nightmare. She lay in her recliner, her heart pounding in terror. Sweat dripped off her fat as she tried to catch her breath. The soft glow of an end-table lamp lit the living room. She forced herself not to look into the shadowed corner. She knew the ghost of Gonzalez would be standing there with his stained hat in his hands, if only for a few seconds. Fighting not to turn her head was like trying to ignore a grizzly car accident as you drove by. An unconscious morbid curiosity compelled her eyes to look at the horror waiting for her. Gasping for air, she turned and peered into the corner.

Chrissie stood there.

In the shadowed light, the pink plastic of the doll's fake flesh seemed to glow. The thing was an obscene vision, with pointed inflated breasts and a knife-like gash for a vagina. Blonde hair framed a plastic face with a mouth twisted into an evil grin. Lifeless, painted-blue eyes showed a look of hate and cold murder.

Oh God, save me! Miss Rosenberg's mind screamed in terror. *Close my eyes and it will go away! Just like Gonzalez. I'm still dreaming. Close my eyes and it will go away!*

She shut her eyes hard and heard the sound of her blood racing in her ears. She prayed that when she looked again the nightmare would be gone. The same morbid curiosity that had compelled her to look in the first place forced her again. She had to see if the nightmare was over.

She snapped open her eyes.

The doll was upon her. Inflated hands reached for her throat. The face of Chrissie twisted into an evil grimace as it bent down to strangle her in the chair. Miss Rosenberg tried to scream but no air came. She was vaguely aware of a pain starting in her chest and spreading out into her arms as the grip of the doll tightened around her windpipe. She remembered the ice pick in the pocket of her flower print dress. In sheer panic, her right hand fumbled for the wooden handle. The pain got worse in her chest and was accompanied with a heavy pressure. She needed to breathe but couldn't get any air. She finally grasped the pick in her hand.

The face of Chrissie, beautiful and horrific at the same time, hovered over hers while the grip of the doll's hands remained tight around her throat. The lurid mouth of twisted pink plastic bent down close to her ear.

"Gonzalez is waiting for you," Chrissie whispered.

The coronary came on in full force. Miss Rosenberg's body shook and quaked in the recliner as her heart exploded. She died with a look of total horror, her mouth wide open as dead white eyes rolled back into her head. The ice pick slid from her lifeless fingers and dropped onto the carpet on the floor.

* * * *

The next morning, Calvin found Miss Rosenberg after he'd knocked and knocked. When there was no answer, he opened the door. Miss Rosenberg was sprawled out in the recliner with her face the color of dull purple and her white eyes staring at him as if she'd anticipated his arrival. Calvin was so upset he ran up and down the hall crying like a baby. Abe Cranshaw called 911 for the second time in twenty four hours. The EMTs came and strapped Miss Rosenberg's covered body onto a gurney and huffed as they hauled her heavy corpse down the wooden steps and out of the boarding house. A detective named Branson asked Calvin a bunch of questions about Miss Rosenberg and how he'd found her. The detective told him she had died of a heart attack, no doubt from the stress of the passing of Mr. Henner. It was unusual to have two deaths in such a short time, but life happens like that sometimes.

"What is going to become of me?" Calvin asked. "Miss Rosenberg was all that I have. Without her, I don't have a place to live no more."

Detective Branson patted him on the shoulder. "I know this is rough on you, Calvin. I'll have a social worker stop in and check on you. I'll drop in from time to time, as well. Would you like that?"

"I guess so," he replied with a wide smile. Calvin liked Detective Branson. He decided the next time the detective visited he would tell him about Gonzalez buried out in the tool shed.

After all the excitement, after the police and medical technicians had left, things began to return to normal at the boarding house on Ninth and Harbor. Calvin spent the rest of the day with the other tenants talking about the recent deaths. None seemed to care about Miss Rosenberg's passing.

After dark, Calvin returned to his one-room apartment. He switched on the dim overhead light and contemplated, in his simple way, a life without Miss Rosenberg. Maybe things would be better for him now, he decided, as he slipped into bed and fell asleep. Sometime in the night, the bed moved and something slid under the covers. Turning on the bedside lamp, he recoiled in shock to see a life-sized doll that looked like a naked white woman with blonde hair lying next to him. Calvin had never seen a naked woman before, real or artificial. He looked in awe and surprise as the head of the doll turned toward him and her mouth twisted into a grotesque smile.

"I am Chrissie," she said in a whispering voice. "Love me."

THE LAST TRICK-OR-TREATER

"Would you like me to tell you a ghost story?" Mr. Morley asked.

"Sure. After all, it's Halloween. " Charlene Carson smiled and leaned forward toward the crippled man scrunched down in the wheelchair. He peered at her with a rheumy glazed look. In the dim yellow light cast by lamps in the musty living room, the old man appeared frail and twisted, his gray wispy hair quickly disappearing due to the chemo. Charlene knew from his medical charts, provided by the hospice agency that he was only fifty-eight, but the ravages of terminal cancer had aged him beyond his years. She tucked the blanket tighter over his lap. "First, are you warm enough, Mr. Morley?"

"Yes, yes," he replied as he waved her away with his hand." Do you have any children, Nurse Carson?"

"I'm not married."

"I never married either." A thin smile pushed through the loose skin of the old man's face. "You're a very pretty nurse. Not like the other broads with rough hands and a rude bedside manner to match. To them, I'm just a living corpse. Someone whose butt they have to wipe. You're different and would make a good wife."

"You're too kind, Mr. Morley." she said as she pushed a lock of blonde hair from her face. *The only men in my life now are dying ones,* she thought. *I work too many hours as a nurse to even think of a boyfriend, let alone a husband.* "Why did you ask if I had children?"

"Because Halloween is a wonderful night to be a child. When I was growing up, it was one of the biggest holidays of the year. I was raised very poor. My brothers and I looked forward to the night with great anticipation. We would trick-or-treat until our feet were raw and our bags were full. When we were done, we would go home and dump our candy out onto the bed and stay up late, eating and trading sweets." He looked down at his gnarled hands.

"Those were the good days of Halloween."

"I love the children dressing up and going door to door to get candy."

"Of all my childhood memories, Halloween is my best," Mr. Morley said.

"Really? I wouldn't have thought so. You told me to turn off the porch light so we wouldn't have any trick-or-treaters. Why didn't you ask me to buy any candy? We could have handed out treats to the children who came to the door. I figured you didn't believe in Halloween for some religious reason."

"Quite the opposite. In fact it is tonight, on Halloween, that I'm going to die."

"Mr. Morley, we both know you have terminal cancer but the doctor says you have another six months. You're going to live to see Christmas and Valentine's Day."

Mr. Morley shook his head. "Tonight I'll die and you'll be here to witness."

"I've been at the bedside of dozens of terminal patients. I can tell you only God chooses when you die." Charlene stood from the couch and adjusted the old man's pillow behind his head. "If you want me to assist with your suicide, I won't do it."

One of his gnarled hands grasped her by the wrist as he looked up to her. "Do you believe in life after death?"

Charlene paused for a moment. Death was part of her job. She thought of the patients who had expired with her by their bedside, the shriveled husks of old men and women taking their last breaths, some surrounded by family members, some alone and holding her hand. She liked to believe they went to a better place after death, but she really wasn't sure. "I have faith in the idea there is a place we go after we die," she answered.

"Your faith is not misplaced, for there is life after death." Mr. Morley released her wrist. "Oh, don't get me wrong; it's not like your Sunday school fairytales where an omnipotent white-haired old man sits upon a throne in the sky above a city with streets of gold. The spirit passes into a lifeless gray realm that is a shadow of our own world. Here, the souls of the departed shuffle aimlessly until passing through the envelope to the next world."

"It sounds very bleak."

"It is what it is. Sometimes a given spirit still has ties to this world because of the unfair or violent nature of its passing. These souls cross over into our realm from time to time."

"Ghosts," Charlene said.

"Precisely. Which brings me to my ghost story." Mr. Morley leaned back in the chair and crossed his hands in his lap. "The story of Scabby Bobby."

"Scabby Bobby? Why on Earth would anyone have a name like that?"

"On the mantle you will find a photo album. Please, bring it to me.

She checked her watch. Just after seven in the evening; three more boring hours to go until she finished her shift and went home to a lonely five-room apartment. At least if she kept Mr. Morley talking the time might pass more quickly. Charlene stood and crossed the living room carpet. Waiting on the mantle of the unused stone fireplace sat a leather-bound photo album. She picked it up and prepared to return to Mr. Morley's side when she heard the laughter of children from somewhere outside the house. Sliding aside the edge of a curtain, she glanced out a picture window to the street. Beneath the streetlight on the corner, a group of trick-or-treaters passed along the sidewalk in a parade of goblins, witches, and other Halloween costumes. They walked on down the dark street without paying any attention to Mr. Morley's old house.

"What did you see out the window?" Mr. Morley asked as she handed him the photo album.

"Children trick-or-treating," Charlene said as she settled back onto the couch. "None came to the door."

"Eventually, one will." Mr. Morley opened the leather cover of the album. "But, I'm getting ahead of myself." One of his yellowed fingernails tapped a black-and-white photograph on the album page. "That's us in 1960. The Rowdy Rangers were what we called ourselves then, just a rag-tag bunch of boys growing up on the poor side of town. We spent our days playing sandlot baseball, riding bikes, and getting into mischief." He slid the album over for her to get a better look at the photograph. In the faded black-and-white picture she saw four boys, about thirteen years old, standing together wearing T-shirts and ball caps, and holding baseball bats. A fifth overweight boy, who reminded Charlene of a fat Beaver Cleaver, stood apart from the motley group.

Mr. Morley tapped each boy's face in the photo with a fingernail. "That's Alex, Paul, Tanner, and me."

"Who's the heavyset kid?" Charlene asked.

"Bobby Riser," he said and let out a long breath, "or Scabby Bobby as we so cruelly named him. Back then, childhood obesity wasn't so common or accepted as it is today. Poor Bobby took the brunt of all our teasing and name calling. He was a disgusting kid, too. He would pick and eat his scabs and, thus, he earned the nickname. He always smelled like sour milk, spoke with a speech impediment, and could not say words ending with a T without severe stuttering. He wanted so badly to be a part of the Rowdy Rangers, but we never let him join. We only tolerated his presence so we could push him around and call him names. We made him do terrible things, too. One biology class, Tanner told him to eat some dead flies lying on the window sill and he did, right in front of the class. I guess he just wanted desperately to fit in and be a part of us."

"Children can be so heartless." Charlene slid the photos back to Mr. Morley.

"I'm not proud of our actions back then," he said and closed the album. He placed his wrinkled hands on top of the cover and gazed back at her. "Three years after that picture, we were sixteen years old and still called the Rowdy Rangers. Our activities had matured as well. Now, we were committing acts of juvenile delinquency such as breaking windows, picking fights, shoplifting cigarettes, etc. It was Halloween night in 1963, and we were going up and down the neighborhood, scaring little kids and egging houses. Finally, it got so late that all the kids were in bed. That's when we ran across Scabby Bobby out trick-or-treating. He came down the sidewalk, dressed in a stupid hobo costume, and carrying a bag full of candy."

"What happened?"

"It was like hitting a gold mine for us Rowdy Rangers when we found Scabby Bobby in a lame hobo mask and too old to be trick-or-treating. We laughed and pushed him around, calling him all kinds of terrible names, until he cried and pleaded for us to leave him alone. Tanner then grabbed his bag of candy and we took off running across a road. Bawling like a baby, Bobby followed, and because of the puny eyeholes in that stupid hobo mask, he couldn't see the truck. I remember hearing the squeal of brakes and looking back as his body flew up onto the hood and then back onto the pavement with a sick thud. I can still see Bobby, lying on the pavement with his head turned sideways and his mask halfway off his shattered face, a pool of red blood spreading outward from his body. We ran off into the night and sat and ate Bobby's candy together in a railroad yard."

"That's awful, Mr. Morley."

"The next morning at school, we heard the news that Bobby Riser was dead. We didn't think twice about it. We never felt bad about Bobby and soon forgot all about him. Our lives continued and eventually the Rowdy Rangers grew up and broke apart. Tanner died in 'Nam in '68. The rest of us former Rangers remained here in this town. One Halloween night I got a call from Alex. He was frantic and screaming over the phone saying Scabby Bobby was standing on his front porch. I thought he was drunk or crazy and hung up. I wanted to forget our past. The next day I read in the paper Alex died of a heart attack. The following Halloween, Paul falls down a flight of stairs and breaks his neck. The police report said he was running from someone in a hobo costume. I knew it was Scabby Bobby and I was going to be next."

"This can't be a true story," Charlene said.

"You said you wanted to hear a ghost story. Here it is," Mr. Morley said, and added, "the next Halloween I waited for Scabby Bobby in the living room of my house. I knew what I had to do. The doorbell rang and there he was in his hobo outfit, his torn mask hanging from his dead face. I handed him a bag of trick-or-treat candy and he disappeared. Bobby had come back from the spirit world to get his stolen candy. That's how I know there is life after death." Mr. Morley's rheumy eyes looked toward the foyer and the front door of the house. "It's been the same every Halloween since. Scabby Bobby comes to the door, I give him his bag of candy and he goes away."

"This is a gag, right? You're setting me up for a joke or something," Charlene looked around the living room. "I don't see any bag of candy to give Scabby Bobby when he shows up."

"I told you on this night I was going to die," Mr. Morley replied. "Tonight it ends."

"You're scaring me, Mr. Morley. I know it's Halloween, but that gives you no right to frighten me. I don't think it's funny."

"An old debt must be paid." Mr. Morley shrugged. "You'll see firsthand evidence of life after death tonight."

"Mr. Morley, I must thank you for creeping me out this—"

The doorbell rang. Charlene gasped in shock.

"It's time," Mr. Morley said. "Go see who is at the door."

She stood as the doorbell chimed again. Entering the foyer, Charlene did not turn on any lights but placed her eye against the peephole in the front door to see who was on the porch. In the absence of a porch light, she could only make out the shape of a short, stocky person wearing a clown or hobo mask; she could not be sure. The doorbell rang again.

This is ridiculous, Charlene told herself. *Get a grip on yourself. It's just some kid out trick-or-treating. After all, it's Halloween, for God's sake.*

The doorbell rang once more.

"It's Scabby Bobby," Mr. Morley's voice called out from the front room. "Let him in."

Charlene unlocked the door but left the chain latched. She opened it the one-inch space the chain allowed. In the dim light of the foyer, a hobo mask filled the gap of the open door; a painted rubber eye with a pencil-sized hole where the pupil should be, stared back at her.

"Trick or treat-t-t-t. Smell my feet-t-t-t. Give me something good to eat-t-t-t," a distorted childlike voice spoke from inside the mask. For a second, Charlene thought she smelled something sour or rotten wafting out from the figure.

"I'm sorry, kid," Charlene said. "We're not celebrating Halloween. Try another house if you want candy."

"Trick or treat-t-t-t. Smell my feet-t-t-t. Give me something good to eat-t-t-t."

Charlene shut the door and locked it.

The doorbell rang again. Twice. Three times and then silence. Pressing her ear against the door, she heard the sounds of slow shuffling feet stepping down the steps from the front porch. Letting out a long sigh, she returned to the living room.

"He's gone, Mr. Morley," she said.

"No," the old man shook his head. "He won't stop until he gets his candy or me."

Charlene sat back on the couch. "I have to say this is a great Halloween trick. First you tell me this ghost story about Scabby Bobby and then you have someone come to the door dressed in a hobo costume to scare me. Who was it? A nephew or the child of someone you knew? Of all the tricks to pull on someone tonight, this has to be one of the best. Am I on television? Is there a hidden camera somewhere?"

"It's no trick." Mr. Morley's eyes looked at her with sadness. "I wish it was, but it's not."

A shadow appeared against the shade hanging in a living room window. The silhouette reminded her of Emmett Kelley, the famous hobo clown from the Barnum and Bailey circus of the fifties. A light tapping shook the glass.

"Trick or treat-t-t-t. Smell my feet-t-t-t. Give me something good to eat-t-t-t."

"Screw this, I'm calling 911!" Charlene said, fishing her cell phone out of her purse. She dialed the number. It rang three times.

"Emergency operator," a woman's voice buzzed in her ear. "What is the nature of your emergency?"

"I'm at a house on 1312 Rockton Street and we have a prowler outside trying to get in. I'm the caregiver of a terminally ill patient who is being terrorized by whoever it is. Can you send someone to check it out?"

"You're aware this is Halloween night? Are you sure it is not some kids out trick-or-treating?

"He is pounding on a window right now!" Charlene held the phone up so the operator could hear. The tapping at the window had grown to a hard rattling knock threatening to break out the glass.

"Trick or treat-t-t-t. Smell my feet-t-t-t. Give me something good to eat-t-t-t."

Charlene returned the phone to her ear. "Does that sound like little kids to you?"

"I'm sending a squad car over to your address. Keep all your doors and windows locked and don't let anyone in the house until they get there."

Charlene hung up the phone. The rattling against the glass grew louder.

"Trick or treat-t-t-t. Smell my feet-t-t-t. Give me something good to eat-t-t-t."

Putting her hands over her ears, she shouted, "Go away!"

The silhouette stepped away from the window. Silence followed.

She knelt beside Mr. Morley in his wheelchair, still clinging to the photo album in his lap.

"Bobby's not going to stop," he said.

"Police are on their way." She squeezed his shoulder. "You said he would leave if he got candy. Is there any in the house? Something we can give Bobby to make him go away?"

"I might have a bag of old candy left over from last year in a cabinet in the kitchen." His aged hand reached out and touched hers and unrelenting terror shone in his tired eyes. "Charlene, I've changed my mind. I don't want to die now. Not like this."

"You're under my care and I won't let anything happen to you."

She crossed the dark dining room and into the kitchen where a lone light bulb lit the faded linoleum floor and the dingy yellowed curtains. Charlene swung open cabinet doors, knocking aside dishes and cups as she searched for the bag of candy. Her heart pounded as she pulled out drawers, spilling their contents onto the floor. A movement beyond the drawn curtains of the dark kitchen window caught her eye. Someone or something shambled through the bushes outside the house.

Where is it? Her mind screamed. *Where is the bag of candy?*

She flung open a drawer and threw aside cooking utensils. Her heart jumped at the sight of a plastic bag of Halloween candy corn sitting in the bottom of the drawer. She snatched up the bag and the contents spilled out all over the linoleum of the floor. Cursing, she checked the bag and found mice had eaten through the plastic. She threw aside the empty bag, fell to her knees, and scooped up the orange candy.

In another room, a door creaked open.

"Tell me, Mr. Morley, is the back door locked?" She yelled.

"I'm not sure. I don't think so."

With shaking hands, Charlene reached into an open drawer and lifted out a large butcher knife. A floorboard creaked as a shadow of someone walking in the adjoining dining room passed across the kitchen walls. The sliding scrape of dragging footsteps across a wooden floor resounded in the next room. Someone had entered the house! The smell of something sour and stale wafted in the air.

Where are the police? They should be here by now.

"Charlene!" Mr. Morley screamed from the front room, "Scabby Bobby's here!"

Butcher knife clutched in her hand, she charged across the dining room to the door of the living room. At the entrance, she froze. A dark form occupied the center of the room. Scabby Bobby stood a little over five feet in height and wore a shabby jacket on top of a muddied clown suit. His round stomach gave his overweight body a pear shape. A cheap rubber hobo mask covered his head. The combination made him look both comical and gruesome. He ambled slowly toward Mr. Morley, his head moving from side to side as if it wasn't connected to his neck.

"Trick or treat-t-t-t. Smell my feet-t-t-t. Give me something good to eat-t-t-t."

"Bobby, I'm sorry," Mr. Morley cried out to the misshapen form. "I can't imagine how much anger and hate it took to bring you back from death. I ask forgiveness for the way we treated you. We were young and stupid."

"Trick or treat-t-t-t. Smell my feet-t-t-t. Give me something good to eat-t-t-t."

"Hey!" Charlene shouted and threw some pieces of candy corn against the back of the figure. Slowly, Scabby Bobby turned around to face her. His head hung to one side on top of an obviously broken neck. The torn rubber hobo mask only covered half of the boy's face; on the other, bones showed through gray, rotting flesh. Broken teeth in a slack mouth formed a grimace of hate.

"Trick or treat-t-t-t. Smell my feet-t-t-t. Give me something good to eat-t-t-t."

"Mr. Morley, get out of here!"

Old man Morley turned in his wheelchair and rolled toward the front door as fast as his diminished strength would allow.

Scabby Bobby shambled toward her.

"Trick or treat-t-t-t. Smell my feet-t-t-t. Give me something good to eat-t-t-t." His horrid mouth worked the words as the stench of something sour hung in the room.

"You want something sweet?" Charlene shouted. "Here it is."

She threw more candy corn pieces onto the floor as she heard the front door slam shut. *Mr. Morley has made it outside,* she told herself. *At least he's safe.* In horror and fascination, she watched as Scabby Bobby knelt slowly to the floor and picked up a piece of candy corn with decayed fingers. Slowly, he put the candy in his mouth and chewed it with his broken teeth.

"Sweet-t-t-t."

The next second, the lights of a police cruiser lit up the window shades of the living room. Charlene turned and ran out of the back door of the house and into the flashing lights painting the patio in alternating shades of red and blue.

"Drop the knife now!" A strong voice shouted as a bright light hit her face.

"Help!" She let the butcher knife fall out of her hand and onto the patio stones. "Someone broke into the house!"

The light left her eyes and a police officer stepped up to her. A black pistol filled his hands. "Are you hurt or wounded?"

"No." Charlene shook her head. "Check on Mr. Morley. He's in a wheelchair and escaped out the front door. I'm his nurse."

"Who's inside?"

"Someone in a hobo outfit. He came in the back door and was in the living room when I left him!"

"You stay out here," the police officer said and turned to his partner. "Frank, you go around front and I'll take the back."

Tears formed in her eyes as the two officers entered the house, awash in the glow of the blinking red-and-blue lights. The night air carried a cold crispness of late October and she wrapped her arms around herself to keep warm. She watched the windows of the home as the officers searched through the interior turning on the lights in the process. There were no gunshots or shouting, just an eerie silence filled with the flashing of the squad car lights and the crackling of the police radio. She sensed people watching and turned to look at the street. Groups of children and adults stared at the police car and the house, the shifting lights flashing across the various costumes they wore.

"Miss," the young police officer said from the back door of the house. She turned her attention away from the onlookers. "What is your name?"

"Charlene Carson."

"I'm Officer Daniels. Will you follow me please, Mrs. Carson."

"It's Miss Carson," she corrected as she stepped forward and his hand guided her back in the house. "Is Mr. Morley all right?"

"You were his nurse?"

"I'm his hospice nurse. Mr. Morley has terminal cancer." Her eyes darted around the rooms of the house now lit by the interior lights. "Did you find the intruder?"

"We found no one."

"But he was right here." She stood in the middle of the living room floor covered with the scattered pieces of candy corn.

"There is no sign of any intruder. We searched the whole house."

"Mr. Morley can verify my story."

"When you fled out the back door, where was Mr. Morley?" Officer Daniels looked at her inquisitively with his dark brown eyes.

"He went out the front door with his wheelchair," she said and glanced through the foyer at the open front door. Flashlight beams shone through the space and men's voices were talking outside on the porch.

"Was he aware there was no ramp for the wheelchair?"

"He just became crippled in the last six weeks as his health deteriorated. He didn't have enough money to put in a ramp for the chair." She began walking toward the front door. "What happened?"

Officer Daniels put a hand on her shoulder. "I don't think you want go out there."

She pulled away from his hold and ran toward the door. "Mr. Morley!"

The scene waiting for her outside caught her breath so hard she couldn't even scream. The wheelchair lay on its side on the porch, one wheel badly bent. Like a broken mannequin, Mr. Morley lay sprawled at the bottom of the porch steps. The beams of a police flashlight highlighted his face twisted unnaturally over his back due to a broken neck. His mouth hung open and his white eyes stared up at her.

She found her scream then.

* * * *

Charlene sat on the couch drinking hot coffee from a police thermos while Mr. Morley's body was loaded into a waiting ambulance. Officer Daniels sat with her and quietly asked her questions. She liked his brown eyes and the way he tended to her needs.

"Do you believe me that some big kid broke into the house?" Charlene asked as she sipped the steaming cup.

"We found foot prints around the yard along with trampled bushes," he said. "Mud was tracked in from outside. Someone was here."

"Who do you think it was?" Charlene didn't tell the police the story of Scabby Bobby. She knew they would never believe her. She barely believed it herself.

"Who knows?" Officer Daniels shrugged. "Some retarded kid or some crackhead in a clown mask. There's a full moon tonight and it's Halloween."

"Halloween," she repeated softly.

"Whoever broke into the house, they are long gone now. We canvassed the neighborhood and found no one walking around dressed as a hobo."

"Am I free to go?" She handed him the empty cup.

"If I have any more questions I can call you tomorrow," he said and smiled. "Or maybe I can call you even if I don't have questions."

"I'd like that."

"Are you good enough to drive home or do you want a black-and-white to take you?"

"I'll be all right." She picked up her purse.

"It was nice meeting you, Charlene."

"And you, Officer Daniels."

"Call me Mark."

Charlene walked out of the late Mr. Morley's house and into the crisp October night air. The world no longer seemed real to her after the events of the evening. Her Saturn was parked under the streetlight. Climbing behind the wheel, she took one last look at poor Mr. Morley's run-down old house before pulling away.

Tonight, Mr. Morley's debt was paid in full.

She drove through the dark middle-class neighborhoods leading back to her lonely little apartment as her mind began to rationalize the things she'd experienced. *Officer Daniels could be right. Maybe it wasn't Scabby Bobby after all. Just some handicapped kid breaking into the house for candy. Mr. Morley's story made me believe the intruder was Scabby Bobby. I know it seems like an incredible coincidence, but it makes more sense than believing an avenging ghost came back from the grave.*

Turning a corner, her headlights caught the dark figure of someone walking across the street. She slowed and cruised past the person now on the sidewalk. It was a kid trick-or-treating. Dressed in a hobo outfit and mask, he waddled down the street under the halogen lights. In one hand, he held a bag heavy with candy. Charlene glanced down at the digital clock in the car's dash: 10:36. *Way too late to be out going door to door,* she thought to herself. *This has to be the last kid out tonight.*

Looking in her rear view mirror, she imagined this must be the way Bobby Riser looked before the Rowdy Rangers stole his candy and he died by being hit by a truck. The way he looked on a forgotten Halloween night in 1963.

"You will see firsthand evidence of life after death tonight." The words of Mr. Morley echoed in her mind.

She had to find out the truth. Pulling the car over to the curb, she parked and got out. A dark sidewalk covered with dead leaves stretched before her. Ahead in the shadows, she heard the footsteps of the kid walking briskly away. She followed with her heart pounding in both fear and excitement. *To know the truth of life after death,* she told herself. *To know as I sit by each patient in the last moments of his or her lives, it will not end there. There is a place beyond death.*

She quickened her pace and began to overtake the slower moving figure. A few feet ahead, the back of the ridiculous hobo mask bobbed before her.

"Bobby," she called out to him.

"Go away," he pleaded. "Don't-t-t hurt-t-t me!"

"I'm not going to hurt you," she said. "I just want to talk to you."

So close she could almost reach out and grab him. She wanted to turn him around and see if he was a ghost or just another kid out late on Halloween night.

So close to the truth.

"Don't-t-t!" he cried out and took off running and bolted into the street.

"Bobby, wait!" she shouted and saw headlights of the approaching truck barreling down the street.

The screeching of brakes echoed across the neighborhood as the pickup truck slid to a stop. Charlene ran out to the front of the truck as the driver jumped out of the cab.

"Jesus!" he said. "The kid came out of nowhere. I didn't see him. What was he doing out in the street?"

Charlene knelt down in the bright glow of the headlights expecting to see Bobby sprawled out on the street, but he was not there. The only thing lying in the road was a bag of Halloween candy scattered across the pavement. Scabby Bobby was gone.

"Where's the kid?" the driver asked as he bent down and looked under his truck. "Where's the kid in the hobo mask that ran in front of my truck? I swore I hit him!"

"There's no kid here," Charlene said.

The man ran his hands through his thick hair in relief. "Oh, thank God. I thought I ran over some poor trick-or-treater. I swear I saw this kid in a hobo mask run in front of my truck. What the hell just happened?"

"You know what night this is?"

"Halloween," the man said climbing back into his truck. "I guess that explains it. Strange things happen on this night."

The truck pulled away leaving her standing alone. She stared down at the candy scattered across the pavement. A light breeze began to stir the dead leaves and several rolled across her feet, as overhead, a full moon peeked around the clouds. Somewhere an owl hooted. She stood silently in the street where a boy had died, not on this night, but on a forgotten night many years before she was born. Tears came to her eyes, for now she knew the truth of death.

"Halloween," Charlene repeated to herself before she walked back to her car.

ATROCITY

Robert Tessman's bladder threatened to stain his pants when he saw the waitress working the counter at the Great Plains Twenty-Four Hour Truck Stop outside of Tulsa, Oklahoma. He could have sworn he'd raped and murdered her forty years ago in Vietnam.

The pretty Asian girl paid no attention to him as she wiped spilled coffee off the other end of the countertop. Tessman returned his gaze back to his coffee cup. *God, is it her? Kim-ly!!! How could it be? I watched her body burn to a blackened husk. There's no way she could still be alive. She would be near sixty today. This girl looks to be barely twenty. She's too young to have been alive during 'Nam. Get a hold of yourself.*

He risked a sideways glance at the waitress. Slowly wiping her way down the counter toward him, she maneuvered around the truckers chatting it up at one thirty in the morning. Her dark eyes met his for a brief second. Tessman jerked his gaze back to his coffee cup.

My God! She has the same face, the same haunting eyes.

He shook his head. *No way, man. It couldn't be. This waitress just reminds you of her. All of them fucking gooks look alike, anyway.*

For a second, his mind flashed back forty years to memories he had long suppressed since returning to the States. He saw himself, younger and skinnier, riding in the back of a bouncing Army jeep with his M16 propped between his legs. A green private, his orders were to assist on some intelligence-gathering mission with Carter and Corporal Morrison, who rode in the front. The Army jeep wheeled into a small collection of huts in a muddy shit-hole corner of the northern part of South Vietnam. Carter, a civilian CIA spook, was into all kinds of covert bullshit and Morrison was his lapdog and did all his dirty work. The year was 1968, right after the Tet Offensive.

* * * *

"What's the name of the village?" he had asked.

"Dum Fuk, for all I know, Private," Carter replied after lighting up another cigarette. "Someone's been using a ham radio to give Charlie information about our troop movements in the area. We're going to find the radio and the gooks responsible."

Corporal Morrison drove the jeep and cut a donut in the mud in front of the circle of huts as squawking chickens scattered before its wheels. As if they took their cue from the poultry, the villagers fled in fear into their huts of bamboo and thatch; except for one. She stood, young and proud, in the door to her simple home and watched their arrival with dark, unemotional eyes. For her, occupying soldiers come and go like the seasons. Beneath the conical bamboo hat tied to her chin, long, black hair fell to her waist. She was near his age and the most beautiful girl he had seen since arriving in 'Nam.

He hated what he did to her.

* * * *

"More coffee?"

Tessman looked up as his recollection faded to be replaced by the stark fluorescent of the crowded truck stop. The girl was standing across the counter from him, looking evenly into his eyes with her dark gaze.

"Huh?" he asked with a wavering voice.

"You want more coffee?"

"No."

"You no want coffee, Private Tessman?" she said in a broken English accent.

"What did you—" His words stopped in mid-question. The girl's eyes became pools of blackness with no white showing around the pupils. Her mouth opened and the stench of gasoline and burning flesh poured out of her in a sickening cloud.

"No! No!" Tessman pushed himself away from the counter.

"Tessman, no want coffee?" she asked again.

Staggering on weak legs, he rushed toward the door of the restaurant. Several customers stared in confusion as he passed by their booths. Behind him, the girl shouted, "Come back, Private Tessman. You no pay! Come back!" It was a voice from the grave.

Exiting the restaurant doors, he ran out into the rainy Oklahoma night air. The sickening-sweet smell of cooked human flesh still tingled his nostrils, causing his stomach to retch. He walked a few more steps before vomiting all over his cowboy boots. Wiping his mouth across the sleeve of his jean jacket, he glanced back through the greasy front glass of the diner. The girl stood at the window holding a coffee pot and staring at him with eyes of inky black. Her mouth worked silently; though he could not hear her words, he could read what her lips said.

"Come back. You no pay."

Threatening to be sick again, he fled across the rain-drenched parking lot until he reached his Peterbilt. Climbing up into the cab of the eighteen-wheeler, he slammed the door shut. In the dark interior, he sat and attempted to calm his panicked breathing.

His hands trembled as he put the key in the ignition and started up the diesel engine. Smoke billowed out of the dual pipes as he slammed the truck into gear and pulled the rig and trailer out of the parking space. He drove past the front of the diner, but didn't look through the lighted windows. The girl might still be standing there, watching him with lifeless eyes. Instead, he wheeled the truck out onto the two-lane blacktop and left the neon lights of the stop behind in his side mirrors.

Under a night sky full of rain-laden clouds, Highway 11 stretched before the headlights of his rig like the wet skin of a giant black snake. Carrying a load of oilfield equipment bound for a well site in the Texas panhandle, he still had several hours of driving before he could call it a night. Carrying an overweight load and behind on his log books, he had decided to take the two-lane instead of the Interstate to avoid any scales and the Oklahoma Highway patrol. Traffic on the highway was very sparse this time of night and soon he had only the throb of the engine and the rain-swept highway as company.

Once the horror at the diner was far behind him, he began to rationalize the event. Exhaustion and road fatigue had caused him to mistake the waitress for Kim-ly. The words the girl said to him and the smell of the burning flesh were just part of his imagination, sparked from a lack of sleep. *You've been driving too long. She wasn't the same girl you killed over in 'Nam. The fucking dead don't pop up in diners in Oklahoma and serve you coffee.*

"Come back, Tessman. You no pay." Her words echoed in his mind.

Fighting back a shiver, he switched on the radio. The low music of a classic rock station out of Wichita filled the truck cab. He eased back into his seat and let the beat of the music calm his mind. Soon, the events back at the diner began to seem distant and unreal. Before him was the grinding solitude of the road that would eventually carry him into Texas. He centered his attention on the endless yellow line running before his wheels. A slow drizzle of rain washed against his windshield as distant lightning flashed sporadically in the darkness beyond his headlights. The steady click-clack of the wipers drew his mind hypnotically into the past and back to the sixties and a fucking place called 'Nam.

Memories long buried returned to the surface. Images of naked gook children standing outside their burned out homes begging for candy bars or cigarettes, medics slipping pieces of a combat buddy into a body bag, the roar of a helicopter and the stink of napalm, a friend with both his legs blown off by a mine, or ... the day he raped and murdered the girl.

* * * *

At gunpoint, they assembled the entire village, forcing the men, women, and children to kneel in the mud. He went with Corporal Morrison inside each home in a search for the ham radio and weapons. Inside the main hut, they found what they were looking for hidden under a floor mat—a radio unit along with maps of the area marked with troop movements. They carried both out of the hut and dropped them in the mud at the CIA spook's feet.

"You see this is what really fuckin' pisses me off! Someone here has been spying for Charlie." Carter shouted at the assembled villagers. He repeated the statement in Vietnamese. The people cringed in fear and kept their heads bowed. Carter drew his .45 automatic from his hip holster and fired three rounds into the radio unit. The sudden shots caused birds to scatter in the nearby jungle and the people of the village to cry and shudder. Grabbing up the maps, he turned to the assembled villagers.

"I want to know who has been using the radio and helping the fucking Commies! If someone doesn't tell me, I'll have my men begin shooting you people randomly. Now tell me who the fuck it is!" He shouted over their heads and repeated it again in their language.

The girl, kneeling beside her elderly parents, rose to stand like a lone willow tree amidst the gathered group of villagers.

"Private, go bring that Commie bitch to me," Carter ordered.

He went and grabbed the girl by the arm. She went willingly, with no emotion upon her face, to stand before the Company man.

"You live in this hootch?" Carter pointed to the hut where they'd found the radio.

"Yes," the girl replied.

"You understand English?"

"I went to Saigon University. I speak some English."

"What is your name?"

"Kim-ly."

"Seven Americans were killed in an ambush near here because someone gave their location to the VC. Was that you?"

The girl nodded her head.

"What we got here is a gook bitch who aids the enemy," Carter said. "Corporal, hold her for me."

"My pleasure," Morrison replied. He grabbed the Vietnamese girl and locked her arms behind her back.

Carter stuck the barrel of the .45 under her chin. "Seven Americans are dead because you helped Charlie. You're going to pay for that."

Kim-ly spat into his face and cursed in her language.

Carter wiped off the spit. "Corporal, you hold her while I give these people some education. They need to learn not to fuck with me. Private, go bring her Mama-san and Papa-san to me."

"What are you going to do to them?" Tessman remembered asking.

"Just follow your orders, soldier," Morrison barked.

"Yes, sir."

He crossed to where the girl's parents were kneeling together in fear. He helped them both to their shaky feet and forced them to walk the distance to stand before the CIA man. Both kept their heads bowed as their bodies quaked in terror.

Carter's eyes had a psychotic glaze as he asked, "Tell me, Private Tessman, have you killed anyone yet since being in 'Nam?"

He shook his head no.

"What do you know, Corporal? We got us a cherry here."

"It's time to get your cherry popped," Corporal Morrison said while holding Kim-ly.

"Killing is easy, Private," Carter said. "Let me demonstrate."

Carter turned with the .45, pulled the trigger, and shot the elderly woman between the eyes. Her head snapped back from the impact of the bullet. Blood and brains blew out the back of her skull and splashed across the thatch wall of the hut. Lifeless, her body slumped into the mud at their feet. Kim-ly screamed out in shock at the death of her mother.

"See. Nothing to it." Carter flashed a crazed smile. "It's your turn, Private. You get to do the old man."

Carter handed him the automatic pistol. The gun felt warm and sweaty in his grip. Guiding his hand, Carter placed the pistol barrel to the side of the old Asian man's trembling head. The man cried tears as he looked down at the body of the woman at his feet.

"Just pull the trigger, Private," Carter whispered in his ear. "Prove you're a man."

He did as he was told. The gun bucked in his hand as the old man's head yanked back and blood flew in a spray. His body slumped across the corpse of the woman in the mud. Feeling both exhilarated and sick to his stomach, he handed the pistol back to Carter and turned to look at Kim-ly. Her eyes were filled with hate and anger.

"Now you're a bad ass, son." Carter clasped him across the shoulder.

* * * *

Tessman sighed to himself and stopped his recollection of that day forty years ago. He turned up the radio to hear the Stones playing "Sympathy for the Devil" in time to the beat of the windshield wipers. A headache throbbed between his eyes, caused by too much stress and long driving. He found a bottle of aspirin and shook out a couple of pills and grabbed a Styrofoam cup with cold coffee in it from the dash to wash them down. The rainstorm had increased in its intensity and he hadn't seen a headlight for several miles.

The song ended and the radio crackled, "From Saigon, this is the American Force Vietnam Network bringing you music for the Aquarian age."

Tessman nearly choked on the cold coffee. He hadn't heard those station call letters since he was in 'Nam. He turned up the radio. It started playing a Jimmy Hendrix tune but he was certain he heard the announcement of the station out of Saigon. He tuned to other channels and everyone was playing the same song. It wasn't possible. In dismay he shut the radio off.

Some weird Twilight Zone bullshit is happening!

His heart pounded in fear as he continued down the highway. He fought to keep the memories out of his head but they returned in spite of his efforts. Too many inexplicable events had happened tonight to remind him of that horrific day. The nightmare he'd fought so hard to forget had come home. The terrible things he'd done had returned to haunt him.

* * * *

"What are we going to do with the gook girl?" Morrison had asked.

"It's time to get a little boom-boom action, Corporal. She spreads her legs for Charlie, let's see if she does it for Uncle Sam."

"Oooo-eeeee!" Morrison shouted and dragged the struggling girl into the hut. Kim-ly screamed and fought against the larger man as he threw her down on a straw mat, tore open her blouse and yanked down her pantaloons. From the door of the hootch, Tessman watched long enough to see Morrison drop his fatigue pants and mount atop the girl. In disgust, he

turned away.

"What's the matter, soldier? Don't feel sorry for her. Just remember that seven of our boys are dead because she spied for the enemy. She doesn't deserve your pity."

The sounds of Kim-ly's screaming and Morrison's grunting grew louder from inside the hut.

"Have you ever been with a woman, son?" Carter asked as he lit a cigarette and handed it to him.

"I've got a girlfriend back in Oklahoma, but we never went that far." He took a long, nervous drag on the cigarette.

"It looks like you're going to get your cherry popped twice today."

"I couldn't," he said, shaking his head. "Not like that."

"A little word of advice—" Carter swatted a mosquito against his neck. "You're in a war, soldier. It ain't fucking pretty. Bad shit happens. You'll be lucky if you live through tomorrow. I've seen many a boy, just like you, who went home in a body bag the next day. I don't think I would want to die out here without ever knowing what getting a piece of pussy feels like."

Corporal Morrison, red-faced and sweating, stepped out of the door of the hut.

"Who's next?" Morrison asked while zipping up the front of his fatigues.

"Go on, soldier. We'll wait for you." Carter nodded toward the open door.

He remembered entering the hut. The heat was as thick as a blanket inside. He walked up to Kim-ly stretched out on the mat. Her torn clothes revealed her nakedness. Lust took over as he looked down upon her pert breasts and her spread legs. Carter was right. He didn't want to be blown apart in 'Nam and sent home a virgin in a body bag.

She stared straight up at the thatch ceiling without emotion as he dropped his pants and lowered himself upon her exposed body. Her dark eyes met his as he pushed himself inside her flesh. The intercourse was short and his orgasm came quickly. During the rape, his dog tags had come free from his shirt. As he stood up, she grabbed and ripped them from his neck.

"Private Tessman," she read his name from the metal tag. In the dim light within the sweltering hut she sat straight up. He watched in horror as her face turned ghostly pale and her eyes transformed to solid black pools showing no whites. In terror, he backed away as his spine turned to ice.

"One day you pay, Private Tessman. One day you pay," she said in an inhuman hoarse voice.

Shocked, he rushed out of the hootch and back into the sunlight.

"How long?" Carter asked the Corporal.

"Fifty-four seconds," Morrison said staring at his wristwatch.

"Just like a grunt, always ready to shoot off his gun," Carter said with a laugh.

He turned to them and said in a shaky voice, "She changed ... her eyes became black ... her voice horrible."

"What the fuck are you blabbering about, Private?" Corporal Morrison asked.

"Kim-ly ... she's something ... something not human."

"That must have been a great piece of ass. This boy is hallucinating."

They both laughed aloud.

"She's like a specter or something," he remembered saying while his trembling hands zipped up his fatigues.

Carter nodded. "She's going to be a ghost, for sure, soldier."

"What do you mean?" he asked as he watched Corporal Morrison remove a metal gas can from the back of the jeep.

"We're going to cook this gook bitch," Carter said as he lit another cigarette with his Zippo lighter.

* * * *

Tessman returned his thoughts to the present. Cold sweat dripped down his forehead as he fought back the images of that day. He looked down to turn the radio back on to see if the ghostly music from a war long past was still playing. Adjusting the volume, he heard an announcer talking about the weather in Vietnam.

No! It can't be! It's not possible!

In anger he shut the radio back off and looked up at his driving. Something caught his eye and he slammed on the brakes. The huge rig lurched as eighteen wheels tried to grab hold of wet asphalt. Crossing the middle line, he saved the truck from jack-knifing by whipping the wheel to the right and straightening out the trailer. The vehicle came to a stop in the middle of the highway.

What did I just see? His heart thundered as he looked back through his side mirrors where a highway sign glowed in the red of his tail lights. From his position, he could only see the back of the sign.

He swallowed hard. *I have to go and find out if what I saw was real.*

He eased out of the cab of the truck and walked on shaky knees through the rain toward the road sign. There was no sound except the idling of the diesel engine and patter of the rain. The landscape on both sides of Highway 11 was wheat fields stretching into darkness beneath a sky of rolling black. He stopped before the sign and looked up to read the words in reflective letters:

Saigon 62km

What the fuck? He blinked against the rain expecting the name on the sign to change to some Oklahoma town. The words remained.

Quickly he ran back to the cab of the truck and slammed the door. He was soaked and his hands shook in fear. *Something supernatural is happening to me. Like a bad dream that I can't wake from.* Putting the truck in gear, he throttled up the engine and continued down the highway. He needed to get somewhere where there was civilization and people; somewhere where reality still existed. The truck raced full speed through the rainy night as he opened up the diesel and smoke poured from the stacks.

The highway whined beneath the eighteen wheels of the rig and trailer as the wipers fought hard against the rain. He hated rain and mud. It always reminded him of Nam.

* * * *

Morrison entered the hut and splashed gasoline over the walls and interior. Kim-ly remained curled up on the floor mat and cried to herself as she was doused in gasoline. Gone was the horrific thing he had seen when he finished raping her. He no longer believed what he saw was real. Morrison returned to the outside, pouring a stream of gas in a trail leading back into the hut.

"All done, boss," he said throwing the can into the jungle.

Carter flicked open the Zippo and handed to him. "You get to do the honors, soldier."

He looked down at the flickering flame of the lighter. "I can't."

"Don't puss out now, son. You're a bad ass, remember?" Carter put his arms on his shoulder and walked him toward the stream of gasoline leading out of the hut. "We got to teach these people not to fuck with Americans."

He looked up from the flame of the Zippo to see Kim-ly standing in the door of the hut. Gasoline was dripping from her clothes and flesh. With her wild black hair and eyes as dark as the abyss, she looked like some Oriental witch. Insane laughter erupted from her open mouth.

"Jesus!" he screamed in terror.

"What the fuck?" Carter gasped beside him at the sight of the girl. "Quick! Light the gas!"

He threw the Zippo into the wet stream of gasoline. In an instant it caught flame and raced toward the creature in the door of the hut that had once been Kim-ly. Her body became engulfed in fire, but she continued screaming her insane laughter and charged out of the hut toward them. Her hair and body were ablaze. Villagers scattered in panic at the sight of her. He remembered running to the jeep in sheer terror. Still she followed, as the flames ate away her flesh. Her scream was choked silent by the fire eating into her lungs. Halfway to the jeep, her immolated form fell to its knees. Broiling fire continued consuming her flesh and she collapsed face first into the mud.

Leaping into the back of the jeep, he watched as Carter and Morrison climbed into the front.

"What was that thing?" Carter asked with the tinge of fear in his voice.

"I don't care. I'm getting the fuck out of here," Morrison replied starting up the jeep. It grinded into gear and spun mud from under its tires as it pulled away from the village.

The air carried the stench of gasoline and burnt flesh. He looked back to see that her smoking body was now a blackened husk. They fled from the village and never spoke again of what had happened that day. Three weeks later, Carter and Morrison were killed by a VC mortar that hit their jeep. Later that year he was shipped stateside after taking shrapnel in his thigh. He was the only one with any memory of that terrible day and had put it far into his subconscious until tonight.

* * * *

Something was in the road just beyond the glow of his headlights! He was going too fast to stop the truck. In an instant he was upon the object. Kim-ly stood like a ghost in the center of the highway. He caught a glimpse of her, eyes as dark as death and skin as pale as snow. Her clothes were ripped and torn and she looked up at him and opened her mouth. The next second, the truck ran over her. Tessman swerved the rig and it went into the shoulder of the road. The trailer slid into the ditch and mired itself in the thick mud before the truck came to a stop.

"Fuck!" he screamed aloud in the cab. *I'll need a tow truck to get out of the ditch!*

Fearful of what he would see, he glanced into his side mirrors and down the road. He saw nothing but rain and highway. *Did he fall asleep and dream the girl in the road?* He popped the latch to the door and jumped out of the cab into the mud. Ever since 'Nam he'd hated stepping in mud. He walked around his truck and searched underneath. There was no body under his wheels. He turned and looked down the dark highway.

A small metal object caught his attention in the glow of the tail lights.

With his breath coming in short gasps, he walked to the item in the road. It was a set of dog tags and he knew, as he picked them up, who the owner would be. Turning them over, he read his name in the red glow.

This nightmare is real.

He looked up. Just beyond the edge of the light from the truck, something lurched down the center of the highway toward him. As it drew near, he saw the old Asian man he had shot forty years ago. Half the side of his head was a bloody hole from where the bullet had cut a path out of his skull. The corpse continued shambling toward him as lightning flashed overhead.

"No! Stay away from me!" he shouted at the horror and raced back to the cab of his truck.

Hopping behind the wheel, he slammed the door. In the dark of the cab, he hung the dog tags from the visor so they dangled in front of him. He watched them swinging slightly as the smell of gasoline and burnt human flesh permeated the air inside the truck. He looked to the passenger seat knowing what impossible thing would be sitting there.

It was Kim-ly. Her face turned toward him. Her eyes were as black as the memory of the atrocity he'd committed against her. She opened her mouth and a cloud of smoke and the stench of wretched cooked flesh poured from her insides. He fought against the urge to vomit up the contents of his stomach as he fell back against the driver door.

"One day you pay, Private Tessman. One day you pay," she said in her broken English.

"Kim-ly, I'm sorry for what I did," he sputtered in desperation as tears ran down his face. "It was the fucking war and the insanity of it all. I was young and stupid. Forgive me."

"You pay now," she replied.

Frozen in total fear, he watched the apparition of the girl fade away into nothingness. His breath caught in his lungs. Searing pain spread through his abdomen and he threw himself bodily against the driver's seat. Horrified, he looked down at his legs to see flames spreading up his jeans. Fire continued up his torso and engulfed his hands and melted away the flesh. Pain like he had never known burned throughout his body. He opened his mouth to scream and the inferno leaped into his lungs, cooking his insides. The last thing he saw before his eyes boiled away in their sockets was his dog tags hanging in front of him.

* * * *

"This poor bastard's got his truck buried ass deep in the mud," said Oklahoma Highway Patrol officer Ted Allison to his partner as he put the cruiser in park behind the black Peterbilt.

"Let's see what his problem is," David Walker said as he climbed out of the passenger seat and shut the door behind him. "We might have to call for a tow truck."

Ted radioed in their position and followed his partner as he walked the short distance to the rig. The morning sun had just crested over the eastern horizon and the rain had ended an hour before.

"Looks like he just slid off the road," Dave observed as they neared the front of the truck.

"He probably fell asleep while driving." Ted reached up to knock on the driver's window and noticed something black and sooty covered the glass. "Oklahoma Highway Patrol, we need to see your license, registration, and manifest," he called out as he knocked on the door.

"The guy's probably passed out in the sleeper," Dave said. "Go ahead and open the door."

Ted swung open the driver's door and stepped back in shock and revulsion. The smell of burnt flesh rolled out of the cab. Sitting in the driver's seat was the figure of what was once a human but now a corpse cooked to a crisp black. Its mouth hung open to show rows of cracked teeth.

"Son of a bitch!" Ted gasped. "What the hell happened to him?"

"Damned if I know," David answered and returned to the car to radio in a possible homicide.

While his partner was away, Ted slipped on a pair of gloves and studied the crime scene. Nothing else in the cab was burned besides the corpse. The upholstery, the steering wheel, the roof were barely singed by the fire that had killed the driver.

"I called HQ," David said as he returned to the truck. "They are sending a sheriff and CSI to investigate."

"You know what this reminds me of?"

"What?"

"Spontaneous human combustion."

"What the hell is that?"

"It's where somebody just erupts into flames and burns right where they are sitting. I saw something about it on the Discovery channel. It looks like this poor bastard just cooked to death behind the wheel."

"That's some weird shit."

Ted reached in and removed the dog tags from the visor. "I haven't seen these since I served in 'Nam."

"What's the name on them?"

Wiping away the soot on the tag, Ted said, "R. Tessman, Private First Class."

THE END OF THE ROAD

1.

"Everything seems to be working fine now," Frank Nolton said as he turned the crank of the condom dispenser and a purple packet plopped into the tray. "I fixed it."

"Good. I don't want to listen to another gay cowboy bitching about the machine ripping him off," said the twenty-something bartender at Phil's Sports Bar and Grill in Springwater, Oklahoma.

Frank tossed him the condom. "There you go. A free Midnight Passion on me."

"I prefer riding bareback whenever possible," the bartender said with a smile as he put the condom in his front pocket. "But, I'll keep it in case one of these nights, some wasted country girl wants to get it on after closing time. It hasn't happened yet, but a man can dream, can't he?"

"I'm forty-three and divorced so I don't get as much action as I used to. If I were your age, though, I'd carry one with me. What's the Boy Scout motto? Always be prepared?" Frank picked up his box of inventory and exited the small restroom of the empty sports bar, his fifth stop today on the delivery route. Chairs were stacked up on the tables throughout the place as sunlight, shining through the beer decals in the widows, lit the dusty air. The young bartender went behind the register as Frank removed his receipt book from his back pocket.

"That's one dozen French ticklers and twenty Midnight Passions. I also threw in a few Magnum ribbed," Frank said as he tore off the ticket.

"Until I worked here, I always wondered who the guy was stocking the rubber machines in all those gas station restrooms or bar crappers." The bartender opened the register and put the receipt under the till. "Now, I know."

"We don't call them rubbers anymore. The term is condoms or prophylactics. Besides, this isn't my regular job. I'm just filling in for someone who didn't show up for work today. Got talked into running his route."

"I know what that's like. They have me pull second shifts in this rat hole all the time." He shut the register. "I'll make sure my boss gets the bill,"

"Works for me. How about giving me a bag of corn nuts for the road?" Frank flipped through the pages of his route book. "According to my log, I got one more stop left. A little town called Omega. Have you heard of it?"

"Omega? I can't say that I have, but I'm new around here." The bartender slid the bag of corn nuts across the bar.

"Damn, I was hoping you could tell me where it is. I've checked the road atlas and can't find any listing for Omega."

"The place is probably so small it doesn't even rate a dot on a map. What kind of name is Omega for a town anyway? It sounds like the last place in the world anybody would want to be."

"The town might not be on the map but the occupants are practicing a lot of safe sex. I've got a whole case of condoms and other goodies to stock up at Smitty's Filling Station there. I checked the purchase order and they had the same order last month. It sounds like Omega is a party town."

"More than I can say for this place," the bartender replied as he began taking down the chairs from a table.

"Thanks for the corn nuts."

"Drive safely, Haven't you heard? We're expecting some severe weather later this afternoon. Tornado watches are already up."

"Thanks for the warning."

Frank left the bar and squinted as he stepped out into the blazing sunshine. Opening the side door to his delivery van, he threw in the box of sex goodies alongside the stock of novelties stored in the back. He tore open the bag of corn nuts and stood to the side of the open door, letting the oven-like heat broil out of the interior. *Another hot muggy day in Oklahoma,* he told himself. *Forty-three years old, thirty pounds overweight, divorced, and barely employed and I'm stuck delivering sex aids to rednecks on the most humid day of the year. You've done a lot with your life, Frankie. Way to go.*

He popped a corn nut in his mouth and crunched it.

After slamming the door shut, he slid behind the steering wheel and tossed the roadmap onto the passenger seat. *One last stop and I can't find where the hell it is. I should just go back to the warehouse and tell Tony I couldn't find the town. It's not my regular job, anyway. This is Marty's route. The slacker!* Frank let out a long frustrated sigh. He knew he couldn't lose another job. The back child-support payments were stacking up. *I'll just drive around, find a gas station, and ask directions from one of the local yokels. Pray I get one coherent enough to point me the right way. If I don't find anyone to tell me where the town is located, I turn around and go home.*

He started the van and pulled out of the gravel parking lot of the sports bar. The sun shone in his eyes as he turned west. Frank dropped down the driver's side visor to shade his eyes and a piece of folded white paper fell into his lap. Unfolding it, he found a crudely drawn map leading to Omega. At the bottom of the page, Marty had signed his name. A star-like symbol Frank couldn't recognize was scrawled next to the signature.

Thanks, Marty; now I have no excuse not to go to Omega, Frank thought as he slipped the map in his shirt pocket.

The map showed a turnoff about fourteen miles to the south. Cranking up the air conditioning and the radio, Frank headed out of Springwater. The ribbon of black asphalt stretched in the direction where huge white clouds were gathering on the horizon. Easing back into the seat, he crunched on corn nuts and listened to a classic rock station blasting out of the speakers as the delivery van ate up the miles of highway. Every song he knew by heart as if the station had decided to play the soundtrack of his life. Each classic rock hit came with an accompanying memory of where he'd been and who'd been with him when he'd first heard the song.

Then the station played "The Pretender" by Jackson Browne.

His mind flashed to 1978 and the concert in an overcrowded arena in Dallas, Texas. For once he had the good seats. So close to Jackson Browne you could see the spots of sweat on his forehead as he plunked out "The Pretender" on his piano in the hazy stage lights. *Who did I go to the concert with? Melanie. My God, it was Melanie, before she became my wife and the mother of my three children. I remember my arms wrapped around her waist as we held up our Bic lighters and swayed to the song.* The concert was a piece of golden memory of a loving Melanie: before the marriage, before the affair, before the divorce, before the child support and custody arrangements, before his life became a stretch of blistering asphalt and a van loaded with cheap sex aids.

"Say a prayer for the pretender," Frank sang aloud along with the song.

He caught sight of the highway turnoff as he drove past. Putting on the brakes with a loud whine of rubber on the hot highway, he brought the van to a halt. Looking back over his shoulder, he saw a crude hand-painted wooden sign nailed to a fence post at the intersection. Words in faded black read:

Omega 7 miles.
A surprising town awaits you at the end of the road.

Below the writing, a scrawled arrow pointed down a lonely stretch of country asphalt. Frank put the van in reverse and backed to the entrance of the turnoff. As the radio station announced a severe weather alert for the surrounding county, he swung onto the one-lane blacktop and drove in the direction of the arrow.

The road to Omega proved to be one the county didn't see fit to keep maintained. The broken and cracked black surface of the highway thumped under the tires, and no one had taken the time to paint a centerline down the middle. Fields and fences rolled past in a brown haze on each side of the van. After a couple of miles, a large black buzzard took flight from the side of the highway up ahead. He slowed when he came upon what the buzzard had been feeding on. The carcass of a dead cow, bloated and swollen, rested on the shoulder of the road; its legs sticking straight up toward the sun. The belly of the animal had burst and maggots squirmed through the gash in the flesh. A sickening knot formed in Frank's stomach and he pushed back the bile threatening to invade his mouth.

His cell phone rang, causing him to jump. Frank grabbed the phone and flipped it open. The call was from his boss in the warehouse.

"Yeah, boss man, what's up?" he asked as he pushed the accelerator and sped away from the cow's carcass.

"Hi, Frank." Tony's voice sounded far away in the receiver. "Where are you?"

"About five miles out from some fly speck named Omega." Frank checked the signal strength on the cell phone display. Two bars and, as he watched, one faded away. "Tony, the reception out here is shitty. I'm probably going to lose this call real quick."

"I'm calling about Marty." Tony said with a solemn air to his voice.

"Marty? You tell that slacking faker thanks for making me cover for him today. I've got storms brewing all over out here."

"I can't." A long pause followed. "He's dead."

"What the hell?"

"Marty's dead.... " The reception on the phone began to break up. "You know that Browning shotgun he wanted so badly for Christmas?"

"Yeah." Frank replied, his mind trying to come to grips with what he was hearing.

"Marty took it out on his deck behind his trailer house ... pulled the trigger ... head blown off ... his wife, Marcy, saw it all ... said he was talking some weird ... insane ... end of the world shit ..."

Frank checked his phone display. No bars were showing. "Boss, you're breaking up. You're not coming through very clear."

"Apocalypse ... demons and monsters ... funeral Wednesday."

The phone beeped in Frank's ear. He checked the display and saw the words: *Signal Lost.*

"Damn it!" Frank yelled and tossed the phone into the passenger seat. He gripped the wheel with both hands as his mind tried to grasp the concept. *Marty's dead?* He remembered being at the trailer house right after Christmas and Marty showing him the Browning shotgun, shiny and new, still lying in its box. *He was so proud of that gun. Said he was planning to hunt turkeys in the fall. Instead he blew his head off in front of his wife.* Wondering if he should turn back or drive on to Omega, he decided to continue to the town, get a beer at Smitty's Filling Station and drink a cold one in memory of Marty.

Poor son of a bitch.

Frank turned off the radio in the middle of another weather alert and listened to the whine of the tires on the road. A deep sadness settled into his heart. Marty's suicide reminded him of the failures in his own life. He just wanted to turn around and drive back home. Find a new reason to live instead of existing day to day. Too many years with too much heartache was behind him. He needed something better before him.

Topping a hill, he saw a red late-model Honda parked on the grassy shoulder of the road. At first, he thought the car was abandoned, but driving nearer, he saw someone sitting in the driver's seat. The occupant opened the door and got out just as he went past. In the rearview he caught a glimpse of a girl with brown hair. She motioned with a wave for him to stop. Frank put on the brakes and eased the van over to the shoulder. Framed in the side mirror, the girl jogging up to meet him appeared to be a young attractive brunette with long legs wrapped in blue jeans, shoulder-length hair, and a tight shirt showing half her belly.

What could she want with me?

He let down the driver's side window just as she reached the side of the van.

"Can I help you?" Frank asked.

Stepping up, she placed her hands in the open window. For one second Frank's mind catalogued her beauty: dark brown eyes, chestnut-colored hair, glistening tanned skin, and a face like a teen model. She looked young enough to be his daughter.

"My car died on me," she said, a little breathless.

"What happened?" Frank looked into her eyes. She had highlighted their seductiveness with a black eye-liner.

"I don't know." She pushed a strand of hair out of her face. "I was driving and then it died. I'm glad you came along. I've been broken down out here for a while," she wiped a hand across her wet forehead and smiled, "It's really hot."

It's really hot, Frank's mind echoed. *Just like you.* He had to remind himself that, to this girl, he probably looked like her dad.

"I guess I can see if I can get it started." Frank opened his door and climbed out into the heat.

"Thank you." She handed him the keys to the Honda.

Together they walked back to the car. As he neared the vehicle, a smell reminded him of something electrical burning.

"You say the car just died?" Frank asked as he opened the driver door of the Honda and climbed in.

"Yes." She stood with her arms crossed and a look of concern. "I was driving down the highway and suddenly it had no power: no radio, no AC, nothing. I just pulled over to the side. You're the first person I've seen coming down the road in an hour. I tried to call someone on the cell but got no signal out here."

"Me neither." Frank put the key in the ignition and turned it. Nothing happened.

"Battery is dead," he said as he popped the hood release.

"That's just great. A brand new fucking car, pardon my language, and it has a dead battery."

He climbed out of the Honda and stood next to the girl. *Damn she is sexy! A beautiful damsel in distress on the side of the road. Things like this just do not happen to me.*

"Were you driving to Omega?" Frank asked as he walked to the front of the Honda.

"Where?"

"Omega. It's a little town about four miles further down the road."

"I never heard of it." The girl shrugged. "I guess I got off on the wrong road. Usually I'm not such a ditz. By the way, my name is Kayla."

"Frank."

He reached down and lifted the hood. The smell of burnt wiring grew stronger. "I'll just check your battery. I might need to jump you." He silently winced after he said those words. I *might need to jump you! That's an understatement if ever there was one.* He wanted to laugh aloud but instead looked down at the battery and the jellyfish-looking creature.

"What the hell?" Frank stepped back so fast he bumped into Kayla.

"What's wrong?"

In disbelief, Frank studied the car battery and tried to come to grips with what he saw. Something had attached itself to the battery top and covered the terminal posts—*something alive?* His first impression was that it was a white jellyfish with octopus-like tentacles. About the size of a softball, the body of the creature appeared translucent and squishy. Whitish tendrils grew out of the thing and covered the black case of the battery. A milky mucous substance seeped from the mass of the alien-looking creature and dripped down into the engine of the car.

Kayla let out a gasp. "What is that?"

"Fuck, I don't know; pardon the language." Frank leaned in closer to take a look. The creature wasn't moving and lay perfectly still. The smell of burnt wiring grew stronger. Sucker-like appendages covered the white tentacles and he noticed a darker mass visible in the center of its translucent body. In horror, Frank thought it reminded him of a human eyeball.

"How did that thing get on my battery?" Kayla whispered.

"I've no idea." Perplexed, Frank stepped back from the car engine. "When the car died, did you hear or see something?"

"I thought I heard a buzzing sound. I figured it came from the engine."

"Are you sure you didn't see a flying saucer or anything weird?" Frank asked as he picked up a dry stick from the ground.

"No," Kayla shook her head. "Why?"

"Because whatever this thing is, it's not from this Earth as far as I can figure. Maybe things like this live deep in the depths of the ocean, but certainly not in central Oklahoma." Returning to the car battery, Frank softly poked the bulbous body of the creature with the end of the stick. It didn't move. Next he lifted a tentacle from the battery case. Still no movement. "I've never seen anything like it."

"Is it dead?" Kayla asked

"It's not moving." Frank slid the stick under the main section of the creature's body and lifted. A sucking sound followed and more mucous material seeped from the body. He noticed the thing had a tentacle wrapped around each battery post.

"Gross," Kayla said.

"How the hell did this thing end up under your hood?"

"I don't know but it's creeping me out."

Frank turned and started walking back to the van. The humid still air made his back run with sweat.

"Where're you going?" Kayla asked, following him.

"To find something to put that slimy thing in." He opened the back of the van, grabbed a cardboard box, and emptied out all the cartons of condoms inside.

"What is all that sex stuff?" Kayla asked as she looked over his shoulder to see the pile of Trojans and Maxims.

"I'm not an old pervert, if that's what you're wondering. I work for a novelty company and deliver to places with condom machines. It's not even my job. I'm just filling in for some guy today."

Walking back to the Honda, Frank handed Kayla the box. "I'm going to remove the creature from your battery. I want you to hold the box until I drop it in there."

"Are you sure this is a good idea? What if it comes alive, jumps up, and attaches itself to my face like that ugly creature in the Alien movie?"

Frank chuckled. "I'll make this quick." He took the stick and slid it under the bulbous mass of the creature. In one swift motion, he lifted it up from the top of the battery case. White tendrils covered in milky slime released the hold on the battery posts. He turned and dropped the creature into the cardboard box with a sickening plop. "See, nothing is attached to your face."

"Really gross." Kayla gave the box back to Frank. "What do you plan on doing with it?"

"I haven't thought that far ahead." He smiled at her. "The main thing now is to get your car started."

Placing the box in the back of his van, he searched for jumper cables in the side compartments. Kayla stood nearby and watched. He wanted desperately to help her get the Honda running but after a thorough search of the van interior he found no jumper cables. He closed the back door.

"You wouldn't have any jumper cables in your car, would you?"

Kayla shook her head no.

"We're not going to be able to start your Honda without them." Frank wiped sweat from his brow. "Go shut the hood, Kayla, and I'll drive you into Omega. It's only a few miles up the road. There's a service station in town so we can get someone to help you."

"Thanks."

2.

Frank started the van and contemplated the events happening to him. Ever since he'd turned onto the road to Omega, the day had become one of the strangest of his life. He'd learned Marty had committed suicide, found a beautiful girl stranded on the side of the road, discovered an alien-looking creature hugging her car battery; and now, the same girl was going to ride with him to Omega. His life had turned into a *Twilight Zone* episode.

He watched Kayla in the side mirror as she shut the hood to the Honda and got her purse from inside. She was long, lean, and gorgeous, the kind of girl he would have dated twenty years ago before the extra weight and age set in. She came back, climbed into the passenger seat and he caught the scent of freshly sprayed body cologne. *She must have just put some on to cover the scent of her perspiration,* Frank thought as he pulled back onto the highway.

"Oh my God, air conditioning! It's like a sauna out there!" Kayla bent down before the AC vent in the van and pulled her top forward to let the cold air blow against her sweaty chest. Frank caught sight of what looked like a Victoria's Secret bra beneath her shirt. He turned his attention to the road.

"We'll get to town and find you a mechanic."

"Thanks, Frank, you're my savior."

"Saving beautiful girls is a hobby of mine." He smiled at her and she returned the favor.

"What are we going to do about our little alien buddy?"

"I've got to get some ice on it. The thing won't last long in this heat. You know, Kayla, this find might be worth some money. We may have an unknown life form here. Somebody might pay to research it."

"We're partners then?" Her eyebrows arched as she looked at him with her brown eyes and held out her hand.

"Fifty-fifty," Frank said as he shook her soft hand.

"I don't even know anything about you, Frank, and here I'm riding in your van full of condoms and an alien jellyfish."

They both laughed.

"Well, I'm Frank Nolton, and I'm forty-three years old, divorced, with three kids. I work at a distribution warehouse. What about you?"

She settled back in the passenger seat and stared out the window. "I'm Kayla Jennings, twenty-three, college student who just broke up with another loser boyfriend. In fact, I was driving home from his place in the country when I took a wrong turn onto this highway. Right now, I think all men pretty much suck."

"Present company excluded," Frank said.

"Of course."

"Where do you go to college?"

"University of Oklahoma," she said and then sat up. "Frank, I just thought of something. I can call the Science Department at the college. I have a friend in the physics department. I'm sure someone there would like to examine our little specimen."

"Good idea," he said and added. "First we take some digital pictures of our find so we can distribute them on the internet. That way we can prove we have full claim to the discovery. Call the news media, newspapers and television to cover our story. Who knows, Kayla, we might end up on network television. Oprah, Geraldo, *Dateline*, *60 Minutes*; we might have to do them all." He turned to look at her. "What would you say to that?"

"Look out!"

He snapped his attention back to his driving and saw a "Narrow Bridge" sign pass by out of the corner of his eye. Ahead, the bridge was gone. A huge hole gaped in the highway in its place. Frank slammed on the brakes and the tires squealed as the rubber slid along the asphalt and over the edge of the hole. Kayla screamed. For a frozen moment in time, the van suspended airborne before the front crashed into the bank of the other side of the creek. Both driver and passenger airbags deployed in dual eruptions of inflated white cushions. The driver airbag knocked Frank back against his seat as the windshield shattered into pieces of broken safety glass. For one heartbeat, the van stood on its nose before the rear end fell hard against the rocks littering the creek bottom. Dazed, he shook his head as the airbag deflated and turned to Kayla. She hadn't bothered to put on her seatbelt.

"Are you okay?" he asked, his voice sounded shaky and unsure.

"I don't know," she replied weakly.

Frank moved his legs. Nothing seemed broken. Releasing his seatbelt, he popped the door handle and swung it open. The pings of the engine and the creak of the van's suspension settling its weight on the rocks were the only noise breaking the eerie quiet. He eased himself out of the wrecked cab and onto the large chunks of broken concrete the van now rested on. A smell invaded his nostrils: the aroma of fresh gasoline. *The gas tank must have ruptured in the wreck,* he told himself. *I have to get Kayla out before it catches fire!*

Staggering over rocks in the bright sunlight, Frank made his way around the collapsed front of the van. The smell of gasoline became stronger and burned his throat and nostrils with its pungent stench. Reaching the passenger door, he threw it open.

"Can you move?" he asked.

"I'm not sure. My hip is hurting."

In shocked dismay, Frank saw flames beginning to spread beneath the crushed hood.

"Kayla, I've got to pull you out now!" He hooked his hands under her arm pits and yanked her from the passenger seat. She let out a cry of pain. He dragged her body across the rocky creek bank as fast as he could away from the vehicle as fire sputtered and crackled in the engine block. With a deafening whoosh, the van went up in an explosion of heat and flames, throwing twisted metal into the air. The concussion from the blast blew both Frank and Kayla to the ground. The thick smell of smoke, burning rubber, and gasoline filled the air.

"Thanks for saving me," Kayla finally muttered, as she caught her breath.

"I told you it was a hobby of mine." Frank sat up. He ached everywhere, as if he had been used as someone's punching bag. He studied Kayla, still sprawled out on the rocks. A line of blood seeped from a shallow gash on her forehead.

"How bad are you hurt?"

She reached up and swiped at the blood on her forehead. "My head is bleeding."

"It's superficial and doesn't look too severe. Where else?"

"My left hip and ribs."

"You'll have to excuse me but I have to check it out." Frank bent down and raised her shirt to expose her taut waistline and bra. A bruise already began to color the bone of her left hip. *God, please tell me her hip isn't broken,* he prayed silently. Her ribs were showing the coloration of sub-dermal bruising.

"I'm going to feel your ribs," he said. "Tell me if it hurts anywhere."

He softly pressed against her lower left ribs. He wasn't certain but he thought he felt one move.

"It hurts!" she gasped.

Frank looked up and surveyed the surroundings. The creek proved nothing more than a trickle of brown water. The bank consisted of chunks of shattered concrete, remnants from the bridge that had once stood there. Overhanging fifteen feet above them was the edge of the broken span. Beyond lay the road leading to Omega.

"I would go get you help but I can't leave you here on these rocks. You'll cook in this heat and a storm is moving in."

She nodded.

"We're going to have to climb up out of this creek. Can you move your legs?"

"I think so," she said and demonstrated she could.

"Good girl." Frank smiled. "I think your hip is just bruised. You may have a broken rib, however. It might hurt like hell, but I think you can walk. See if you can sit up."

Painfully, she rose to a sitting position. "Okay, I got this far," she said letting out her breath.

"Do you think you can stand?"

"With your help," she replied putting an arm around his shoulder. Carefully, he lifted her to her feet where she stood on her own strength.

"How about climbing up this bank to the road?"

"I feel better now. I think I was more dazed than hurt," she said and then pointed to the van engulfed in flames. "I left my purse and phone in the van. Damn it, we lost our alien specimen, too!"

"We can't worry about that now. We've got to get you to town and have someone look at your injuries."

She shook her head. "No one is going to believe us, Frank, about the thing on my battery."

"I know."

Slowly, they scrambled over rocks and dirt to reach the surface of the road. Fire crackled below them as the flame consumed the van. A cloud of black smoke from the burning tires rose into the blue sky. Frank climbed over the edge of the broken bridge and reached down to help Kayla up. Carefully, he lifted her to the surface of the road.

"I should pay more attention to my driving," he said.

"It wasn't your fault. How come nobody bothered to put up a sign saying the fucking bridge is out?"

"Good question."

Once back upon the highway, Frank turned his attention toward Omega. A white grain elevator and a water tower stood ahead in the distance. He estimated they were still a couple of miles from the town. On the far horizon, more clouds were gathering in preparation for a serious storm. Something else caught his eye. Parked in some trees off to the side of the road was a piece of heavy road equipment: a large ditch digger with a bladed metal scoop. Intrigued, he walked over to the machine and checked the blade on the shovel. Fresh cement dust peppered the tines.

"What is it?" Kayla asked as she limped behind him.

"I think this was used to smash up the bridge," he said, and then turned toward her. "Why would anyone do that? There is only one road leading in and out of town. If the bridge is under construction, why wasn't there a roadblock put up?"

"Who can say? I just want to get to town and find something cold to drink."

"It's damned weird. Things don't add up. Why isn't someone investigating the van explosion and the fire? Look at the cloud of smoke rising in the sky. I'm sure they could see it from town. If they knew the bridge was out, wouldn't they suspect someone had a wreck? There should be a sheriff or volunteer fire department coming to investigate."

He looked back down the road. No vehicles were heading in their direction.

"I haven't seen even one car coming or going on this highway," Kayla said. "What do we do, Frank?"

"We walk into town and find us a land line phone. We call the highway patrol and report the bridge being out and the accident."

"After that?"

"We find whatever sorry excuse for a bar they have in Omega. Then we get shitfaced drunk while discussing our lawsuit against the town and the dumb asses that tore up the bridge."

Kayla smiled. "Sounds like a plan to me."

"Do you think you can walk that far?"

"If there is a cold beer at the end, I could walk it on my hands."

"You're my kind of girl," Frank said and added, "a beer drinker."

* * * *

Now on foot for the last two miles to Omega, Frank fought off the numbing exhaustion threatening to take over his body after the adrenaline surge due to the wreck. He couldn't imagine how tired Kayla felt. She walked beside him with a slight limp but he knew she was suffering pain from her broken rib. No longer as glamorous in appearance as a model—her clothes muddied and torn, her hair matted with sweat, and dried blood crusted the side of her forehead—she still gave off the air of a sexy young woman. *A strong girl,* he realized, *to keep going after so much has happened.*

Angry billowing clouds continued to mass on the horizon as their color began to shift from white to gray. Lighting flashes pierced the wall of the approaching tempest, heralding a powerful storm front heading in their direction. He had lived in Oklahoma long enough to know how dangerous a storm can be out in the open. Frank hoped they would reach the town and shelter before the first wave of bad weather reached them.

"How long have you been divorced?" Kayla asked breaking their silence.

"About three years," Frank replied. "I was married sixteen."

"What happened?"

"I guess you can say our marriage ran out of steam." He glanced in her direction. "I ended up having an affair with the wrong person. The divorce was the end result of my mistake."

"Do you ever want her back?"

"Every hour of every day."

"Did she remarry?"

"No." Frank shook his head.

"You should call her and try to reconcile. Ask for her forgiveness."

He thought about his ex-wife for a second. His relationship with Melanie had disintegrated down to shared custody of the kids and shouting matches over his being late on child support. Whatever happiness they had had together was long gone. "If it was only that easy, Kayla. I hurt her bad when I had the affair. I don't think she'll ever forgive me."

"You don't know unless you try." She touched his arm lightly. "After all this is over, promise me you'll make that call. Trust me, Frank, it's what she wants."

"Okay, you got a deal."

They walked along the shoulder of the blacktop under a row of telephone poles with high-voltage electrical wires strung between them. Frank studied the homes and buildings of Omega and still didn't see any vehicles or people moving about. It seemed like they were heading toward a ghost town.

Kayla stopped. "Do you hear that?"

"What?"

"There is a very low hum in the air. So faint it's almost imperceptible, but it's there."

"Your ears are better than mine." Frank concentrated and listened. Kayla was right. He could hear—no, feel—a low, throbbing hum centered in his chest. The humid air vibrated with almost imperceptible energy.

"I think it's coming from the wires overhead," Kayla said as she looked up. "Have you ever heard electrical cables hum like that?" Her fingers reached out and grabbed hard onto his arm. "Oh my God!" she gasped.

Frank followed her gaze and his mouth dropped open in shock. At a junction box where high-powered conduit cable connected to the telephone pole, more of the jellyfish creatures clung together in a mass of milky mucous and writhing tentacles. Exact in appearance to the one he removed from her car battery, the life forms appeared even more alien when moving and alive.

The weird occurrences since he'd turned down the road to Omega made Frank feel like he was walking on ice getting thinner and thinner with each strange happening. The sight of the writhing mass of unearthly creatures caused the ice to break. His reality shattered along with his belief system. He sat on the ground, put his head in his hands, and tried to get his mind to cope with this new forced reality. "This can't be happening. What I'm seeing can't be for real. I must be in a dream or a coma."

"Frank, stand back up and let's keep moving."

"It's no use. This is a dream or a nightmare. None of this is real."

Kayla slapped him hard across the top of his head.

Shocked, Frank looked up at her. "Why did you hit me? That hurt!"

"It's no dream if you can feel pain. Believe me, I know, because my fucking rib hurts like hell. Sorry to hit you, but I need you here with me." She wiped tears from her eyes. "Whatever shit we're in is for real, so deal with it."

"It's just too hard to believe. Its like we've walked into a bad sci-fi movie." Frank stood and dusted off the seat of his jeans. He returned his attention to the creatures squirming on the telephone pole overhead. In disbelief, he watched as another of the life forms appeared among the writhing mass, the teleportation accompanied by a quick buzzing sound.

"What are they doing?" Kayla asked.

"I think they're feeding off the power just like the one on your battery."

"That makes sense. Now, forget about them. What are we doing?"

"Same plan as before. We get to a working phone and call the highway patrol, call the governor, hell, call the president. I don't know what's happening in Omega but someone needs to be told."

3

Walking as quickly as possible with Kayla limping by his side, Frank covered the distance to the outskirts of Omega. Above them, the bizarre alien jellyfish swarmed in greater numbers around the high voltage cables and the scene took on a surreal aspect. *Like something out of a madman's fevered dream*, Frank thought. He tried not to look too closely at the unearthly mass of creatures, for fear the sight would send him skittering off the slippery slope of sanity for good.

The weather began to change for the worse. The temperature dropped a full twenty degrees and the wind picked up strength. Clouds darkened and rolled nearer as the distant rumbling of thunder intensified in its frequency and magnitude. On the edge of town, a large billboard sign stood by the side of the road; it read:

Omega
Pop. 1489
The Unity Church welcomes you.

Across the printed words someone had scrawled a strange symbol in black spray paint. Frank remembered where he'd seen the symbol before—on Marty's crude map showing him how to find Omega.

"I don't believe it," he said, removing the folded map from his pocket.

"What don't you believe now?"

"Marty knew about this place. He knew something about what is going on here."

"Who's Marty?"

"The driver I'm subbing for today. I got a call from my boss when I turned down this road. He told me Marty committed suicide. He had been acting strange the last month, always talking about Revelations and the end of the world, crap like that. I figured he was going through some sort of depression. He must have known something about Omega and the strange events we're witnessing. Look at the symbol he marked at the bottom of the page. It matches the one on the billboard."

"What does it mean? It looks like an inverted star with something in the center."

"I've no idea."

A sudden gust of wind swept down the road followed by a startling clap of thunder signaling the storm's arrival. Dirt and grit stung their eyes and they turned their backs to escape the wind's fury. Boxes, trash, and dried brush tumbled down the main street through the center of the town.

"We'd better find a place to get out of this weather," Frank shouted above another loud blast of thunder.

The first two buildings at the edge of the town were Smitty's Filling Station and a one-story house on the other side of the highway. They ran for Smitty's, which proved to be a small Conoco station combined with a convenience store. Two sets of gas pumps stood beneath a metal canopy rattling in the wind. Parked in the lot on the side of the building sat a rusted old tow truck. Reaching the front door, they found it locked.

"Damn!" Kayla shouted above the howling wind. "It's closed!"

Frank peered through the glass. A pay phone hung on one wall of the store.

"Not for long," he said.

Walking back to the tow truck, he searched the bed until he found a tire iron. Fighting against the fierce wind, he returned. "Stand back."

She nodded and took a couple of steps back. Frank swung the tire iron, shattering the glass in the front door. Immediately an alarm bell rang as he reached in and unlocked the bolt.

"Open for business." Frank said above the sound of the burglar alarm. "Go inside, but be careful of the broken glass."

Kayla entered the store, her shoes crunching across the shards of glass on the tiled floor. "Aren't you afraid the cops are going to bust us?"

"Let them," he said, entering behind her. "Then we can tell them about the wreck and they can call the highway patrol."

Crossing over to the cooler doors, Kayla peered through the glass at the bottled beverages inside. "Should we add shoplifting to our list of crimes committed? My money burned up with my purse in the van."

"No need to do that." Frank placed the tire iron across the register counter. "Let's just leave it at breaking and entering." He pulled his wallet out and laid a twenty-dollar bill on the cash register."Help yourself and I'll take a Budweiser while you're at it."

As Kayla opened the cooler door, Frank turned to the pay phone on the wall. He reached into his pocket and fished out some change. "Jesus, I haven't used one of these in years." He dropped a couple of quarters into the coin slot and placed the receiver against his ear. There was no dial tone.

"Shit!" He slammed the receiver back in the cradle.

"Don't tell me," Kayla said, handing him a Budweiser in a bottle.

"You guessed it. The phone's dead." Frank took the offered bottle and took a long draw, tasting sweet beer rolling down his parched throat.

"What do we do now?" Kayla asked.

"We wait until the police come to check on the alarm we tripped."

"To partners in crime," she held up her beer bottle and smiled.

"To partners in crime." Frank clinked his bottle against hers.

The storm outside the Conoco station grew in fierce intensity. Wind ripped at the canopy over the gas pumps and the clouds transformed the sunny day into dark twilight. A plastic trashcan went rolling down the street. Kayla stood at the front door looking out at the weather and sipping on her beer.

"The weather is getting worse. What do we do if a there's a tornado?"

Frank walked behind the register and found a small travel pharmacy stocked with aspirins and other meds. "The safest place will be in the walk-in cooler. We'll just hide in there." He pulled out a bottle of Tylenol and tossed it to Kayla. "Take some of those. It'll help you with the pain.

"Thanks." She shook out four tablets into her palm and downed them with a swig of cold beer. "I've never seen a tornado. I'm from Wisconsin and only came to Oklahoma for grad school. I didn't go back this summer because I thought I would stay here with my boyfriend."

"I was in a tornado once. May 3, 1999. A category five went through Oklahoma City. I was working for a medical warehouse then. I remember it was dark in the afternoon just like it is now."

"That doesn't give me much confidence." Kayla stood staring out the broken door and the raging storm. "Tornados scare me."

Frank shrugged. "I've brought you this far, I'm not about to let some twister blow away my beer-drinking buddy."

She turned to him and smiled as lightning flashed against the side of her face. "You're my knight in shining armor."

A knight in shining armor, he repeated to himself. *No woman ever thought of me in that way. Would his ex-wife think so? Not Melanie. Not after the mistakes I made with her and the marriage.* "Let's just say I'm your knight in tarnished armor."

"I wish more men were like you. You're a good man, Frank."

"For an old guy."

She smiled. "For an old guy."

The noise of a sudden downpour pounded the metal canopy and roof of the store.

"Great, here comes the rain." Leaning forward, Kayla peered harder through the storm. "There's someone with a flashlight on the porch of the house across the street."

Looking out the large front window, Frank saw an elderly man waving a flashlight for them to come to his house. The stranger shouted to them but the storm drowned out his words.

"Are we going over there?" she asked.

"He's the only person we've seen since this nightmare started. He might have some answers and a working phone. Besides, the sound of this alarm bell is driving me crazy. Let's run across the street and see what he wants."

"We're going to get wet. It's really raining hard."

"We'll run between the drops."

"Very funny."

Lightning flashed brightly and the rain pelted them as they charged across the dark street. By the time they reached the old man's front porch, hail began peppering the yard and the roof of the house. Frank ran behind Kayla up the stone steps to the porch. The man waiting for them was almost comical in appearance. Dressed in a bathrobe, pajamas, and house slippers, he looked like a caricature of an elderly man drawn for a cartoon show. Rain covered his glasses and his bald head was framed by wisps of gray hair blown wildly by the wind.

"God's sake, let's get you out of this terrible weather," he said loudly above the rush of the wind.

He opened the front door and Frank followed Kayla inside. They entered a warm living room lit by shaded lamps. An elderly woman, dressed in a paisley dress, stood in the center of the carpeted floor and looked at them with intense concern on her aged face. A television blared in one corner and Frank caught sight of a weather alert on the screen.

"Shut the door, Abe," the woman said. "The weatherman just reported all people in the Omega area should prepare to take shelter immediately. Something about a hook echo and a wall cloud."

"That won't go well. This is church night, Martha."

"Do you have a phone we can use?" Frank asked above the noise of the television.

Abe said to Martha, "Woman, turn down that TV so I can talk to these people."

Muttering to herself, Martha hobbled over and turned the volume down on the television.

"Now, what did you say?" Abe asked as he removed his glasses and wiped the water off the lens.

"We need to use the phone. We had an accident down the road and have to call the highway patrol."

"Phone's out," Abe replied. "I heard the alarm across the street and saw you two had broken into Smitty's station. I thought you two were a couple of store robbers and tried to call Sheriff Turley. That's when I found out the phone isn't working."

"You have a sheriff in town?" Kayla asked.

Abe nodded and slipped his glasses on his head. "Sheriff Turley's our only police officer. Martha told me I shouldn't leave you two at the mercy of the approaching storm, even if you're store robbers. We decided to invite you two to our shelter."

"It's God's way," Martha said.

"It's God's way," Abe repeated.

"We're not thieves. We'll pay for any damages done to the store. We only broke inside because we needed to use a phone to report the accident to the highway patrol." Frank glanced at the silent television. The screen presented a radar image of the approaching storm front. The map showed a dark stain spread across the center of Oklahoma. Outside, hail hammered the roof and the metal canopy of the station across the street with a continuous beat. "Thanks for letting us into your house. We're dripping water all over your floor."

"Don't fret about that, son. Now you're here, you can come help me. I've got some things that need taken down to the basement. My old back won't let me do it. We'll all have to stay down there until the storm blows over. Leave the women to talk up here while we get prepared below."

"Poor girl, you must be soaked to the bone," Martha said to Kayla as she removed a quilt from the couch. She wrapped the blanket around Kayla's shoulders. "Sit here on the couch while I fix some hot cocoa."

"Thank you." Kayla slowly eased her injured body onto the couch cushion. She smiled weakly back at Frank. "I'll be fine."

"Martha will take care of your wife," Abe said putting his arm on Frank's shoulder.

"Oh, she's not my wife. I just met her on the road here. Her car broke down."

"You're not married?" Abe asked as he led the way through a kitchen to a closed door with an ice chest and blankets stacked in a pile to one side.

"Divorced."

"I'm sorry to hear. Martha and I have been together fifty-eight years." Abe opened the door and flicked on a light switch. Wooden steps led down to a cluttered basement lit by a yellowed bulb in the ceiling. The sound of the rain and hail pounded against the basement windows. "People don't marry anymore like they used to. Grab that ice chest and haul it down here for me."

Abe flopped down the steps in his house shoes as Frank picked up the ice chest and followed. At the bottom, the old man pushed a few boxes aside to make some room. Frank placed the ice chest in the cleared space, and as he did so, caught the wafting smell of burnt electrical wiring hovering in the air. His stomach tinged with a touch of fear. Something didn't seem right. Like the strange creatures clinging to the high-voltage wires, everything about the town of Omega, up to this point, was out of touch with the real world. He realized this old man might be part of the nightmare as well. Uneasy, he turned his attention to the only other occupant in the basement.

"You've been doing work on the wiring down here, Abe?"

Lightning flashed in the basement windows, highlighting the shape of the old man watching him from behind his thick glasses. "No, why do you ask?"

"I smell something like burnt wiring," he said sniffing the air again. The smell came from the old man. "Tell me, what were those weird looking jellyfish creatures we saw coming into town?"

"Saw those, did you?"

"What are they?"

"Tryllobytes."

"Tryllobytes?" Frank stepped a short step back from the old man. He felt his heel hit the bottom step of the wooden basement stairs. "Where did they come from?"

"From the Fray," Abe replied. "A time-space fabric exists between the worlds of different dimensions. Sometimes this cosmic fabric becomes frayed and creates a place where two worlds have a rip between them."

Frank studied the old man. His hands extended down his side like bony claws. His wide eyes showed the hint of madness as he stared at him with the yellow light reflecting off his balding head. "A fray in the fabric between dimensions, you don't say?"

"Thanks to Reverend Masterson and the Unity Church, Omega is such a place where a Fray exists."

"So the tryllobytes come from this fray?"

"They're like damned cockroaches. They get into everything but it is a necessary drawback of opening the Fray." Abe replied. "They are the heralds of the Sentients."

"Sentients?"

"The teachers of cosmic knowledge and lore forgotten long before man walked the earth. The Sentients return to teach us the ways of God. Haven't you ever gone to church, son?"

"Abe, did you take your medicine today? Because you're scaring the hell out of me."

"There is nothing to be afraid of, son. I can show you the way. Accept the gift of the seed and you will become part of the One." His appearance of being a frail old man faded away into something evil and alien. The line of his wrinkled mouth began to lengthen unnaturally and stretch beyond anything human. Something became visible within the huge gap of his transformed mouth. A white slug-like creature with legs like a centipede emerged from the roof of his palette.

"It's God's way," the Abe-thing croaked in a voice almost beyond human comprehension. Lightning flashed. Frank fell back onto the steps paralyzed by a fear he had never known before. The unearthly being grabbed onto his arms with bony clawing hands as its mouth opened wider, dripping milky mucous. Utilizing multiple white tendrils, the slug-like creature emerged further from Abe's widened maw. As he succumbed to a terror-induced madness, Frank's scream lodged in his throat, unable to escape.

Upstairs, Kayla screamed instead.

Hearing her piercing cry, Frank snapped out of his paralysis. He kicked out hard in panic. His heel struck the old man in the stomach knocking him back. The Abe-thing released its hold on his arms as the slug creature retreated into its mouth. Terrified, Frank crawled backwards up a few wooden steps as the old man followed grabbing at his legs.

"There is no escaping the One," the thing spoke. "It's God's way."

"Screw you!" Frank's next kick caught Abe in the face, shattering his glasses. "Keep the fuck away from me, you inhuman shit!"

He kicked him in the face, repeatedly, smashing nasal bones and breaking out the man's dentures. Undaunted, the old man continued coming up the steps and grabbing at him with his bony hands. Reaching the top, Frank kicked out desperately with all of his strength, catching Abe under the chin with the heel of his shoe. The old man lost his balance and crashed back down the stairs and landed at the bottom with his head hitting hard upon the stone floor. In the next second, an unearthly howl emitted from his mouth as his body shook violently. Horrified, Frank watched as Abe's back arched in an impossible bend accompanied by the sound of brittle bones snapping. In a spray of white mucous, tentacles ripped through his pajama top and exploded out of his chest. The grayish mass of squid-like tentacles flapped in convulsions before Abe's body fell back and went still. In the light of the dim bulb, the old man's frail form disintegrated into a milky fluid spreading out across the basement floor.

Frank fought back against a fresh wave of nausea and the taste of bile in his throat.

Kayla screamed again.

Praying he wasn't too late, he raced out of the basement door and into the kitchen. He instinctively searched for a weapon and found a wooden rolling pin hanging on a peg by the stove. Grabbing it up, he charged into the living room and into the middle of a horrific sight.

In the light of the television, Kayla struggled against the form of Martha looming over her on the couch. The old woman's mouth twisted into a sickening hole out of which slimy mucous dripped. Martha looked up as he entered the room and made a repulsive gargling noise. Swinging the rolling pin with all of his might, Frank hit the woman between the eyes. The impact sent the horror off the couch where it fell back against the television. Lights flickered in the room as the creature made a low-throated groan. With surprising speed, the Martha-thing charged back toward him. He swung again with the pin and smashed it hard against the side of its head. Skull bones fractured from the blow and the creature fell across a coffee table, sending hot cocoa flying into the air. Rolling onto the floor, Martha landed on her back and emitted an unearthly scream before her body arched and the front of her paisley dress exploded into a mass of writhing tentacles. She fell still then as her body liquefied into a white slime.

Frank dropped the rolling pin and knelt down beside Kayla on the couch. Her eyes were wide with fear and she muttered to herself under her breath. He touched her forehead and her skin felt cold and clammy. *She's going into shock,* he told himself as he wrapped the blanket tighter around her body and hugged his warmth against her.

"Come on Kayla, stay with me," he said.

"The old woman … her mouth … something in her mouth …" she breathed as she trembled against him.

"You told me to snap out of it. Now you've got to do it."

"Monster … grabbed me … mouth opened."

"Kayla, I've never struck a girl before, but—"

Frank slapped her across the face just hard enough to shock her. The dim look left her brown eyes and she refocused her gaze upon him.

"Sorry." He smiled.

"Oh, Frank," she said wrapping her arms tightly around his neck. "You saved me again."

"It's that damned hobby of mine."

He held her while she cried against his chest as he smoothed back her chestnut colored hair. In a release of raw emotion, her slim body shook against his. The two of them reduced to their most primal selves: a man and woman clinging together for survival. At that moment, Frank came to a revelation: *This is what it's all about, the truth about marriage, mating, childbirth, and family; the reason for all the love and heartache. From the dawn of time, man and woman held desperately to each other to survive, through thick or thin, against the storms, disasters, and uncertainty of a world fraught with danger.*

"What are we going to do now?" Kayla looked up at him with her teary brown eyes.

"I don't know but I promise I'm going to get you out of Omega alive."

4

The storm's fury sent sheets of rain mixed with pea-sized hail in a continuous assault against the roof and walls of the house. Thunder shook the windows in their frames as lightning crackled and the lamps flickered in the living room. On the couch, Frank hugged Kayla close. Glancing over to a wall clock above the television, he read the time: 4:35 in the afternoon. Outside, the cloud cover had transformed the bright summer day into near night. *It is almost unnaturally dark,* Frank thought, *even for a severe storm in Oklahoma. Any second and the lights are going to go out due to the lightning.*

"I'm so cold." Kayla shivered against him. "Sorry to turn out to be such a whiner."

"Don't worry about it." He pushed a strand of wet hair from her face. They were both soaked from running through the rain minutes earlier. "You've been through a lot, girl. Once the storm blows over, we're out of this screwed-up town. I've had enough of this alien invasion bullshit. We'll walk all the way back to the main highway, hitch a ride to some place safe, and call the highway patrol from there."

She smiled. "Sounds like a plan, partner."

Her brown eyes met his and he fought back an urge to reach over and kiss her, to press her lips and her body against his. *Get a grip, Frankie. You've got aliens masquerading as humans and a dangerous storm to deal with. The last thing you need is to be lusting over this girl. Keep a clear head until we're both safe and far from here.* Frank pulled away and wrapped the blanket tighter around her shoulders.

"Was it something I said?"

"You're a hot college girl and I'm an old divorced guy who hasn't had sex for six months." He stood and turned away from her. "Let's just say, I'm not the best man to be cuddling with right now. Best to stop while I'm still your knight in armor."

"Where are you going?" she asked as he walked to the kitchen door.

"Down into the basement. Abe's flashlight is there and I want to get it before the lightning knocks the power out."

"You can't leave me up here alone, Frank." Her eyes darted for a second to the large stain of fluid on the carpet that had once been the form of Martha. "Not with that … what's left of that old woman." She started to rise from the couch. "I'm going with you."

"It's no better down there. I left Abe a puddle of goop all over the basement floor. Just give me a couple of minutes. Stay up here and watch some TV."

"Okay," she said and grabbed up a television remote from the coffee table. She flicked through the channels. "There's storm coverage … storm coverage … and storm coverage." She threw the remote back on the coffee table and said, "There, I've watched it."

"First you turn into a whiner and now a smart-ass." Frank smiled at her.

"I'm going with you and that's all there is to it," she said, easing herself to her feet. "You're the only sane thing I've encountered all day and I'm not going to leave your side."

Lightning crackled, and just as he'd predicted, the house went dark as the electricity went off. Kayla let out a short cry of alarm and limped over to him. Frank held out his hand and she took it as more lightning brightened the living room windows.

"Just stay close to me," he said.

"Don't worry about that. This house is seriously freaking me out."

Frank led the way through the shadowed kitchen and to the open door to the basement.

Wooden steps led down to the gloom below.

"I'm going to get the flashlight."

"It's too creepy down there for me," she said. "I'm very claustrophobic. I'll just stay up here instead."

"I'll be right back." He released her hand and turned his attention to the steps leading down into the basement. Taking care not to slip and fall, he descended the wooden stairs slowly as lightning flashed through the basement windows, illuminating the dark in strobe-like brilliance.

"I can't see you. Are you still there?"

"I'm at the bottom of the steps."

"Keep talking to me so I can know where you are."

He looked around in the gloom. A glistening pool of white liquid bubbled across the tiles of the floor and dripped into a water drain. Lightning lit the room and, in horror, he saw Abe's broken eye-glasses resting in the center of the puddle. He also spotted the flashlight on a nearby shelf. "What's your major in college?"

"I'm in my first year of pre-med."

"A doctor, huh? Are your parents rich? It takes a lot of money to get through medical school."

"My daddy owns a printing company in Milwaukee."

Not wanting to step into whatever substance Abe had melted into, Frank stretched out from the bottom step and wrapped his hand around the flashlight. "Daddy's rich little girl? I bet you're spoiled as all hell. I've got the flashlight, Kayla."

Only the sound of thunder answered him.

"Kayla?" Frank flicked on the flashlight and shone it up the stairs. At the top stood a man dressed in a rain-slicked green poncho. His hand was clamped over Kayla's mouth. In the other, he held a sawed-off pump shotgun against her chin. She looked down at Frank with brown eyes filled with fear.

"Daddy's little girl isn't talking right now," a grim voice said from the dark of the poncho hood. He swung the shotgun from Kayla's chin and pointed it at Frank. "You're the prick that broke into my store."

"Listen to me. I can explain. We only needed to use the phone. We didn't take anything and I left money on the counter. I'll pay for any damages."

Frank noticed new sounds other than the storm against the house—footsteps moving across the floor overhead, men's voices, the slamming of doors.

"Did you find 'em, Smitty?" A voice asked from somewhere beyond the edge of the flashlight's illumination.

"Yeah, they're here," the man in the rain poncho answered. "Take the girl"

Smitty shoved Kayla to the side as the shadow of another man grabbed her and dragged her out of sight.

"Frank … oh, God … Frank!" she shouted before she disappeared from his view.

"Please, don't hurt her. She had nothing to do with it." Cold desperation swept through him as he weighed his options. *I could throw the flashlight at Smitty and charge up the steps to wrench the shotgun from his hand. It might have been possible when I was younger and thinner. If I try it now, Smitty will blow my ass back down the stairs before I get halfway there.*

"Is that your girl?" Smitty asked keeping the shotgun aimed on Frank. "If it is, you've got you a nice piece of tail there."

"I met her on the road here. She's been injured in a car wreck. She needs help." In another part of the house, he could hear Kayla cursing her captors. "There is no need to point that gun at me. I'm not a robber. I told you we would pay for any damages."

"You're a murderer." The man reached up and pulled back his rain-hood. He was tanned and gaunt, with long dirty-blond hair and an OU ball cap on his head. "You killed Abe and Martha.

"Did you see their bodies? They melted into some sort of slime. They weren't even human, did you know that? There is some sort of unearthly shit happening in your town. Some sort of invasion from another world." He knew his words sounded crazy but Smitty showed no reaction. He looked hard into the man's eyes glistening in the light. There was coldness behind his stare, like the eyes of a snake. "Maybe you aren't human, either?" Frank added. "What is it, Smitty? Are you a part of the human race?"

"Come on up and get your ass into the living room." Smitty motioned with the gun.

Frank climbed the stairs. Once he'd reached the top, Smitty took the flashlight from his hand and shoved him toward the front room. Six men waited for him there. They were typical small-town Oklahoma types dressed in ponchos and raincoats. All were armed with shotguns and hunting rifles. The group reminded Frank of a band of rustlers he'd seen in a western once. One of them even held an oil camping lantern to light the room in a flickering yellow glow. Kayla sat on the couch and looked up at him with tear-filled eyes as he entered. She said nothing, but Frank could read the near panic in her gaze.

Smitty thrust the barrel of the gun against his back. "Go join your girlfriend."

"Why are you doing this?" Kayla asked as he crossed the room and sat by her side. She grabbed his arm and leaned her head against his shoulder. "We've done nothing wrong."

Smitty grinned. "You broke the law," He stepped forward and pointed the shotgun at Frank. "You know what that means?"

"Then take us to jail. Let us talk to the sheriff," Frank said.

"Man, we ain't taking you to jail." Smitty smiled as the group of men chuckled amongst themselves. "We're taking you to church."

Kayla snapped her head up and looked at Smitty. "Don't you know we're in a severe storm? The weather report ordered all people in Omega to take shelter immediately. Are you all such stupid rednecks you can't see the danger coming?"

"The One will protect us. It's God's way."

"It's God's way," the other men in the room echoed.

Frank squeezed Kayla's hand. "Save your breath, girl, I doubt if they're even human."

Smitty rushed forward and struck Frank hard in the jaw with the butt of the pump shotgun. "We're better than human! Our race walked this planet while you're ancestors slithered in the muck of the oceans!" An insane glint showed in the man's eyes. "We are part of the One and the true rightful inheritors of this world. You primates only served as piss-poor stewards until our day of return. That day is now."

Recovering from the blow, Frank turned to gaze back to Smitty. "You're a fucking slug," he said with the iron taste of blood in his mouth.

Smitty smiled. "You'll be one of us, too, in a very short time." He motioned to the rest of the men in the room. "Take them."

The group stepped forward and pulled them to their feet. Frank managed to keep a hold of Kayla's hand as they led the way out of the house and onto the front porch. The wind had died down considerably and the rain was now a slow drizzle. Overhead, the sky was a ceiling of low rolling dark clouds. Broken tree limbs and torn off leaves littered the front yard. With engines running and headlights cutting through the rain, two SUVs waited by the roadside. At gunpoint, the men forced them across the lawn to the vehicles.

"You take her with you," Smitty ordered the group escorting Kayla. "I'll take this prick with me."

"No!" Kayla cried out as they were pulled away and forced to release each other's hands.

Shoving her into the back of the SUV, the armed men slammed the door shut. Kayla's eyes met his for a second through the rain drops splattered on the windshield. She mouthed a silent: "Frank."

Anger and frustration raged within him. *I see no way I can protect Kayla*

now. I don't care if I die. Hell, I've already made a mess of my life but if I could only redeem myself by saving this young girl. Now it looked impossible to do even that. Some knight in shiny armor.

"Get in," Smitty said as he forced him into the back seat of the SUV. Once inside, he sat next to Frank and shoved the shotgun against his ribs. Two other men took the front seat. "Follow them to the church."

The SUV pulled out from the curb and circled behind the lead vehicle holding Kayla. The lights were out in the town of Omega and the streets were shadowed and littered with storm debris. Through the side windows, Frank watched the darkened storefronts of downtown main street slide by.

"I'm not even supposed to be here. I was talked into delivering a case of condoms to your station, but I wrecked the van and got involved in this fucked-up mess," he said.

"You?" Smitty turned his cold eyes to face him. "Where's Marty? He is scheduled to be baptized by Reverend Masterson today."

"He decided to remain human, after all."

"No matter, you can stand in his place."

"Just tell me one thing. Why would you alien bastards need condoms?"

Smitty smiled. "It's our new bodies. We love the way they work."

Frank turned his attention through the front window to the tail lights of the SUV carrying Kayla about fifty feet in front of them. From an alley to the left, he saw the sudden flash of red-and-blue lights. In the next second, a police car came roaring toward their vehicle. The cruiser missed Kayla's SUV but turned its front toward the side of the one Frank rode in.

"Damn!" Smitty shouted. "Turley!"

Frank braced himself the second before the push bar on the front of the police car broadsided the SUV. The two vehicles collided with a jarring impact, knocking Frank and Smitty together. The shotgun tumbled into the floorboards. Rammed by the powerful police car, the SUV skidded off the street and crashed into a storefront, shattering glass and twisting metal in the process. In the seconds of confusion following the collision, Frank pushed Smitty away from him and fumbled for the latch of the passenger door. The door opened and he fell out of the vehicle. Illuminated by the continuous flash of lights from the police cruiser, Smitty cussed and tried to find the dropped shotgun.

Scrambling to his feet, Frank took a second to get his bearings. The SUV had smashed through the front glass of a small supermarket. The red-and-blue police lights flashed across shelves of potato chips, canned goods, loaves of bread. Behind him, he heard the sudden crack of gunfire and the shattering of glass. He realized the shots weren't directed toward him. Voices shouted and more shots followed. With his wet tennis shoes slipping on the waxed floor, Frank ran toward the back of the store. He ducked behind the end of a row of shelves and risked a glance back at the crash site.

Backlit by the red-and-blues, Smitty was now out of the SUV and walking down the center aisle of the store, his shotgun at the ready. His cold eyes searched the dark. Frank ducked back behind the end of the shelf. He had never known such fear in his life. His heart thundered as his hands shook. Desperately, he searched for something he could use as a weapon. His gaze centered on a solitary grocery cart a few feet away. Against his back, his hands groped frantically along the grocery shelf until his trembling fingers wrapped around a large jar. Bringing it to him, in the dim light he realized it was a container of applesauce.

If I'm going to survive, I've got to act now.

He stood and threw the jar with all of his strength at the figure of the advancing Smitty. Reacting instantly, Smitty pulled the trigger on the shotgun and blew apart the jar in mid-air into a cloud of broken glass and applesauce. Frank dove for the grocery cart as Smitty pumped another round into the shotgun. Screaming at the top of his lungs, he flung the cart down the aisle and it slammed into the gunman just when he'd brought the shotgun to fire again. The impact of the cart sent the shot off target and buckshot blew apart bags of dried noodles and beans to the right of Frank's head. Charging forward, he reached Smitty just as he pumped another round into the chamber.

Frank had only one thought. To live, he had to get ahold of the shotgun. Just as Smitty brought the gun once more to bear, Frank latched his hands around the weapon. The two struggled, wrestling back and forth with the shotgun between them. The gun went off and blew out overhead fluorescent lightbulbs that rained pieces of white glass down upon them. The floor was slick with applesauce and they slid back and forth, each struggling to get control of the weapon. Frank still held on as Smitty shoved him backwards. Canned goods on the shelf behind him went scattering everywhere.

"Let go!" Smitty yelled with his hard, gaunt face a foot away from his.

"Fuck you!" Frank slammed his forehead into Smitty's nose in a desperate head butt. Nasal bones cracked and the grip on the shotgun loosened.

Twisting the gun hard, he sent the shotgun out of Smitty's hands and skittering along the store's tiled floor.

Enraged, Smitty screamed as white mucous poured out of his shattered nose. His hands wrapped around Frank's throat in an insane stranglehold. Reaching around him, Frank grabbed up a heavy canned good and swung it against the side of the man's face. The OU hat went flying off as Smitty's head snapped to the side from the blow. He struck again. This time the man's head made a squishy noise from the impact. Still choking Frank, Smitty narrowed his cold gaze. His facial features began changing into something inhuman as the smell of burnt electrical wiring invaded Frank's senses. With a gurgling noise, the mouth stretched beyond human limits as a mass of writhing tentacles erupted from the maw in a nightmarish retch. The head began to misshape and alter into an unearthly squid-like creature. Eyes became dark pools of inhuman intelligence as more tentacles erupted out of the thing's rib cage and back.

Frank screamed in primal terror ripped from a dark beyond his own sanity. He dropped the can and recoiled in revulsion from the nightmare still gripping him. The Smitty-thing reached out for his own face with gray tentacles dripping white slime. The writhing mass opened more to reveal a mouth of serrated teeth. Frank screamed again.

A shot rang out. The creature's head blew apart and showered Frank in chunks of slimy gray meat and white mucous. The horrific decapitated monster released its hold around his throat and dropped to the tiled floor where it shook violently in spasms highlighted by the surreal flashing police lights. Finally, the thing became still and melted into a spreading pool of white liquid.

Exhausted, Frank slid to the floor. A shadow blocked the light.

"The squid-heads are the worst," a strong voice broke the eerie silence.

Frank turned his attention in the direction of the speaker. A tall figure of a man stood in the blinking glow. Older then Frank, he had a strong, stern face highlighted by a moustache as white as snow. A Winchester rifle slung over one shoulder and a white Stetson cowboy hat adorned the top of his head.

"Who—who are you?" Frank's voice sounded broken.

"Sheriff John Turley." The man cocked the Winchester rifle like a cowboy from an old western.

Relief flooded Frank and he felt like he was about to cry. He looked down at his clothes covered in white slime and the pool spreading across the checkerboard tiles of the floor.

"What the hell is happening in your town, sheriff?"

"The end of the world, son, if we don't stop it." Turley held out his hand to help Frank to his feet.

5

"The sad this is Smitty was probably ten times smarter as a squid-head than he ever was as a human," Sheriff Turley said and turned to walk down the grocery aisle of the deserted store to where the shotgun rested some fifteen feet away. Frank watched with a detached sense of reality as the sheriff picked up the gun and checked to see if it was loaded. The cowboy boots of the tall man echoed on the floor tiles as he returned with the weapon.

"What's your name, son?"

"Frank Nolton."

"Well Frank, it's like this, do you know how to fire a shotgun?"

"I used to hunt with a twelve-gauge when I was a teenager."

"Good." Turley handed him the gun. "It's sawed off so you just have to point and pull the trigger. I've got more shells for it in my car."

"I don't understand. Why are you telling me this?"

"You've just been deputized, Frank."

"Deputized?" He looked down at the shotgun in his hands." What the hell is going on?"

"By now, you've probably realized Omega has got a major problem. I destroyed the bridge this morning in hopes no one from the outside would come into town today." The tall lawman began reloading his Winchester with bullets from a gun belt around his waist. "How did you get here?"

"I crashed my van into the creek bed and walked into town. I didn't come alone. There was a young woman with me. Those things took her and she needs our help."

"Forget about her. She's probably already infected. I guess you know this town is overrun with an ungodly alien presence."

"I'm not giving up on Kayla." Frank shook his head. "We've got to do something, sheriff."

"We're going to kill every last one of those unholy abominations that have ruined my town."

There was the crunching of broken glass toward the wrecked entrance to the store. A young man stood in the blinking lights of the police cruiser. Wearing blue jeans and a tee-shirt with Boston University logo, he looked like a hippie college student from the seventies, complete with shoulder-length brown hair and scraggly beard. Over one shoulder, he hefted a backpack.

"Are we done with all the shooting?" the young man asked. "Guns scare the hell out of me. Can I come in now?"

"Come on," Turley said. "I want you to meet Frank Nolton. He killed one of the squid-heads."

"Cool." The young man motioned with a wave. "I'm Wes Corbin." He placed his backpack on a checkout counter and studied Frank for a moment. "Man, it's a pleasure to meet a fellow human in this fucked-up town."

"Wes is an expert on what is going on in Omega. Found him online."

"Sheriff, you better get to your car radio. The highway patrol wants to speak to you immediately. I stalled them as long as I could," Wes said.

"Fill Frank in on everything. When I come back, we move."

Sheriff Turley walked out of the wrecked front of the store as Wes unzipped his backpack. Sliding out a slim laptop, he placed the computer on the shelf and switched it on. Frank stepped forward to join him as the monitor screen brightened and began loading Windows

"How did you know I was human and not one of them?" Frank asked.

Wes pointed to Frank's right hand. "Dude, you're bleeding red blood. Their blood looks like pale powdered milk."

He looked down and discovered two of his fingers were bleeding where the nails were torn. *It must have happened during the fight with Smitty over the shotgun. I'm too numb to even feel the pain.*

"Did the sheriff deputize you as well?" Frank asked.

"Yeah, he's all into that Marshall Dillon frame of mind. You know, good guys wear white hats sort of shit?"

Windows finished loading and Wes hit a key. "I'm going to have to give you the abbreviated version of this, man. There's not much time." On the monitor an image Frank recognized popped into view; the symbol of the star with a flame in its center which he had first seen on Marty's note. "I'm in my third year as anthropology major at Boston U. I'm currently writing a thesis on ancient man's view of the cosmos and the origins of religion. I spent two years pouring over obscure texts and drawings. Old books and strange writings no one even remembers anymore. In my research, I kept coming across this cult known only as the Church of the Fiery Star. That's the symbol this fucked up church uses."

"I've seen that symbol. It's painted on a billboard outside of town."

"Yeah, I know," Wes said and grabbed a bag of chips off a nearby shelf and tore it open. "I painted it, man." He crunched on a potato chip. "Anyway, I'm doing all this intense research tracing back weird writings and shit on this church. The earliest reference I can find is on a cult in Peru. Fragments of ancient pre-Incan texts detailing a belief in a cosmology filled with extra-dimensional alien gods who once walked on our world when our ancestors were living in the soup of the oceans. I'm thinking to myself, those ancient Peruvians were smoking some excellent drugs, man, until I ran across more references to this church in the writings of the Victorian age, including Aleister Crowley and other noted occultists. That's when I found this." Wes hit a button and the image changed into pages of a handwritten book. "The Book of Ebon. It's a rare forbidden book tucked away in some old library in Massachusetts. I scanned the thing into my laptop. You want to freak your mind out, try reading this wonderful text in the middle of the night."

"What does this have to do with Omega?" Frank said as he watched Wes flip through pages of the book on the monitor screen. Page after page of strange symbols and drawings flashed across the screen.

"I'm getting to that, man." Wes stopped cycling through the scanned pages. The image on the screen was a crude technical drawing of some sort of machine. "This book was penned by a Reverend Bell in Rhode Island around the end of the nineteenth century. He claimed the writings came to him in a dream from another dimension. The church he founded became involved in ritual killings and sacrifices. The Reverend and his entire congregation were either killed or run out of town. No one knows exactly."

"What's the machine in the drawing?" Frank pointed to the screen.

"Some sort of device used to open a portal between dimensions."

"An old man named Abe told me something about the Fray, a tear in the fabric of dimensions."

"Precisely, that's what it's supposed to do. Open a portal to another dimension. It's all weird science, man, like something out of a bad B-movie. Anyway, after Reverend Bell disappears, another preacher steps into the story. This fuckhead," Wes tapped the keyboard and the photograph of a handsome looking man in his early fifties appeared. Close-cropped white hair and a lined graven face with dark eyes highlighted the man's features. "Reverend Damien Masterson. This guy is a Billy Graham from hell. He preaches all hellfire and brimstone end-of-the-world shit with one difference. He's going to bring about the end the world. A real psycho nutjob."

"The Unity Church," Frank said.

"You got it, man. The guy is spouting the teachings of Reverend Bell and gets into some major trouble in Massachusetts. He disappears from the radar screen for a few years and surfaces here in Omega."

"Why here?"

"It's got something to do with the Fray. Omega is sitting on one of the places where the space between dimensions is the weakest. So, when I'm doing my research online for my thesis on this obscure cult, I find out some sheriff in a small town in Oklahoma is using Google for info on the Fiery Star emblem. That's how I got in touch with our Roy Rogers here. He emails me with suspicions about the new reverend in town and the church he is presiding over. Strange happenings are taking place, like church meetings in the dead of the night and trucks arriving in town carrying weird equipment. Townspeople acting odd, that sort of stuff."

"Like *Invasion of the Body Snatchers*."

"Worse," Wes nodded and ate a handful of potato chips. "When these slug-things enter your body they hijack your DNA and begin transforming you into one of them. You don't have to be asleep and they don't make a double of you. These things are so perfect at what they do, anyone on the outside would never know you were carrying one inside. All your emotions, feelings, sexual desires are all the same. Except you're no longer human and now serve the One."

"Abe mentioned something about the One."

"As far as I can figure, the One is some sort of granddaddy alien entity in another dimension. I don't have all the answers, and I don't want to know all the answers. This shit fucks with your mind." Wes closed the laptop. "Talking online to the sheriff, I figured out Reverend Masterson has surfaced again and this time he is going to open the Fray once and for all. Once the portal is opened, these squid-heads will pour into our dimension. I flew in from Boston and met Sheriff Turley because I knew there was not much time and it was going to happen today."

"Why today?"

"It's the Equinox, man. You know, the longest day of the year. They need to do their ritual on a celestial event like that."

"They took a girl with them. Her name is Kayla."

"I hope she wasn't family or something, man. Once Reverend Masterson baptizes her in the new church, she's no longer human."

"He may not have time to infect her. I'm going to get her out of there."

"Dude, we can't let any of those alien fucks escape. If even one makes it outside the town limits and begins infecting others, this horror will spread exponentially. I calculate in eight months, the squids will have spread through the world and mankind will be on the verge of extinction. Why do you think we haven't called in the Highway Patrol or National Guard? It poses too great a risk to spread the infestation. Man, you've got to let her go."

"I can't."

Sheriff Turley stepped in through the broken glass door at the front of the store.

"We hit them now," he said. "The OHP is reporting that an F5 category tornado is headed right for Omega. This town is about to have a major tornado event!"

Wes grabbed up his laptop and quickly stuffed it into his backpack. "It must be the dimensional machine Reverend Masterson is using to open the Fray. It's intensifying the storm."

"I like to think the one true God is about to wipe these blasphemous aliens from the face of the Earth," Turley replied. "They are all gathered in the church. We hit them with everything we got and let the tornado do the rest."

Frank followed the sheriff out of the grocery store and into the street lit by the red-and-blue flashing lights of the police car. Outside, a soft breeze carried an electric hum and the smell of ozone. To the East, a wall of rolling angry black clouds twisted in the sky. Wes went behind him and jumped into the back seat of the sheriff's cruiser. Opening the front door, Frank slid into the vehicle as Sheriff Turley climbed behind the wheel. The police radio blasted with voices announcing emergency codes and visual sightings of the tornado.

"Under your seat there is a box of shells for that pump," Turley said above the radio as he started the engine. "You better load that shotgun, son. You're going to need it."

Reaching under his seat, Frank pulled out the box of ammo. "What are we going to do? Just go in shooting?"

"Pretty much." Turley turned the cruiser onto the street. "No time to be subtle. We shoot our way inside and kill Reverend Masterson and as many squids as we can before the tornado hits."

Wes spoke from the back seat. "We've got to destroy the machine, man"

"That, too." Turley replied. "Frank, you can't be afraid to pull the trigger. You're going to be faced with shooting women and children. Don't think twice about doing it. They are all infected with the alien infestation. They're not human anymore."

"I don't know if I can do that." He slipped the last of the shotgun rounds into the chamber. "I don't know if I can shoot a child or a woman."

"If you don't, they'll kill you," Turley replied as he stepped on the gas and accelerated the patrol car through the darkened streets of Omega.

Frank stared out the side window of the car. *Can I kill women and children, even if they are infested with an alien intelligence? I don't think I can do it. Kill Kayla? I don't think I can do that, either. I just pray I don't have to.*

"Well you two freaks may think you're gunslingers from Dodge City," Wes spoke up from the backseat. "I've got something better than shotguns and rifles."

Frank looked over his shoulder and peered through the metal screen separating the backseat from the front. From the floorboard, Wes sat a plastic milk crate on his lap. Inside were six glass wine bottles with rags stuffed into the necks of each.

"Molotov cocktails," Wes smiled. He pulled out a Bic lighter and flicked the button. "Flame on, man. I've always been a bit of a pyro."

"Don't light up in here," Turley said. "You'll blow us all to hell."

"Just warming things up for the reception we'll receive at the church."

"What do we do about the tornado?" Frank turned back to Turley.

"The church has a basement that serves as a storm shelter. We'll blast our way through and hide in there."

This is insane, Frank thought. *I've got to go along with this in the hopes I can save Kayla.*

The police car raced through the dark streets. Peering through the rain splattered windshield, Frank saw a greenish glow rising up into the black clouds overhead. As the car rounded a corner, the structure of a white country chapel came into view. The building sat in the center of a groomed lawn. A peaked roof with a white steeple topped the clapboard church. Stained glass windows glowed with an unearthly greenish light from inside the place of worship. Two large arched wooden doors waited at the top a short flight of stone steps. In the dark, turbulent clouds overhead, fingers of green lightning flashed through the sky.

"Dear God," Frank muttered aloud.

"God has nothing to do with this church, son," the sheriff said as he swung the patrol car around in the street in front of the manicured lawn. He stopped the car with its front facing the doors of the chapel.

"It's like I said," Wes spoke from behind Frank. "The dimensional machine is intensifying the storm. Look at the green lightning."

"They shouldn't screw with Oklahoma's weather because it will fuck you up," Frank said.

"Reverend Masterson's machine has caused his own destruction." Turley picked up the Winchester rifle and laid it on the top of the dashboard. "The fool probably doesn't know an F5 tornado is heading his way."

"What's the plan, sheriff?" Frank rested the shotgun across his lap.

"No real plan, son," Turley said as he reached into his front pocket and removed a can of Skoal. Taking a good pinch, he placed the chewing tobacco under his tongue and passed the can to Frank. "Help yourself."

"No, thanks." Frank shook his head.

"What about you, college boy?"

"You got any weed instead?"

Turley chuckled. Putting the tin back in his front pocket, he asked, "Are you married, Frank?"

"Divorced."

"Wes?"

"Are you kidding, man? I'm a geeky college guy who spends his spare time perusing through books written by long-dead madmen. I can't even get laid."

Turley placed both hands on the steering wheel and stared out at the hellish looking church. "I was married thirty-six years to a wonderful woman until I came home to find she was something inhuman. I caved in her head with an iron skillet and sat and watched the woman I shared my life with melt into a puddle of white crud. Emma played the organ at the church on Sunday morning. She always wanted me to go to church with her, but I always made excuses. She's gone now and Reverend Masterson is to blame."

"There's a girl in there I promised to protect," Frank said. "She's innocent and doesn't deserve to die."

"Son, they were all innocent and none deserved what they became. This was a good town filled with good people." Turley reached down and grabbed the microphone off the police radio. "This is Sheriff Turley of Omega."

"Captain Wilson of the OHP. Sheriff, did you get your people to shelter?" A voice asked.

"We'll be in the basement of the Unity Church," he said. "Once the tornado passes send emergency responders to that location."

"Will do, sheriff. May God be with you and the town of Omega."

"Roger that and out." Turley hung the microphone up. "Well, boys, its time to test out this fancy ramming prow and high-dollar suspension the taxpayers paid for when they bought this patrol car."

"Are we just going to drive through the front doors?" Frank asked.

"Yep, that's the plan. Wes, hang onto those bottles of gas and brace yourself." Turley stepped on the accelerator and the police car jumped the curb and raced across the expanse of lawn.

In the back seat, Wes let out a loud whoop. "Who you going to call?" he shouted. "Squid busters!"

6

Frank held on tight to the shotgun as Sheriff Turley's police cruiser sped across the expanse of lawn toward the steps and the double front doors of the Unity Church. He took a breath and, for a second, thought about how frightening and bizarre his life had become. In the expanse of one day, he'd found himself fighting an alien invasion in a small town in Oklahoma and saving a beautiful college girl. Now, he was heading toward a confrontation with whatever inhuman abominations waited in the church. The worst part was he knew Kayla was in there as well. He had promised to get her out of Omega alive and he was going to do it or die in the process.

"We're coming up on it, boys!" Turley said. "God be with us."

"Yeah, Baby," Wes shouted, doing some lame impersonation of Austin Powers.

The front wheels of the police cruiser hit the steps of the church with a loud whump sound. The powerful suspension of the car absorbed most of the impact and the vehicle barreled up the entry stairs. The next second, the push bar on the front grill shattered through the double doors and the police cruiser roared into the main chapel of the church. A woman's body thudded up onto the hood and spider-webbed the front windshield before she flew over the roof of the car. Frank got a glimpse of the pastel blue dress she wore. The police cruiser continued into the church as people screamed in panic and scattered in front of the oncoming car. Some were too slow and went under the wheels making sickening thumps. Frank thought for one horrifying heartbeat, *Oh my God, what if they're not aliens! What if they're just people! What have we done?*

Then he saw the pulpit through the cracked windshield and he knew they had driven into the center of madness.

Reverend Masterson stood naked before the church. His hands outspread in supplication and his eyes rolled back in his head leaving only dead white in their place. Thick conduit-like cables ran from open wounds on his flesh and fed into some towering machine rising behind him. At the sight of the strange device, Frank remembered something he had seen in a Frankenstein movie as a child: a Tesla coil. Crackling bolts of greenish energy pulsed up and down the tower of the machine, lighting the front of the church in an unearthly glow.

The police car slid to a stop. "Let's make them pay for my Emma!" Sheriff Turley grabbed up his Winchester and swung open the driver's door.

Frank pushed open the car door on his side. With shotgun in hand, he leapt out onto the wooden floor of the church. Crowds of churchgoers cowered before him. Women, children, and elderly huddled in fear amid the rows of wooden pews. He searched in desperation for Kayla but could not see her.

"Turley!" A hoarse voice hissed from the pulpit. Masterson's eyes were now back to showing dark hatred as they focused on the sheriff. He stepped forward dragging the conduit cables behind him. "You dare to defile the sanctity of this church!"

"You call this unholy breeding ground a church?" The sheriff cocked his Winchester rifle and fired. The shot echoed amid the humming of the tall machine as the bullet caught Masterson in the center of his chest. "Go to hell, you alien heathen."

The reverend staggered back a couple of steps from the impact of the bullet and then looked down at the fleshy hole where his heart had once been. His eyes focused back on the sheriff. "Do you think your primitive weapons will hurt me? I strode upon the sand of this planet when your ancestors swam in the slime! Look upon my face, for now I am a god!" His head leaned back and laughed a cold chuckle. His nude body began to twist and distort.

"Then how about a little fire, scarecrow?" Wes shouted as he emerged from the rear seat with a burning rag sticking out of a Molotov cocktail. He threw the bottle as hard as he could at the pulpit and it landed before the steps exploding in a pool of flaming gasoline. Reverend Masterson stepped back from the fire.

"Kill them, my children!" His voice boomed in the church.

Frank caught sight of movement out of the corner of his eye. Letting out a hissing gurgle, a woman in her mid-thirties leaped through the air toward him. Her head began to change shape and tentacles vomited out of her mouth. Pulling the trigger by shear instinct, he shot her in the head, which exploded into meaty chunks of grey meat and white fluid. She fell on the wooden floor before his feet, kicking in spasms as more tentacles ripped from her chest.

"Where are you, Kayla?" Frank yelled as he worked the pump on the gun.

The crowd of church-things swarmed forward. Repeated cracks of the Winchester resonated in rapid succession. Frank spun to see an elderly man in a black suit rushing to grab him. The man's mouth hung open as a white centipede-like creature slithered out. Frank pulled the trigger and the blast blew a hole through the man's mouth and gray fleshy matter out the back of his head.

"Kayla!" He shouted again. He turned to scan the interior of the church, which had erupted into pure chaos. Wes had another Molotov in his hand. He tried to lob it into the crowd but was overwhelmed. The bottle dropped at his feet and fire exploded. He screamed in terror as flames engulfed his body and set several of the church goers alight with its splash. Pirouetting in a dance of burning death, the young man collapsed to the floor. Firing his rifle, the sheriff was clearing his way through the mob in an effort to reach Masterson and the pulpit.

Something grabbed Frank's leg and he looked down to see a boy of about eight hissing up at him. The child's head began to transform into something else. Frank drove the butt of the shotgun down into the boy-thing's skull, which cracked like soft balsa wood. The thing collapsed onto the floor and twisted in convulsions of gray tentacles and milky fluid.

"Kayla!" he yelled above the confusion and cocked the shotgun.

"I'm here, Frank!" Her voice called out from somewhere in the crowded church.

"Where?" He pulled the trigger again and the face of a portly man exploded. He kicked the headless mass away from him as his back fell against the side of the police car. Jacking another round into the shotgun, he scanned the crowd. The carnage had turned into a scene out of a madman's vision of Hell. Churchgoing townspeople were shifting forms into things non-human. The Winchester boomed and Frank turned for a second to look at the pulpit. Sheriff Turley had made it to the base of the flaming carpet on the steps.

"You dare to defy me!" Masterson croaked in an inhuman voice. The reverend's body began to transform into a hideous misshapen hulk. In shock, Frank watched as the madman grew both in size and bulk until he towered above the sheriff. A massive squid-like head with a mouth of writhing tentacles replaced the reverend's graven face. More greenish-gray tentacles erupted from the thing's chest and back. The ropy appendages lashed around the sheriff, who screamed in insane terror as the monster lifted him into the air.

"Look upon the face of a Sentient, human, and know you are doomed!" The Masterson-horror croaked in a voice barely discernible as he ripped the sheriff's body in half and threw the two bloody parts aside.

Now in the presence of the Sentient, the crowd of church-things ceased their attacks and bowed their heads in respect to the horror standing on the pulpit. Frank used the lull in the battle to open the back door of the patrol car and climb in. He began to reach into the box of shotgun shells and reload the pump when he noticed the milk crate Wes had used to carry the Molotov cocktails beside him. There were four more bottles left and Wes's lighter on the seat beside the crate.

"Hey, stranger, can a girl get a ride?" Kayla stuck her head in the car door.

"You scared the shit out of me!" Frank put aside the shotgun. "I nearly shot you! Hop in!"

She slid into the passenger seat and smiled. "Saving me is becoming a full time job now."

"We're not out of here yet." He glanced through the spider-webbed front windshield to see the Masterson-horror staring at the patrol car with intelligent octopus-like eyes of pure malevolence. White slime dripped from its open mouth and tentacles.

"That thing looks really pissed," Kayla said.

"The keys are in the ignition. Start the car for me," Frank said as he flicked the lighter and lit the four rag tops to the Molotov bottles.

Kayla leaned over and turned the ignition. The police car's engine roared into life. Frank slid out of the back seat holding the milk crate containing the four bottles with flaming rag fuses.

"What are you going to do, Frank?"

"The reverend is about to get a lot hotter under the collar. Put your seat belt on."

Outside the patrol car, he put the crate on the hood. The howling of the wind whipping against the walls outside the church began increasing in volume. The raging storm resonated with a noise like a thundering freight train, a sound he remembered well from May 4, 1999. He turned his attention to the thing staring at him from the pulpit.

"Hey Fucking Ugly, what the hell you looking at?" Frank shouted at the alien horror.

The face tentacles twitched on the creature. "Bow before your new god, human. Soon your race will be devoured by the Sentients," the horrific voice croaked.

"Why don't you eat this instead?" Frank grabbed the milk crate and threw it with all his might at the pulpit. The plastic box of gasoline-filled bottles crashed against the chest of the monster and flames splashed along its greenish-gray torso. The monstrosity let out a horrendous bellow as it ripped the conduit cables from the flesh of its body.

"Fool! Do you think fire can hurt the form of a Sentient?" The Masterson-horror stepped off the pulpit and began walking toward Frank and the patrol car. Flames began to die down across its blistered flesh. As it approached, the monster's clawed feet trampled the church-things who did not get out of the way, as it batted others aside with its massive claws.

Frank stepped to the open driver door of the police car. The intensity of the noise outside the church grew in volume.

"You Sentients are not all that smart, are you?" he shouted at the looming alien being.

"You dare to insult your new god?" the monster croaked.

"You missed one important fact, dumb-ass. You forgot about Oklahoma's weather!"

Frank dived behind the steering wheel of the police car and jammed the shift into reverse as he slammed the accelerator to the floor. Tires squealed white smoke on the wooden floor.

The tornado hit the church then. The stained glass windows burst inward in imploding cascades of multi-colored glass as the wind ripped off the chapel roof. It disappeared into the spinning black clouds overhead in debris of splintered wood. The last thing Frank saw before he backed out of the church was the Sentient emitting a horrible death scream as the cyclonic winds sucked it up and slammed it into the energy field around the machine in a shower of greenish sparks.

The car bounced down the front steps and slid into the lawn as the church imploded into a maelstrom of flying chunks of clapboard, wooden pews, and alien bodies sucked up into the dirt and twisting funnel cloud. The roar of the tornado thundered as it devoured the country chapel as if it were made of matchsticks.

"Holy Shit!" Kayla screamed.

Frank slammed the police car into drive and spewed grass behind the tires as he spun the car around and away from the huge twister. Powerful winds whipped at the vehicle as branches and leaves pummeled its sides. Against the furious gale, he fought to keep the car on the road.

"It's behind us!" Kayla shouted as she looked out the back window.

Driving as fast as he could, Frank sped the police car onto the main street of Omega. In the rearview mirror, the massive cyclone destroyed the town's buildings behind the fleeing vehicle. High-tension wires were ripped from the ground as buildings imploded into chunks of rubble swept up into the storm. Parked cars were being knocked aside like toys by the path of the twisting funnel cloud.

"Look out!" Kayla shouted.

A telephone pole fell in the street before them. Frank whipped the wheel to the left and drove up on the sidewalk, knocking aside a newspaper machine and a fallen store awning. They bounced back onto the main street as the powerful wind threatened to pick up the police car. He stepped harder on the gas and raced over rolling limbs and blowing trash pushed by the wind. It was nearly impossible to see with all the dirt and debris in the road before them. Out of the corner of his eye, he caught a sign to his right that read:

You are now leaving
Omega City limits.
Thank you for visiting.

Frank knew they were now on the one road in and out of Omega. In the side view mirror, he saw the funnel cloud tear through Smitty's Filling Station. The metal roof awning went spinning end over end in the air. The tornado swept left and right along each side of the highway, ripping fence posts and trees from the ground and sucking them up into the spinning cloud of dirt and debris. He pressed harder on the accelerator and put more distance between the car and the funnel cloud. They were coming up quick on the destroyed highway bridge.

Kayla grabbed his arm. "We're not going to crash into the creek again, are we?"

"Once per day is my limit. Unhook your seat belt. When I stop the car, I want you to get out as fast as you can and hide under the broken bridge."

She nodded. "Sounds like a plan."

The wrecked bridge loomed on the highway before them. Frank stomped on the brakes and spun the wheel so the patrol car slid sideways on screaming tires. It came to a rest at the edge of the broken bridge span.

"Out!" Frank shouted. "Run!"

Kayla dived from the passenger door as he leaped out on his side. The ominous howling of the approaching tornado was deafening. Frank took a second to look back at the massive swirling funnel cloud towering into the blackened sky. It was less than fifty yards away and the energy of its turbulence pummeled him nearly to his knees.

"Dear God," he shouted against the wind.

"Frank!" Kayla screamed at him above the storm's fury. She looked out from under the bridge and her eyes, filled with fear and concern, met his. "Get your ass down here!"

Charging and slipping down the dirt bank of the creek bed, he ducked under the bridge span. The freight-train roar of the storm grew louder.

"Hold onto me!" He reached up and grabbed a piece of iron rebar sticking from the broken concrete.

Kayla wrapped her arms around him and pressed her body to his. "Sure thing, partner."

The tornado hit the bridge and the wind buffeted them where they lay together. Frank held on with all his strength to the bar as the whipping wind threatened to tear them away from their shelter under the bridge. The roar of the funnel was like a hundred freight trains passing at once. Dirt and dust filled his eyes and lungs. He felt Kayla's grip slip away from around his body. Then she was gone.

"Kayla!" He screamed but the fierce wind shoved the sound back into his throat.

7

As quickly as it came, the tornado passed, leaving a path of destruction in its wake. The howling winds began to die and the thundering roar of the funnel cloud diminished as the storm continued along the road out of Omega. Wedged under the bridge embankment, Frank spat out dirt and shook dust from his eyes and hair. A broken tree branch lay across his legs and he kicked it off and sat up.

"Kayla," he called out. There was no answer. Fear rose up from his stomach and into his throat. *She's gone. The storm snatched her away from me. To come so far and through so much, only to lose her in the end.*

He slid from under the bridge to find the creek littered with storm debris. Tree limbs, telephone poles, fence posts, and remnants of what was once the town of Omega were scattered along the creek bed. Strewn amidst the larger pieces of wreckage were clothes, trash, and broken lumber. Frank crawled over a washing machine blocking his way.

"Kayla!" he shouted louder.

"Frank," her voice replied weak and barely audible. "I'm here."

"Where?" His heart jumped at the sound of her voice. He scrambled further down the debris-laden creek bank. "I can't see you."

"There's something on top of me," she said from beneath a large part of a wooden wall lying against the slope of the littered bank. The section came from a destroyed home. Mounted in its side was a kitchen window complete with flowered curtains.

He climbed down to her. "Oh God, girl, are you all right?" Grabbing the broken wood and siding, he lifted it up and threw it into the creek bottom.

Covered in dust and twigs, she looked up at him with a dirty face. "Can we go home now?"

Joyous tears began to well in Frank's eyes as he knelt beside her. "Are you hurt?"

"Duh! A fucking house fell on me." She sat stiffly up as red dirt fell from her clothes. "I feel like the wicked witch in the Wizard of Oz."

Frank fought back his tears. "I thought I'd lost you."

"The tornado pulled me down the bank and the next thing I know this chunk of a house is laying on top of me." She leaned into him with tears streaking down her smudged face. "Thanks to you, I'm still here."

Putting his arm around her, he touched his forehead to hers and looked deep into her brown eyes. "My hobby, remember?"

"I think this is the part where I kiss you," she sobbed.

He pulled back a bit. A horrific thought filled his mind. *What if this wasn't Kayla anymore? What if she had been baptized in the alien church? What if she was one of them? She could be carrying the slug-thing in her mouth.*

"What's wrong? You don't want to kiss me?" she whispered. "Don't give me that bullshit about you being a divorced man and not having any for six months. Kiss me, Frank. You deserve it."

With his arm around her, he squeezed the area where her rib had been broken in the van wreck earlier in the afternoon. She didn't wince. "Your rib doesn't hurt anymore?"

"No." She looked at him evenly. There were no answers in her eyes.

"Why?"

"Because my ankle is fucking killing me."

He moved down to her feet. "Why didn't you say so?"

"I didn't want to be a whiner."

He pulled up her pant leg to see a large wooden splinter sticking out of her ankle with blood … red human blood … streaming from the wound.

"How bad is it?" Kayla winced, and looked away. "Am I bleeding badly?"

"Yes," he said and then laughed. "It's the most beautiful thing I've ever seen."

"I don't find my bleeding out all over the fucking creek funny."

"Just sit still." Frank pulled up the flowery curtain from the kitchen window of the wall wreckage. Tearing off a strip of cloth, he tied it tightly around her calf in a makeshift tourniquet. "That should help staunch the blood flow. Are you hurting anyplace else?"

"Why, so you can laugh at those, too?" She shook her head. "I'm probably covered in scrapes and bruises, but beyond that I think I'm fine."

"You're one tough girl."

"Thanks. What's the plan, now?"

"Same as before. We walk back down the road to the highway."

"I don't think I can walk."

"I'll give you a piggy-back." He reached down and took her hand. "You're so thin, you probably don't weigh more than a hundred and ten pounds soaking wet."

"You just keep telling yourself that," she chuckled.

He hefted her up onto his back. He was exhausted but the joy of surviving the storm and finding Kayla alive had given him new strength. Slowly, he picked his way along the debris and up the creek bank on the other side of the bridge. The road leading back to the highway stretched before them. With Kayla riding on his back, he began walking the long way back.

The tornado retreated into the dark clouds leaving only a light drizzle behind. The mist dampened them both as they plodded along the blacktop.

"Nobody told me fighting alien gods and saving the world was this much work." Frank said wearily as he continued down the road.

"Is anyone going to believe us about the alien invasion and the Unity Church?" Kayla said.

"Who cares? We survived, and nothing else matters."

"By the way, here comes the cavalry."

Frank looked further down the road. The flashing lights of highway patrol cars and ambulances raced toward them in a caravan of emergency vehicles. Overhead, an OHP helicopter flew in the direction toward Omega; its rotors beating against the rainy sky. With sirens blaring and lights flashing, the line of emergency vehicles slid to a stop in front of Frank and Kayla standing in the middle of the road. An Oklahoma Highway Patrol car was the lead vehicle from which a state trooper buzzed down a window.

"I'm sorry, guys; the bridge is out." Frank said.

"Did you just come from Omega?"

"Yes." He lowered Kayla carefully to the asphalt surface of the road. "Can I get some medical attention for my passenger here?"

EMTs carrying equipment cases and rolling a stretcher rushed to

Kayla's side. They promptly lifted her up onto the stretcher as one of the emergency medics asked, "What's the nature of your injuries?"

"My ankle and rib hurts like hell," she said. "I think I've lost a lot of blood."

Frank squeezed Kayla's hand. "I'll let them work on you now."

"Stay near," Kayla replied.

Frank walked to where a group of highway patrol troopers and emergency responders gathered in a huddle. A map of the area was spread out on the hood of a patrol cruiser and one man, in his late fifties, shouted commands into a radio. "We need county here with bridge equipment, stat. That's right, the tornado knocked out the bridge. I need more 'copters for medical evacuations, now."

"You're not going to find many survivors," Frank stated.

The man put aside the radio. "Were you there when the storm hit?"

"The town was gathered in the church and the tornado destroyed it. The girl and I barely escaped in the sheriff's police car."

"I'm Captain Williams." The man offered a strong handshake.

"Frank Nolton."

"Aerial reconnaissance reports Omega has been flattened by the tornado. You're damn lucky to be alive, Frank."

"Tell me about it."

"Sheriff Turley is a personal friend of mine. Did you know what happened to him?"

"He died bravely trying to save his town. He was a good man. I'm sorry."

Someone tapped him on the shoulder and he turned to see it was a young EMT. "We're about to load her up and take her to the hospital. She wants to talk to you."

Before he walked away, Captain Williams said. "Don't go far. We don't have a map of Omega. I may need you to assist us with more information about where the church is located in the rubble."

Frank nodded and then made his way through the responder vehicles and OHP patrol cars. In the flashing glow of yellow emergency lights, Kayla was strapped to a stretcher; white bandages were wrapped around her ankle and the side of her forehead. To the side, EMTs waited to lift her into the back of an ambulance.

"Hey, partner," she smiled and took his hand. "Are you going to ride with me to the hospital?"

Frank shook his head. "I'm going to hang around here and help the OHP. I'll catch up with you later."

"I've got something to tell you." She pulled him closer and whispered in his ear, "You saved me and the world, Frank. You should be proud."

"Not bad for a condom salesman," he replied.

"Not bad at all."

"I think I'll take that kiss now," he said with a smile.

Their lips met. For a moment in time, the world fell away and the horror they faced together faded in their embrace.

"Thank you." Kayla breathed when the kiss ended. EMTs lifted her up into the ambulance and were about to close the back doors when she called out, "Don't forget to call your wife, Frank. You promised, so make that call."

The doors shut and the ambulance siren wailed as the vehicle pulled out from the shoulder of the road and headed toward the highway. Frank stood on the wet asphalt and watched the flashing lights disappear into the misty rain.

Call Melanie? What would I say? What could I say? He let out a long, weary sigh and returned to Captain Williams giving orders to his men.

"I need to call my wife," Frank announced.

"Here, use my cell." The highway patrol captain handed him a phone and went back to directing the emergency operation.

Frank punched the numbers into the phone and pressed send.

"Hello?" her soft voice answered after three rings.

"Melanie, it's me."

"Frank?"

"Yes."

A long pause hung between them.

"I'm sorry for what I did to you and the family, Mel. I was so stupid. I love you and the kids so much. Can you forgive me?"

"I love you, too," she said with the tremble of tears in her voice.

"Can we start over and try again, babe? Can we make it work this time?"

"Come home, Frank."

JACK THE KNIFE

The newspapers called him Jack the Knife. He liked the title, though Jack wasn't his real name. He just used it to sign the bottom of the letters he sent to the police

Jack butchered women but didn't think of himself as a butcher. He was a sculptor with a large hunting knife as his tool and soft female flesh as his medium. He would take a living woman, and, with knife in hand, change her into a thing of beauty. After her breasts were sliced off, her throat cut open, and her genitals slashed to ribbons, then, and only then, did Jack feel any arousal toward a female. He would stand looking over his masterpiece and feel the rush of blood to his penis. The newspapers got his title wrong. His name should have been Jack-Off the Knife.

Driving through the dark streets, Jack hunted for number thirteen.

His utility van had the insignia of a plumbing company on the side because Jack worked as a plumber during the day. Night is when he became the hunter. He stalked the poorest parts of the inner city. There, whenever he slowed to a stop, hookers came to the van and asked for a date. Reaching in through the open driver's window, they rubbed his crotch in some vain attempt to arouse him. Jack didn't like to do whores. They were too easy. As a child, he'd once seen a hawk swoop in and snatch up a pigeon on the ground. Bundled in the hawk's talons, the pigeon never fought back and accepted its inevitable, gruesome death. Whores were like that. They barely put up a fight or screamed when he began work with his knife. It was as if they'd accepted the fate of their ruined lives long before he'd arrived. Housewives and soccer moms were the best. He once snatched a mom out of a supermarket parking lot, leaving behind her kids screaming in the SUV. Under the knife she begged, cried, and prayed. She was so beautiful, Jack got off three times.

In the rearview mirror, he caught a glimpse of his pudgy round cheeks, prominent forehead, and short curly red hair which reminded people of a clown's wig. His eyes stared deep into his reflection in the mirror as he heard the words of his sick pathetic excuse of a mother echo in his thoughts. *Bozo the clown,* she'd called him while lighting her crack pipe, *why don't you go and join a fuckin' circus? You ugly freak! A fuckin' ugly clown!* Then she would laugh and blow the crack smoke in his face.

Jack smiled to himself. "Who is laughing now, Mother?" he spoke aloud as he steered the van around a corner.

Mom had been number one.

For a second, his eyes caught the headlights of a car turning behind his van. *Have I seen those headlights before?* Jack asked himself. *I think I saw them behind the van earlier.* He had to be cautious. In the last week, the police had found some of his pieces of rotting art along Highway 90. The letters he sent gave them subtle clues where to look for his little masterpieces. He loved to play a cat and mouse game with the police. It made the hunt even more enjoyable. Since the discovery of his latest victims, the police had set up a task force composed of crime scene investigators, serial killer profilers, FBI special agents, etc. His story aired on America's Most Wanted, CNN, Fox, and all the major networks. The sad pictures of his victims, a pitiful photo parade of crack whores, white trash, and an occasional suburban housewife were paraded on national TV.

Jack the Knife was now big news. Now, more than ever, he had to be careful.

He decided to skip hunting in the inner city. Another crack whore would not do. It had been nine weeks since his last kill and the urge needed to be filled badly. He drove away from the slums and headed uptown. The park was his secondary hunting ground. If he was lucky, he might catch a jogger still out this late in the evening. Female joggers were such elusive prey and always a challenge. They were too fast for him to chase on foot. His three hundred pounds of fat couldn't keep up if they ran. He had to snatch a jogger in one swoop. Catch them by surprise, take them down quickly, and drag them into the bushes. It was the hawk and the pigeon analogy again.

Fifteen minutes later, he cruised through the narrow lanes crisscrossing the city park. The night was still warm and he spotted a few runners plodding on the concrete jogging trail twisting under park lights and dark trees. He pulled the van to the side and parked in the shadows beyond a streetlight. With the sounds of the engine pinging as it cooled down, Jack contemplated his next move. Staring out the passenger window at a copse of dark trees, he knew the jogging trail wound near those trees on the other side of the hill. If he hid himself and waited, maybe he would get lucky, and a girl would come jogging by. It was risky, he knew. Nine months ago, he had snatched his third victim from this park. She was a tall, lanky blonde named Janell or Janet, he couldn't remember. Anyone jogging now in the park might be on extra alert to look for someone in the shadows. The police may have staked out the park as well.

He was going to have to chance it. The urge was too strong. It twisted in his mind and gut like a cold snake. He reached beneath the driver's seat and pulled up a toolbox, not the one he used on his plumbing job, but the other one he used for hunting. Inside the box he took out his latex clown mask, the large hunting knife, and a roll of duct tape. The final thing he removed was his hand-held stun gun. He pushed the button on the side and blue fire sputtered between the two contact studs, lighting the interior of the van in a flash of arc-blue. *The batteries are still strong,* he told himself. *Good.* He stuffed all the items in the various pockets of his jacket and left the van.

Trudging up the hill to the stand of trees, Jack waited in the darkness to catch his breath. He hid his large body behind the thickest trunk he could find and patiently watched the jogging trail. After a few minutes, the shadowed form of a young female jogger rounded a bend and came running his way. Jack felt the rush of excitement of having new prey in sight. He decided to move closer to the edge of the trail, bringing him nearer to the girl when she rounded the next bend. In the process of changing to the new position, his heavy foot snapped a dry tree branch on the ground. The noise alerted the girl jogger and she changed her path and left the jogging trail to give the dark trees a wide berth. Jack's heart sank as he watched her run out of his reach. The move saved her life.

He decided to return before his van was spotted by a patrolling police cruiser. He left the trees behind and trudged down the hill toward where he'd parked. Halfway down, he stopped.

In the streetlight behind his van, a woman with long blonde hair knelt on one knee. She wore a jogging jacket and tight shorts and was massaging one of her calf muscles. Jack caught his breath. She looked exactly like the woman he'd snatched nine months earlier in the park. *What was her name? Janelle?* This woman was victim number three all over again. Same hair, same jogging outfit and tennis shoes, same body build, age, etc. Jack had to blink his eyes. He thought, for a moment, he was staring at a ghost as he kept walking down the hill. The closer he got, the more he became convinced it was the same girl. *How could this be?*

The girl looked up. *She has the same face,* Jack realized. *The very same girl!*

"Oh, you startled me," she said as she continued rubbing her calf muscle. "I didn't think anyone else was here. Damn leg cramps."

"It's the heat," Jack responded in his calm voice. "It causes the muscles to cramp up."

The girl didn't run, Jack noted. *She isn't afraid of me. Could I be so lucky as to find the same girl again?* Confused but curious, he stepped closer to her as he reached into his pocket and put his hand on the stun gun. His thumb rested against the ignition button. The other hand wrapped around the handle of the hidden knife.

"Can you walk?" he asked.

"I don't think so. Maybe in a few."

"Where is your car?" Jack looked around for any other vehicle. He couldn't see any but his van. What was more important, he couldn't see any unmarked police cars. It didn't feel like he was being set up by the police. "Maybe I can help you get to your car?"

"That would be nice." The girl smiled, the same smile as victim number three.

Jack had a sense of being trapped in some strange déjà vu. He just needed to get closer to hit the girl with the stun gun. Fifteen feet more and he would have her and be free to perform his sick desires.

"If you hop in my van, I'll drive you—" He never finished the statement.

The girl produced something like a gun out of her pocket. There was a whoosh sound and two metal studs pierced his chest. *Taser!* Jack realized too late. The next second, a high voltage shock passed through his body. He fell heavily to the sidewalk and flopped about like a fish out of water. The girl raced forward and kicked him hard in the ribs, knocking the air out of him. Jack curled into a fetal position and tried to breathe.

"How did you like that, you sick fuck?" The girl grabbed him and rolled him over onto his stomach. "Not used to a girl that fights back, huh?" She twisted both his arms together and zipped a set of plastic strip-cuffs tightly around his wrists. "I got your fucking ugly fat ass now!" He felt her knee painfully between his shoulder blades. Next, the barrel of a black automatic pistol pressed against his temple. "You do what I say or I swear I'll blow your fucked-up brains into the gutter."

"Don't kill me, please."

"Your van keys," the girl demanded.

"In my pants pocket."

He felt the girl fish around in his pocket and produce the keys. The next second, he heard a beep signaling the van being unlocked by remote.

"Get up, you fat son of a bitch and get in the van. Now!"

Jack struggled to his feet as best he could with his hands tied behind his back. The girl swung open the van's cargo door and hit him across the back of the head with the pistol. He fell into the vehicle's interior. Hopping in behind him, she slid the cargo door shut. Jack rolled over to look at the girl in the dark interior. His head throbbed from the pistol hit and his wrists were hurting from the cuffs. Pieces of metal pipe littered the floor of the van and dug into his shoulders and back.

The girl reached up and turned on an interior light. She squatted in the hold of the van, gripping a Glock Model 23 pistol. Hate registered in her blue eyes as she stared back at him.

"Aren't you going to read me my rights?" Jack asked.

"I'm no fucking cop!" The girl leaned forward with the pistol. "You recognize my face? Don't lie or I'll blow your brains out right here."

"Yes." Jack backed away from her as best he could. Some of the pipe shifted beneath his heavy weight.

"That is because you killed my sister, you sick motherfucker!" She aimed the gun at his head. "My twin sister!"

"Janelle?"

"Yes, Janelle." The girl leaned forward and emptied his jacket pockets. She removed the hunting knife. "Is this what you used on her?"

"Yes."

"You know what I'm going to do with this knife?" She stuck the blade under his nose. "I'm going to cut your dick off and stuff it down your throat. That is if I can find your little pecker in all the fat."

"Don't kill me. Take me to the police station. Turn me in."

"You would like that wouldn't you? Live the easy life in prison until they stick the needle in you. Not good enough for me." She fished into his other jacket pocket and pulled out the latex Halloween clown mask. "What do we have here?" She shoved the mask under his nose. "Is this what you wear when you get your perverted jollies?"

"Yes."

The girl laughed. "You don't even need this fucked-up mask. You look like a fucking ugly clown without it!"

Jack began to whimper. "Don't call me a clown."

"You don't like that do you? You don't like being called a clown. You're a nut job."

"Fuck you." He felt murderous rage boiling inside him. If only he could get free, he would butcher this bitch for calling him a clown. Cut her really good.

"Christ, you're ugly!" She slid the latex mask over his head. "That is much better."

"How did you know it was me?" Jack spoke through the mouth hole of the clown mask.

"I was in Iraq when you killed my sister, asshole." The girl placed the pistol on the van floor and reached into her jogging jacket to produce a pack of cigarettes. She lit one and then picked up the gun. "Second tour. I worked for the Department of Defense. Counter-insurgency intelligence analysis. I've seen shit that makes Abu Ghraib look like a kindergarten class." She blew out white smoke. "I got word my sister was missing stateside. I already sensed she was dead. Twins have a psychic bond to each other, you know? Then the police received a package from Jack the Knife which had a woman's left nipple inside. DNA tests proved it was my sister's but I already knew. I felt it all the way to Baghdad, my sister had been murdered. I returned to the states on a psych leave."

Jack shifted his heavy weight against the pipes digging into his back. The thumb of one hand felt the rough thread of a pipe end. He wriggled enough to place the plastic cuffs around his wrists against the pipe thread.

"Quit moving, you freak." The girl took another drag on the cigarette. "Once stateside, I began looking for you. I had military clearance with the DOD and, thanks to Homeland Security; I had access to FBI, CIA, and law-enforcement data bases since we are all one happy family now. I used satellite recon and shit the FBI couldn't even get their hands on. With all that combined intelligence, I began to piece together a profile for Jack the Knife. I began to sniff your ugly ass out."

Jack continued quietly rubbing the plastic against the pipe thread.

"I've followed you for days waiting for you to make your next move. I knew it was just a matter of time." She put the cigarette out. "Okay, asshole,

I'm done talking to you. I'm going to put a bullet in your brain and let the cops sort it all out." She brought the pistol up in a two-handed aim at his forehead. "Time to kiss your fat ass goodbye, you fucking ugly clown!"

"Wait!" Jack shouted. He needed to buy some time until he wore through the plastic cuffs. "Don't kill me."

"You didn't give the same chance to my sister."

"I can take you to your sister. I can show you where the rest of her body is," Jack blurted. He sensed the girl contemplating what he said in her blue eyes. "You can give her a proper burial. Right now she is food for the maggots. The police may never find her if you kill me."

"Tell me where she is."

"I'll take you to her. I don't want to die like this in the back of the van. If you're going to kill me, do it in the place where I did your sister."

"Okay," She grabbed the keys to the van. "You tell me where to go. If you screw with me, I'll shoot you on the spot."

Jack nodded causing the garish clown mask on his face to bob up and down.

"You know where my grandmother's farm is?"

"Fuck yes, I did the profile on you, remember?"

"Take me to the old work shed on her property."

The girl nodded and picked up the pistol, knife and keys. She slid into the front seat, placed the pistol in her lap, and adjusted the rear view mirror so she could watch him. Jack heard the engine start up and slide into gear. He leaned back on his hurting wrists and tried to breathe in the clown mask. He had bought a little more time to live. It was very uncomfortable, but he rubbed the plastic cuffs against the pipe thread as the van pulled away from the park and left the city.

* * * *

The ride out to the farm took another twenty minutes, most of it bumping along country dirt roads. Jack bounced in the back of the van as he tried to keep rubbing the plastic cuffs up against the pipe thread beneath him. The circulation to his hands was cut off due to the cuffs and the weight of his obesity pressing down on them. He had little room to rub the cuffs over the pipe threads and couldn't tell if he'd made any progress cutting through the plastic. The latex clown mask was hot, making it difficult for him to breathe. Sweat ran down his face and into his eyes. He just wanted to get free so he could kill this bitch for putting him through this torture.

The girl drove in silence and chain-smoked the whole way. She watched him constantly in the rear view mirror. Her cold blue eyes were the eyes of a hunter. One thing in his favor—he felt the lump of the stun-gun in his coat pocket against the side he was lying on. His roll of fat had hidden it from the girl when she searched his jacket. If he could just cut his hands free and reach it.

The van turned sharply and Jack rolled to the side as the pipe shifted beneath him. He knew they'd pulled onto his grandmother's farm. Through a side window, the old rusted bodies of cars and trucks grown over with weeds became visible. The van slid to a stop on gravel in front of the fabricated metal work shed, his workshop for his special brand of art.

"End of the road, shithead." The girl stamped out a cigarette in the ash tray and grabbed up the gun. "This is where you buy it."

"In that workshop," Jack breathed through the mask. "That is where I did your sister."

"I see a lock on the door."

"The key is with the car keys," Jack said as he fought for air in the mask. Salty sweat stung his eyes.

The girl's cold eyes studied him for a minute and Jack knew she was weighing her options carefully. She finally opened the door and climbed out. In the headlights, she ran forward and unlocked the corrugated metal door to the work shed and pushed it aside. He searched frantically for another piece of pipe with thread and found it with his bound hands. He rubbed the plastic cuffs furiously over the pipe thread. The plastic gave way just as the girl returned to let him out of the side of the van. Reaching into his pocket, he grabbed the stun-gun and hid it behind his back. The side cargo door of the van swung open and she stepped back with the gun on him.

"Okay, you sick freak, get your fat ass out."

The van shook side to side as he tried to get his bulk out of the vehicle. Pipes rolled underneath him making it difficult without the use of his hands. The girl, frustrated with his struggling, lunged forward and grabbed the lapel of his jacket to throw him out of the van. That was her mistake. He hit her in the abdomen with the stun-gun which made a sizzling electric shock sound.

"Shit!" The girl cried out as she doubled over from the shock of the stun-gun. He hit her again and again with the hand stunner until she collapsed onto the ground. Jack kicked her pistol away and it went skittering along the rocky gravel. The girl tried to crawl toward the gun. He reached into the back of the van, grabbed a piece of pipe and swung it against the back of the girl's head with a loud thunk. She collapsed face first into the dirt.

Jack whipped the clown mask off and leaned against the side of the van to catch his breath. When he could finally breathe again, he stepped forward and kicked the girl in the ribs. She made a low murmuring sound. *Good,* Jack thought, *she is still alive.*

"You fucking dyke bitch!" He shouted down at the prone girl, sweat flying from his red face. "You're going to pay for calling me a clown!"

He went over and shut off the headlights. Picking up the knife, mask, and pistol, he stuffed them in his pockets before grabbing the girl by the back of her jacket. He dragged her along the ground into the work shed and slid the corrugated door closed with an ominous clang.

* * * *

Fifteen minutes later, Jack had the girl prepped for sculpting. He'd stripped her naked and handcuffed her hands to a metal ring connected to pulleys over her head. Under the stark fluorescent shop lights, her flesh looked stark and pale. Her legs were spread wide and chained to metal rings mounted to the floor. Unconscious, her head hung down, framed by her long blonde hair. A light trickle of blood ran from her nose and down her chin. Her nude body, in perfect shape without an ounce of fat, was the opposite of Jack's, who had stripped naked as well. Rolls of fat hung and shook on his obese body as he walked around the hanging girl. He admired his good luck to have his fortune change so drastically. He opened a bottle of smelling salts and passed it under the girl's nose.

"Wake up sleeping beauty," he said with a girlish giggle.

The girl's eyes opened and her left eye was red and blood-filled from internal bleeding. She took a second to look around and realize her surroundings.

"Oh, fuck no! Fuck no!" Her face contorted in terror as she struggled against the metal handcuffs. "Fucking hell, no!"

"I must thank you," Jack said as he slid the large metal wash bucket along the floor and under her hanging body. "I've never done twins before."

"Jack, listen to me. Don't do me this way. Please," she pleaded as she struggled against her bonds. "You have the gun. One shot between the eyes. Not like this, please. Christ, don't do this to me!"

Jack turned his back to her and slid on the clown mask. "You called me a clown earlier." He turned around to face her. "Tell me what kind of clown. Am I a funny clown, or a scary clown?"

She looked at him with pleading eyes. "I served your country in Iraq. I fought terrorists, Jack. I deserve a quick and clean death, please."

"Frankly, my dear, I don't give a damn." He chuckled as he picked up the large hunting knife from a workbench. "You beg more than your sister did. Let's see if you can scream louder!"

"Stay away from me, you sick fuck!" the girl yelled as she fought desperately against her bonds.

Jack stepped in front of her with the knife. "If it's any consolation, I'm going to honor the promise I made earlier. I'll take you to your sister's body when I'm done."

She stopped struggling and looked at him with eyes brimming with hate. "You putrid fat dickless ugly clown!" She spat on his clown mask. "Is this the only way you can make it with a girl?"

"You say I'm dickless." He brandished the knife in front of her face. "Maybe this is more your size."

"Nooooooo!" She screamed as he rammed the hunting knife blade between her legs.

Giggling like a school girl, Jack began sculpting as the girl bucked against her chains. Everything he removed with the knife made a fleshy plopping sound when it dropped into the metal wash bucket. Her breasts, fingers, ears, all ended up floating in blood spilling into the basin. The end came when he slit her throat and let the girl's final life blood shower down upon his naked obesity. He stepped back and walked around her to admire his newest masterpiece. Her head hung down lifeless as blood continued dripping into the wash basin beneath her. Jack felt his erection rising. He leaned his mask-covered face against her cooling flesh and masturbated.

When done, he whispered softly through the clown mask's mouth, "I love you."

*   *   *   *

Daylight came to the farm. Jack, now fully clothed, dragged the girl's mutilated body to the collection of junked vehicles parked in the weedy grass behind the work shed. Here were the victims the police hadn't found yet. They sat behind the steering wheels of parked cars and trucks like corpses waiting at a drive-in for the dead. Jack found the pickup truck where the girl's sister, Janelle, rotted in the front seat. He opened the rusty door and slid the corpse of the girl beside her sister in the cab.

"Just like I promised, I took you to your sister." Jack shut the truck door. "You two are so cute together. Just like identical bookends."

He walked back into the work shed. Grabbing the pistol, clown mask, and hunting knife, he climbed into the van. Through the dusty front windshield, he stared at the open door of the work shed. *If the girl was able to track me to here, it means the police aren't far behind. They will find my little art gallery soon.* Jack squeezed the clown mask in his lap and contemplated a course of action. Finally, he had the answer. *I have to move. I have to make my masterpieces at a new location in a new city.* Reaching down, he pulled up a CD case, removed a disc, and slid it into the player. The stereo in the van began playing as he put the van in reverse and pulled away from the farm.

"Hit the road, Jack. Don't you come back, no more, no more, no more, no more. Hit the road, Jack, don't you come back no more," he sang off key with the chorus as he drove away in search of new hunting grounds.

NIGHT FRIGHT

A scream sliced the silence. I know this scream. It's my own. The nightmare returned again tonight. Or is it for real? I cannot tell anymore. I lie next to my wife with my heart pounding and cold sweat dripping from my forehead. I'm paralyzed with mouth and eyes hanging wide open as if I'm really a corpse. Even though I screamed, my wife still sleeps. Maybe the scream was only in my mind and never escaped from my frozen mouth?

I'm trapped in the limbo between waking and sleep and the Thing is standing over the foot of the bed. "Thing" is the only term I have for this manifestation. It appears out of the dark of the bedroom, accompanied by an unholy demonic choir singing from the depths of hell. A light begins to grow behind the figure and the shape shifts from a shadow to a tall-cloaked being with a face hidden by a hood. A towering Angel of Death, wrapped in a hooded shroud, whose face I cannot see. Nor do I want to see it. For I know, in my soul, it is the face of Death. To look upon its horrible visage will cause my heart to burst from terror. A hand reaches out from the folds of the wispy shroud. It consists of long fingers of blackened bone and touches my right foot. I feel the sharp fingertips of the thing through the blanket over my feet.

I scream again.

"Bad dream, honey?" My wife turns in the bed to look at me with her sleepy, brown eyes.

I look at the end of the bed as the Thing fades away like ghostly spider webs.

"Yeah," I answer. My forehead is wet with sweat. Under the blankets, my body feels clammy and the touch of the Thing's fingers on my foot still lingers. "Did you hear me scream?"

"I heard you making some weird gurgling noise. I didn't know what was wrong with you."

"Just a bad dream." I roll closer to her and wrap my arms around her slim body.

"I know babe, but this is the second one this week." She snuggles closer to me. "Is it the same dream?"

"Yes." But I lied. It is not the same one I had earlier in the week. The nightmare is becoming more intense and real. The cold sensation where the thing touched my feet through the blanket still tingles on my skin.

"They say dreams turn bad when you're upset or feeling guilty about something." She turned to look in my eyes. "Your not having an affair on me, are you?"

"No," I reply. "Don't be ridiculous. Go back to sleep."

"You might check online about information on what causes bad dreams. You can find out about anything on the internet," she said sleepily.

"I'll do that." I slide out of bed and left her drifting back to dreamland. My wife is right. You can find out anything online. I wasn't going to be able to sleep for a while, anyway.

Downstairs, I sit in the chair in front of the computer and light up a cigarette. Going online, I use the search engine for info on nightmares. Instantly, a dozen pages related to sleep therapy and dream institutes pop up. I browse through them, but after two more cigarettes, and a lot of reading, I find nothing helpful. None of the information seems to relate to my specific problem. I am about to give up my search when a banner advertisement catches my eye: The Nightmare Hotline. I click on the banner and it takes me to a website. I scan through info about how you can call operators on the hotline 24/7 and they will discuss your bad dreams and teach you how to cope with them. Expecting there to be a charge, I check the phone number and it's toll-free. I stare at the number for a long time as I puff down another cig.

Do I dare call the number? It's toll-free but the service will probably ask for a charge once I make the call. Still, what can it hurt? I'm starting to feel sleepy again and a chill runs down my spine at the prospect of having another visitation by the Thing in my bedroom. I grab my cell phone and dial the number.

Three rings. A young woman's voice picks up. "You've reached the Nightmare Hotline. I'm your operator, April. How may I help you?"

Her voice seems detached. In my mind's eye, I imagine a bored college psych major sitting on a bed in her dorm, with a cell phone against her ear, as she paints her toenails.

"I was just wondering what kind of service this hotline provides."

"We are here to help you interpret and cope with any bad dreams or nightmares you may be having."

"Is there a charge?"

"It's a free service. The hotline is the brainchild of Dr. Albert Whitaker, a dream therapist and prominent psychologist." I got the impression she was reading from a cue card.

"What do you get out of it?"

"We gather information about your nightmare for our research database. Dr. Whittaker believes there are basic similarities to all nightmares and, by gathering a large database from thousands of sufferers, he may be able to help others recognize those similarities and learn to take control of their nightmares."

"I've got to agree to be part of a research project?"

"Yes."

"Okay, what do I have to lose?"

"From this point on I'll be recording this conversation for our research purposes. Do you agree?"

"Fine."

"Your name?"

"Michael Robertson."

"Age?"

"Thirty-five."

"Married or single?"

"Married seventeen years."

"Are you under any medications for schizophrenia, sexual dysfunction, depression, or insomnia?"

"No."

"Do you suffer any chemical addictions, such as illicit drugs or alcohol?"

"I smoke too many cigarettes," I answer lighting another Camel.

"In your personal life, are you currently experiencing grief from the death of anyone near to you? Are you under a lot of stress? Suffer from anxiety or deep depression?"

"No, to all the above." I began to get annoyed at the girl's monotone questions.

"Since you're married, are you currently having or feeling guilt over an

extramarital affair?"

"Why would you need to know that?"

"It's for the research project."

"No, I'm not involved in an affair."

"Very well. Tell me of your nightmare as best you can remember."

I tell her everything about the Thing in the bedroom, my inability to move as it touched my foot, the unholy music and the glowing light—all the frightening details about the experience. As I relate the awful dream to a complete stranger, I look around the shadows in my living room. The presence of something watching me seems to hover just beyond my senses.

"Pretty crazy dream, huh?" I say into the phone when I finish.

Silence.

"Hello, are you there?" Maybe the call got dropped.

"Mr. Robertson?" The girl's monotone voice now seems tinged with concern.

"Yes, I'm still here. What can you tell me about my dream?"

"You experienced what we call a Night Fright, a state of intense paralyzing fear existing between the waking and the sleeping mind."

"Yes, that sounds right." I say as I remember how paralyzed my body was during the dream. "What can I do to control these Night Frights? The one I keep having is getting more intense."

"Your dream is a special situation, Mr. Robertson." The girl's voice seems tinged with worry.

"What special situation?"

"We have your number on our caller ID. I'm going to pass it onto Dr. Whittaker who will call you shortly. Is that all right?"

"I guess so."

"I suggest not going to sleep until then."

The line goes dead. I put the phone down and stare at it. What the hell is going on? My nightmare is a special situation? What did she mean by that? Maybe the whole thing is a gimmick? The next call I'll get will be the good doctor offering therapy for a price.

I take my cell with me and walk over to sit on the couch. My eyes are heavy with the need to go to sleep and I can't keep from yawning. I've been putting extra hours in at the factory all week and I'm bone tired. Putting the phone on the coffee table, I lie back and smoke another cigarette, watching the smoke curl up toward the ceiling. Minutes pass and I feel my eyes starting to close.

The phone rings loudly and I snatch it from the table.

"Hello?"

A man's cultured voice spoke into my ear. "Is this Michael Robertson?"

"Yes."

"I'm Dr. Albert Whittaker of the California Dream and Sleep Therapy Institute. Did you recently call our Nightmare Hotline?"

"Yes. I told one of your representatives the nightmare I've been having. She said I was a special situation," I replied, waiting for the doctor to drop the hammer and start talking expensive therapies and credit card numbers.

"What you experienced could be nothing but a simple bad dream or …" The doctor's voice trailed off.

"Or something else?" I replied.

"I don't want to alarm you, Mr. Robertson, but have you been contemplating death?" The man's cool voice spoke in my cell.

"Why do you say that?"

"During our research, we've discovered a similar dream experience preceded the death of the dreamer."

I swallow hard. "You're kidding me, right?"

"This is still preliminary research, but we've documented a certain dream experience shared by the terminally ill and suicidal schizophrenics."

"The Angel of Death?" I can't believe what I'm hearing over the phone. This is insane.

"It's nothing so supernatural, Mr. Robertson. The mind knows it is about to die so it manifests a certain iconic image representing death from the subconscious. We all have one. What troubles me is why you're having this dream. Are you in good health?"

"Yes."

"Have you been considering suicide?"

"No."

"Then it is perplexing as to why you would be having this encounter in your sleep."

"What can I do about it? Never sleep again?" I'm starting to feel apprehension growing inside.

"Of course not. The mind needs sleep to function and eventually you would succumb to the need. There might be another way to deal with your problem. At the institute we've been experimenting with lucid dreaming.

Do you know what that is, Mr. Robertson?"

"No."

"In layman's terms it is the ability of the dreamer to gain control of the dream and alter it."

"Is that possible?"

"Oh yes, we've had many subjects who find lucid dreaming quite enjoyable. They have entire adventures in their subconscious while sleeping. They gain control of their dreams by using simple memory images and shift the dreams to their desires. Some find it the most joyous experience of their lives. I can teach you how to gain control of your dream of the Angel of Death and banish it."

I laugh quietly to myself. This is what I was expecting, the real purpose of the phone call from this smug sounding doctor in California.

"You want money, don't you?"

"If you flew out to the Institute for a weekend, I could teach you lucid dreaming skills so you could control your nightmare of death."

"I have to admit, you got a pretty good scam going here, doctor. First you have the sucker call your hotline and then you come on the phone scaring the poor person half to death before you offer some course at your institute on dreaming. You had me going there. I'm hanging up now."

"Wait, I'm not after money. I'm trying to help you avoid a potentially dangerous situation. The next time you have the death dream, think of a beloved pet you had during childhood. You may be able to banish the nightmare."

"Good-bye." Disgusted, I end the call.

So it turned out to be nothing but another internet scam for money. I check the clock on the wall: 4:33 AM. In less than three hours I've got to be at the factory and put in another double shift. Now, I'm going to have to work it with no sleep. I've wasted half the night over a stupid bad dream. I tap out a cigarette from the pack and light it up. Lying back on the couch, I blow smoke and watch it curl toward the ceiling. I should go upstairs and climb into bed next to my wife but I want one more smoke first. My eyes grow heavy as long minutes pass in slow procession.

Before I realize it, I slip back into the half-dream state. I'm paralyzed and unable to move as I lie on the couch. The living room looks the same as when I was awake but my eyes stare at a shadow in the corner. I know what is coming as the formless darkness begins to shift. I try to scream but my mouth hangs open in absolute fear and makes no sound. The shadow is shifting, taking shape. Oh God, I don't want to see it! The Thing is returning. From some deep corner of my unconscious I remember the recent conversation with the doctor on the phone.

The next time you have the death dream think of a beloved pet you had during childhood.

I clutch at the thought like a drowning man grabbing at straws. The pet I remember the most from my childhood was a brown mutt named Queenie. The memory of her brings feelings of happiness from when I was eleven years old. I stare in fear as the Thing is forming into the horrific grim reaper and approaching the end of the couch.

"Queenie," I say aloud, not in the waking world, but in the half-dream world I am now part of.

Instantly, the Thing retreats back into the shadows and fades away. In my amazement, Queenie is standing in its place and just the way I remember her before she got run over by a car on one sad summer day. The beautiful dog I spent so many warm afternoons playing with in my backyard; she'd always trotted along side of my bike when I went out riding. She bounds across the living room floor and leaps right up on my chest where I lie on the couch. Joy at the sight of the long lost dog from my childhood washes over me. In the dream world, I laugh like a child. She looks at me with her big, brown eyes and her panting mouth opens.

"Fire," Queenie says.

In shock, I wake from the dream. Around me the living room is engulfed in flames. Fire is spreading up the curtains and across the ceiling. The room is filled with black, boiling smoke and I choke on it. My wife has always warned me about falling asleep while smoking. Oh God, my wife! I roll off the couch away from the intense blast furnace of flames devouring the ceiling above my head.

"Madeline!" I scream as loud as I could as I choked on the smoke. "Madeline, get out of the house!"

I remember my cell on the coffee table. I grab it and dial 911

"Emergency operator," I hear in the receiver.

"My house is on fire!"

"I'm sending the fire department now. I have your address." The operator's voice says in a subdued urgent tone. "You must exit the house now."

"I can't. My wife is trapped up stairs," I reply in a hoarse whisper. I choke on the smoke entering my lungs. "I have to save her."

Dropping the phone, I crawl across the floor toward the stairs. I know if I stand, the flames above will ignite me like a giant matchstick. Tears are rolling down my face and I can't see anything in the thick smoke. Oxygen is being sucked out of the room by the raging inferno overhead and it is impossible to breathe.

"Madeline!" My voice is so hoarse it is nothing but a croaking whisper.

Somehow, through the thick smoke and the crackling flames, I reach the foot of the stairs and collapse.

"Madeline!" I attempt to shout but I'm not certain any sound comes out of my smoke filled lungs. "I'm so sorry."

With teary eyes, I look up the expanse of carpeted steps and I now know I'll never reach her. Flames have spread along the ceiling and are catching on the second floor as well. There is nothing but black poisonous soot to breathe. I realize I'm going to die.

At the top of the steps, I watch in horror and fascination as the cloud of smoke begins to shift and take form. I know what is returning. I begin to hear the unholy demonic choir as a golden unnatural light shines through the black smoke like a beacon. Floating toward me down the steps is a tall cloaked being in a hooded shroud. A towering Angel of Death whose face is hidden in the shadow of the hood. Skeleton hands of blackened bone reach slowly up to pull the shroud back.

It is no dream.

This time, I get to look upon its face.

THE BUTCHER BROTHERS

Jeb Butcher let out a rebel yell when the cement block he dropped from the overpass smashed through the windshield of the blue New Yorker traveling below on Texas State Highway 113. The car continued for a short distance before it ran into the ditch and rolled four times. In a billowing cloud of brown dust, the vehicle ended on its crushed roof with four tires spinning in the air.

"Ooo-wheee! I got that booger between the eyes!" Jeb shouted, stepping back from the overpass railing. "She's lying in the ditch, legs up, like a dead armadillo."

His big brother, Earl, sat behind the steering wheel of the rusted pickup truck. Finishing off a can of Keystone Light beer, he let out a loud belch. "Well, get your dumb ass in here! We got to get down there before somebody else does first."

Jeb raced back to the truck and hopped in the passenger door as Earl ground the stick shift into gear.

"You know whose car I think it was?" Jeb asked as the pickup rattled down the access lane to the highway below.

"Who?"

"Doesn't them old Clayborne spinsters drive a blue New Yorker?"

"Yep," Earl nodded. "Clara and Bertha Clayborne, that's their car. They were probably on their way to Sunday bingo night at church. I never did like that Clara Clayborne. The old bitch was my sixth grade teacher and flunked me. That's why I never went back to school."

The truck reached the highway and slid to a stop on the shoulder of the road behind the wrecked car. Both brothers jumped out and slammed the doors behind them. From the back bed of the truck, Jeb grabbed up the blood-stained machete and the burlap feed sack while Earl rushed forward to the side of the overturned auto. Bending down his large frame, he peered through the shattered passenger window.

"Goddamit!" Earl took off his greasy ball cap and slapped it against the bottom of the car.

"Now what?" Jeb joined his side and handed him the machete.

"Bertha's all mashed up! Her brains are spread all over the place. She's no damn good to us!"

Jeb glanced at the driver seat and saw it unoccupied. "Where's Clara then? She had to be drivin'."

"Her ass got thrown free, I'm bettin'" Earl cupped his hands to his mouth and shouted, "Clara, are you out here somewhere?"

A low pitiful groan came from behind a stand of sagebrush about twenty-feet from the crash.

"I'll be shittin' if she ain't over there." Earl pointed in the direction of the sound.

Jeb followed his brother. In the bottom of a shallow gulley, Clara Clayborne lay sprawled out on the dusty ground. Clad in a ragged and bloody paisley dress, she looked more like a broken old mannequin then a prim retired schoolteacher. Her spindly legs stretched out in odd angles and her bruised face looked up at both brothers. During the wreck, she had lost both her glasses and her dentures. Aged eyes tried to focus against the bright sunlight.

"Damn, woman, don't you know you should wear your seatbelt?" Earl asked as he stood over her, blocking the sun.

"Earl Butcher, is that you?" she asked in a weak voice. "Take me to a hospital. I'm hurt bad. I think my legs are broken."

"You remember the shit you gave me in school?"

"Please, I need an ambulance."

"Sorry, no can do." Earl raised the machete over his head. "Mama's hungry."

The blade came down and severed the old woman's head from her shoulders. Her eyes rolled back showing the whites as her toothless mouth opened one last time in shock. Blood spurted from the open neck stump into the brown Texas dust.

"Brother, use that gunny sack and catch this." Earl bent down, picked up the woman's head by her gray hair, and tossed it in Jeb's direction. He popped open the feed sack and Clara Clayborne's head dropped inside.

"Two points," Jeb said, closing the bag.

"Let's get the hell out of here before someone else comes upon the wreck."

They threw themselves back into the truck, and with a grinding of the gearshift, took off back down Highway 113. Earl drove as Jeb sat in the passenger seat. Clara's head in the sack rested on the floorboard between his feet. Once out of sight of the crash, Earl slowed down, reached into an ice chest behind his seat, and pulled out another cold Keystone Light.

"I had hoped we would be riding home with more than one kill." Earl popped the top of the beer. "Mama ain't goin' to be happy. If Mama ain't happy, nobody's happy, retard."

"Don't call me that." Jeb crossed his arms and glared at his brother. "I hate it when you call me that." He decided to change the subject. "Earl, why do you think Mama came back?"

"Because she's Mama, that's why." He took a long sip of beer. "Not even the cold, hard ground is goin' to keep Mama down."

"But she was dead, Earl. We buried her good. She shouldn't have been able to come back from the grave. I'm sayin' it ain't natural."

"I'm sayin' she came back because her love for her favorite son was so strong, not even the grave could hold her."

Jeb looked out the window and remained quiet as he watched the brown landscape roll by. He could never win an argument with his brother. Earl was bigger and stronger, and claimed to be smarter, though Jeb doubted it. He spent his twenty-three years of life being the target of Earl's constant humiliation and degradation. He was sick of it.

Memories of the unbelievable events of the last week began to replay in his mind. Seven days ago, he had gone with his brother to Bubba's Salvage Yard over by Killeen to find a new clutch plate for the truck. They were gone most of the day. When they returned home, they found Grampy waiting on the porch of the farmhouse. Tears filled his rheumy eyes.

"Boys, your Mama passed while you were gone. She died in her sleep," Grampy said as they climbed out of the truck.

They both raced into the house. In the living room, they found the four-hundred-pound body of their mother sprawled out in her favorite chair. Her mouth hung wide open as it always did when she slept, though, this time, it was evident she wasn't taking a nap. Sticking out from below the hem of her faded print dress, bloated legs were already starting to turn black. Jeb leaned in close to check if she was breathing and saw flies buzzing inside her mouth.

"Yep, she's dead all right," he announced to Earl.

Earl broke down and bawled like a three-year-old kid. His big brother had always been Mama's favorite, a fact he constantly shoved in Jeb's face at every opportunity.

"What do we do now?" Jeb asked after the family members had assembled in the kitchen. "We can't leave her like that. She's already starting to stink more than usual."

Earl wiped his tears and blew his nose. "Well, we got to have a funeral for her. I guess I've got to go to Killeen and tell the mortician to come and get Mama."

Sitting at the kitchen table, Grampy said, "Wait a minute, boys. Let's think this thing through. Earl, you got money to pay for one of those fancy city funerals?"

"How much is one goin' to cost?"

"I'd say twelve hundred dollars, or more."

"I don't have that much. I guess I got to sell the truck to get the money."

"You couldn't get half the money for that old piece of junk."

"Then what do you suggest?" Jeb asked.

"Well, she ain't going to get any better. I say we bury her out back. Earl, you dig a grave with the tractor, and make it a big one. We put your Mama in it and we give her a proper Christian funeral. This way we save over twelve hundred dollars and Mama gets to still stay close to her boys."

So they did as Grampy suggested. Earl used the backhoe to dig a hole in the dirt under the shade of the big elm tree out back. Both brothers then went inside to get Mama and soon realized she was far too heavy to carry. Instead, they had to drag her bloated corpse through the house and out the back door to her final resting place. Grampy phoned cousin Dottie, the only relative they knew who could read, to come over and recite passages from the Bible. They tied the huge corpse to the A-frame Earl used to pull the engine block out of his truck and lowered Mama into the dirt hole. Grampy and Dottie watched in tears. After Earl used the tractor to cover her over, they said their last words and left Mama in her final resting place.

Or so they thought.

That night, Jeb woke to the sounds of heavy footsteps and the floorboards creaking in the living room. At first, he thought it was Mama walking around in the house until he realized they'd buried her earlier. He shot out of bed and turned on the light. Earl was still asleep and snoring loudly in his bed across the room.

"Earl, get up!" Jeb whispered and shook his brother's beefy frame.

"What is it?" His brother asked, accompanied by the smell of stale beer.

"Mama's ghost has come back to haunt us. I hear her walkin' through the house."

"Quit being a retard. We buried Mama for good."

It was at that moment Grampy let out a scream. Earl rushed into the living room and switched on the light. Jeb followed and stopped cold to gawk at the nightmare scene before him. Mama had come back from the dead, but she was not a ghost. Fresh brown dirt clung to her unkempt hair and faded print dress. The flesh of her obese body had turned a shade of rotting black and she smelled worse than ever. Grampy lay at her feet with his head cracked wide open exposing gray brain matter. Kneeling over the fresh corpse, Mama reached into the opening in the skull and scooped up a handful of Grampy's brains just as easily as she used to reach into the cookie jar for a fresh chocolate chip.

"Brains," she said in a croaking voice before she gobbled down the jelly-like mess.

"Mama, you came back!" Earl shouted. Tears of joy began to form in his eyes.

"I don't think that's Mama anymore," Jeb remembered saying.

"Bullshit, that's Mama and she came back to be with her favorite son."

"Yeah, well she's eatin' Grampy's brains."

Mama looked up with eyes covered in a lifeless hazy glaze.

"Brains," she said in a hoarse, gravelly voice as she stood and began walking slowly toward them. Her bare feet left tracks of brown dirt across the hard wood floor.

"Brains."

"Earl, go get your shotgun." Jeb stepped back.

"Go to hell, retard. I'm not goin' to shoot Mama."

"Brains." The floorboards groaned beneath her weight as she shuffled closer.

"Then what do you propose to do with her?" Jeb asked.

"Have her follow you out back to the work shed. We can lock her in there. That way we can keep her until she learns to be herself again."

"I don't want to."

Earl took off his ball cap and smacked Jeb across the head. "You'll do this, retard, or I'll knock the snot out of you!"

Jeb decided it was safer to evade a four-hundred-pound undead woman then to face Earl Butcher when he got angry. He darted around the massive shambling form. Sensing his movement, Mama's grubby hands, with black, broken nails, attempted to grab him as he went by.

"Brains," she uttered in an eerie broken voice.

Jeb ran into the kitchen and Mama followed with lurching footsteps.

"Damn, Earl, she's after me. She wants to eat my brains, too!"

"That's all right. Just keep her occupied until you get out by the shed!"

"I don't like being brain food!"

Out the back door, he fled with Mama behind him, her flabby arms outstretched before her.

"Brains."

Jeb reached the work shed only to find a padlock on the door. "Earl, the door is locked!"

"Here, catch the keys, dumb-ass!"

The key ring flew over Mama's head and landed in the grass before the door. Jeb snatched them up as the shadow of the massive undead woman fell across him. He tried the lock.

"It's stuck!"

Mama lurched forward to just a few steps away; her rotting stench nearly made his supper come up.

"Wiggle it, retard!" Earl shouted.

"Don't call me that!" Jeb jimmied the key back and forth and the padlock finally snapped open just as Mama reached him. He threw open the door and jumped aside as his brother charged forward and shoved the obese horror into the work shed. Slamming the door, Earl locked it again as Mama began pounding against it from the inside.

"Brains."

"What are we going to do with her now, Earl?" Jeb tried to catch his breath.

"We get Mama what she needs. She never hesitated to bring us something to eat when we were growin' up. We are goin' to do the same for her now."

"Earl, she wants to eat people's brains."

Earl shook his head, which meant he wasn't open for arguing about the subject.

They searched the grounds. An open maw of raw earth was in the place of the covered grave where Mama had been put to rest. Amazingly, she'd managed to claw her way out of the dirt. Not wanting to let a good grave go to waste, they placed Grampy's frail body in the hole and buried him.

The murders started the next night.

Under the shadow of darkness, Jeb accompanied his brother as they snuck into the neighboring farmhouse. They surprised old man McFadden and his wife Ethel while they slept in their bed. Earl decapitated them both with the machete. They carried both heads back to Mama and she cracked them open like coconuts and devoured the brains like strawberry jam. Once she fed, Mama grew quiet for a few days but began to look much worse. Her skin turned darker and flesh began to fall off in places. The gagging stench from inside the shed grew so strong it made Jeb want to retch. The hunger soon began again, too. On her bad days, she would pound against the door demanding brains repeatedly for hours on end. This would continue throughout the day and into the long night until it drove both of them crazy and they went out on the hunt for kills.

The grind of the gears against the worn clutch-plate brought Jeb out of his horrific memories and he focused back to the present. Earl turned the truck into the dusty drive leading up to the Butcher farmhouse.

"Earl, this has gotta stop," Jeb said. "We can't go around hackin' every head off in the county just to bring them home for Mama to eat. We're goin' to get caught and go to prison."

"It's for our Mama, or did you forget?"

"That thing livin' in the shed ain't my Mama!"

Earl shot him an angry look. "Mama was right. She should've thrown your retarded ass down a well when you were first born."

"I'm no retard!"

"You're a retard. Born retarded and always goin' to be retarded."

"Shut up, fucker!"

Earl slammed on the brakes of the truck, causing it to slide to a stop in front of the farmhouse.

"You're going to get an ass-whoopin' now, boy!" He jumped out of the driver door and raced around the hood to the passenger side. An insane angry look flashed in his eyes. "I told you about using that foul language!"

"Stay away, fucker!" Jeb tried to lock the door but he was too slow. Swinging the door open, Earl grabbed him by the collar of his pearl-snap shirt, pulled him from the truck cab, and dumped him into the dirt.

"Retard!" Earl kicked him in the ribs. "Retard!" He kicked him again. "That's why I'm Mama's favorite son, 'cause you were born a retard!"

Jeb rolled up into a ball on the ground and hugged his hurting ribs.

"I'm going to feed Mama now." Earl grabbed the bloody burlap bag off the floorboard of the truck. "You'd better stay away from me the rest of the day if you don't want more of the same."

Toting the bag with Clara's head, his brother headed out back toward the work shed. Jeb rose painfully to his feet and spat blood and dirt out of his mouth. He knew what he had to do. This nightmare had to stop. Limping through the front door, he entered the house and crossed the living room to the hall closet. From a top shelf, he pulled out Earl's double-barrel shotgun and opened the breach to make sure both barrels were loaded.

"Fuck you, Earl," Jeb said as he clicked the breach back on the shotgun. "I'll show you who's a retard."

He passed through the house and out the back door into the farmyard where Earl had just finished unlocking the door to the work shed.

"Mama I brought you some lunch," Earl said. "You remember old Clara Clairborne, don't you? She was my sixth-grade teacher so that means she's smart and educated. I figure that's some good brains for you to eat."

With the shotgun at the ready, Jeb sneaked closer, making sure his brother didn't see his approach. Reaching into the burlap bag, Earl pulled out Clara's bloody head and swung open the work shed door. Flies and the stink of rotting flesh wafted out of the doorway in a sickening cloud.

"Brains," a hoarse voice muttered from the dim inside.

"Yeah, that's it, Mama. Your favorite son will never let you down. I'll always take care of you."

"Brains."

"Here you go, Mama." He tossed in the head. "Eat now."

Not knowing that Jeb stood behind him with the shotgun pointed at his back, Earl closed the door and was about to lock it. From inside the shed, came the sound of shambling and the crack of a skull being broken open.

"Brains," said the inhuman voice from inside.

"Don't lock the door yet, Earl," Jeb said. "Mama ain't done eatin'."

Earl spun with a look of surprise across his sweaty face. His eyes widened when he saw the two barrels of the shotgun pointed directly at him.

"What do you think you're doing?"

"Something I should've done a long time ago."

"Put that shotgun away before you accidentally pull the trigger and someone gets hurt."

"No. Like I said, Mama ain't done eatin' yet. You get to be the second course. Now get your ass in that shed."

"You're crazy! I'm not going in there!"

"You're Mama's favorite, remember? Here's your chance to prove it."

"Little brother, put the gun away. That's a dangerous weapon and shouldn't be in the hands of a retar—"

Jeb pulled the trigger on one barrel. The shotgun bucked in his hand as the blast hit Earl in the left knee. Buckshot blew apart the kneecap and shattered the leg from the knee down. Earl screamed in pain and fell to the ground.

"I told you not to call me a retard."

"Oh Jesus, you shot me, you dumb-ass! I'm your big brother, for Christ's Sake!"

"You've always treated me like shit, too. I still got one more shot left, Earl. Unless you want it in your other leg, I'd be crawling into that shed."

Earl reached back and grabbed the work shed door. He called out, "Mama, it's Earl. I'm comin' inside with you now. Don't hurt me. I'm your favorite son, remember?"

"Brains," said the hideous voice inside the shed.

"Get on in there." Jeb raised the shotgun.

"I'm coming to join you, Mama," Earl shouted as he swung the door open and crawled backwards. "Now don't get crazy, I'm your favorite, remember?"

"Brains." Bloated hands of rotting flesh reached down and grabbed his brother by the head and yanked him further into the shed.

"Oh God!" Earl screamed. "No, Mama, I'm your favorite! Don't, Mama!"

Jeb stepped forward and shut the door as the sounds of struggling accompanied with the crack of bones came from within. Earl's pleas disintegrated down to mindless screaming.

"I told you, Earl, you were going to be the second course to Mama's meal." Jeb slid the padlock through the hasp and clicked it closed. "Don't you remember what Mama used to say? Two heads are better than one."

THE CURSE

I take a long puff of the cigar and blow out the smoke in a whirling cloud of gray mist. In the red light of the room, the smoke cloud obscures the image of the woman before me. Everything about her appearance is mysterious; her pale face, lined and yet still youthful, does little to reveal her age. Shoulder-length straight black hair and a hawkish nose poised above thin red lips add to the exotic mystery of this strange woman. Her piercing dark eyes study me across the small table. She advertises herself as a fortune teller and a psychic. Does she know I'm here to kill her?

"Why do you wish to speak to Madame Zara?" she asks in a voice grown weary from repeating the same question to countless customers over the years. She places each ring-laden hand flat on the table beside the translucent crystal ball sitting between us. I take a second and stare within the orb. The polished crystal distorts the images of us both into something from a hallucinogenic dream.

"I want to discuss something with you," I reply and flick cigar ash into the cheap carpet covering the floor. The room's decoration is in Hollywood schlock down to the garish red lights and the crystal ball on a black tablecloth. Everything about the place was to impress the tourist half-wits stupid enough to be lured into the ratty parlor. After a session with Madame Zara, they leave with nothing but some vague predictions and a lighter wallet.

"Sir, it is not advisable to smoke in here. It disturbs the spirits I must contact to read your fortune properly." She speaks in some European accent that is probably as phony as everything else in the shop. I don't really care, however. She'll be dead soon.

"I'm not here to have my fortune told." I stamp out the cigar against the sole of my shoe and put the stogie in my shirt pocket. No reason to leave more evidence behind than necessary.

Her dark eyes return to studying my face. "Then why are you here?"

"You've been giving spiritual advice to a young lady named Mary Hensley?"

"What communication I have with customers is strictly confidential," she replies in an even voice.

"Oh, I know you have because I've got the one-hundred-dollar-per-session check receipts to prove it. I'm the man who's been funding your so-called advice." I remove a pair of black leather gloves from an inside pocket of my jacket..

"You're Mr. Hensley?" she asks as she studies me slipping on each glove.

"Bingo." Maybe the broad was psychic after all.

"I only give spiritual advice." I could see a tinge of nervousness upon her placid features. Her eyes never leave the gloves now on my hands.

"Yeah, I know. Your advice to my wife was she should leave her cruel and abusive husband. You predicted if she didn't get out of the house she could end up in the hospital or dead soon. Congratulations, your prediction came true. I strangled the bitch two hours ago."

Her eyes narrow but registered no other emotion. A moment of tense silence passes between us. Finally, she sighs. "You're going to kill me, too." It was a statement and not a question.

"Yes." The same murderous rage that drove me to strangle my wife begins to twist in my gut and pound against my forehead. "I'm going to teach you to meddle with my marriage. It's because of your advice my wife had to die! You think you're so smart, telling her to get a divorce. I'll never let her get her hands on half of my money! You know what she got instead?" I remove a length of nylon cord from a pocket and pull it tight between my gloved hands. "This cord around her neck. She's outside in the trunk of my car. You're going to get to join her!"

"You're insane, Mr. Hensley." She stands away from the table and begins stepping back toward the rear door of the parlor.

"Maybe, but you're the one who's going to be dead."

"Do you think I'm just a simple charlatan? You are very mistaken. I'm the seventh daughter of a seventh daughter. I come from a very powerful gypsy family in the old country. A curse I'll cast upon you, Carl Hensley, if you try to harm me."

I laugh out loud. "Don't even try to scare me with that carnie sideshow bullshit!"

She moves toward the back door. I rush forward with the cord taut between my hands. She evades my attempt to put the rope around her neck, but I block her exit and back her into a corner. I'm a big man who used to play linebacker for a semi-pro football team. Her slim body is no match for my strength. She tries to duck and run toward the front door, but I shove her against the back wall. Towering over Madame Zara's huddled form, I prepare to put the rope around her neck.

"Don't.!" Her strange eyes remain focused on mine. "Don't do this!"

"I'm not going to lose the money I worked so hard for," I say in a low voice. "I'll kill anyone who tries to take my fortune!"

The hate in her eyes intensifies as her face distorts in anger. "I curse thee!" Her face suddenly turns upward as her voice changes to an angry screech. "I call upon the forces of darkness to revenge the life you now rob from me! Blood for blood!"

I whip the cord around her throat.

"A curse upon thee! A curse—"

I pull the rope tight and cut off her words. She struggles against the cord cutting into her neck with much more determination than my wife did. Her black fingernails claw up at my face and scratch my cheek in bloody lines. Gurgling noises escape her clenched mouth and her eyes, bloodshot with hate, never stop staring at me. The toe of her shoe kicks hard against my shin forcing me to shift her position. I swing her from the wall and slam her down on the table in the room. The rope tightens more and her struggling weakens. In a last desperate move, she reaches out for the crystal ball, perhaps to grab it as some sort of weapon, but it slips from her fingers and rolls off the table and onto the floor with a thump.

Her struggling stops as she falls limp.

I keep the cord tight for a couple more minutes than release the hold and lean back against the wall. Sweat drips from my forehead and the too-familiar pounding between my temples begins to subside along with the rage. I let out a long breath. The deed is done.

The corpse of Madame Zara is sprawled across the table before me. I take a second to study her. She is quite dead. Her eyes rolled back exposing the whites. A blackened tongue hangs out from her open mouth and her face has the color of a fresh bruise. Cutting deeply into her neck, the cord has left nasty ligature marks purpling her flesh. Once again, I feel nothing at the site of someone I've murdered, only a cold emptiness. What if I can't stop killing? What if this is just the beginning and I'm destined to go on strangling other women? What if I'm criminally insane? Shouldn't I feel something?

I stop my train of thought. I have to clean up the crime scene and move the gypsy woman's body before she is discovered. Rushing across the room, I peek out the curtain on the front door window to check the parking area. Only my Mercedes is visible and no other cars or customers in sight. I turn over the Open sign hanging in the window to show the shop is Closed. I don't need tourists stumbling in while I'm moving the woman's body. Murder, I've discovered, is messy work. There is always plenty to clean up afterwards. I turn to start fixing the crime scene when my foot strikes against something on the floor.

Looking down, I see it's the crystal ball. For some reason it looks different, darker and cloudier. Curious, I pick the orb up with my gloved hands. My eyes are inexplicably drawn to stare into the interior of the polished crystal. A cloud of smoky mist is forming inside like ink spreading in water. What the hell? The dark coloring changes the orb to pitch black while in my grip.

Then something else catches my attention. The smell of sickly-sweet incense assails my nostrils accompanied with the sound of low indiscriminate laughter. I look away from the crystal ball toward the body of Madame Zara. What I see there makes me forget the orb and drop it to the floor. Like black smoke, something rises from the body of the gypsy woman. Tendrils of darkness escape her open mouth and float toward the ceiling. In the harsh red light, a mass of seething shadow forms above the corpse. What is it? I blink my eyes in disbelief. It's not possible, but there it is.

Fear rises from my gut and sticks in my throat. Something is wrong, terribly wrong. The mass of darkness increases in size and begins to take shape. A face is emerging from its center. White eyes with no pupils appear in the billowing mass of inky blackness. The laughter grows louder.

"Blood for blood," an almost inaudible voice speaks from the impossible shadow.

I jump back and my gloved hand fumbles for the door knob. Tendrils of obsidian black stretch toward me from the impossible thing hovering in the room. The door opens and I stumble out into the Florida sunshine, which offers no heat to the cold chill of my clammy skin. In panic, I slam shut the door and spend a second of confusion as I stand there on the step. What did I see hovering above the dead gypsy woman? Was it even real or something I imagined due to the stress of murdering two women in less than three hours? Am I losing my sanity?

I don't have the nerve to reopen the door and enter the parlor again to find out. Instead, I rush to my Mercedes and slip behind the wheel. Throwing my gloves to the passenger seat, I sit and study the front of the fortuneteller's shop as my mind ponders a course of action.

My original plan was to stuff Madame Zara's body into the trunk alongside the body of my wife. From there, I would sneak them aboard my twenty-five-foot cabin cruiser, docked at a nearby marina. Setting off into the Gulf, I would dump both bodies into the ocean for a burial at sea. Simple and neat. The anomaly I witnessed in the parlor changes everything. I'm not able to take the gypsy woman's body with me and I don't have time to clean up the evidence at the crime scene. The murder has been sloppy and possibly traceable back to me by the police. Whatever the course of action, it's not wise to sit here in front of the shop waiting for someone to see me.

I start the Mercedes and pull out of the parking lot and into the street. I turn down a coastal highway, headed south toward the marina where my boat is docked. The late afternoon sun has peaked and on a gradual descent into the blue-green waters of the ocean in the west. Behind the wheel of my car, driving through the beautiful Florida sunshine, my terror at what I have encountered at Madame Zara's begins to subside. I don't have any answers to what I have seen, but I begin to suspect it was a trick of the darkness and the stress of the moment. I still have to deal with the body of my wife, however.

Cape Coral is a collection of suburban style homes, shopping malls, restaurants, and boat docks, with a few palm trees thrown into the mix. I drive through the town and out into the marina sector. At a stoplight, I wait in a line of traffic and watch sailboats tacking across the bay. Everything seems normal, but due to the impossible terror I have experienced at Madame Zara's, my gaze searches the scenic landscape around me. In the side mirror of the car, I spot something in the sky. The cold fist of fear clutches my heart because I know instinctively what I'm seeing. The shadow-thing I left at the fortune teller's parlor is in the sky behind my Mercedes; it is following me in the broad daylight, like a shroud of black cloth, being pushed by a wind!

I use the automatic control to shift the mirror to better see the hideous shape of the shadow flying in the blue sky. My mind cannot comprehend what my eyes are seeing. How is this possible? Why none else sees the nightmarish object, I couldn't fathom. I look at the line of cars behind me and see normal people going about their business waiting for the light to turn. Pedestrians are walking along the sidewalks. No one pays any attention to the horror following me! Why?

The light turns green and I drive into the access road leading to the marina. I know the shadow-thing is still following even though I've lost sight of it for the moment. In the process of searching for the object in my mirror, I nearly drive off the pier and slam on the brakes. Mary's body shifts in the truck with a loud thump. Mr. Cranston, the white-haired dock master of the marina comes running up to the side of the car.

"Everything all right, Mr. Hensley?" His tanned face shows lines of concern.

I power down the window. "Frank, what do you see in the sky behind my car?"

He scratches his thick, white hair. "I don't quite get you?"

"Do you see something strange in the sky?"

He stares up for a long second. "Well, I see some gulls and a few clouds."

"Is that all?"

"Was I supposed to see something else?"

I look through the back window. The billowing shadow-thing is drawing nearer. Its mass greater defined and I can see it consists of writhing tendrils like snakes drawn in black ink, shifting and formless.

"You can't see that horrible thing behind me?" my voice suddenly bellows in desperation.

Mr. Cranston steps back. "What thing?"

"Never mind." I put the car in drive. Am I the only one who can see it?

"Will you be taking the boat out today, Mr. Hensley?" The old man's voice sounds nervous.

"Not today."

"Well, give my regards to Mrs. Hensley."

I squall my tires and leave the marina behind. I have to get away from the horror pursuing me. Far away. No boat would be fast enough. Winding back through the streets of Cape Coral, I begin to formulate an alternative plan. After killing Mary, I had placed ten thousand dollars in cash and my passport in the glove box of the Mercedes. Insurance in case the police got too close to nailing me for the murder. I had already transferred two million dollars in liquid assets from my home construction company to a secret account in Barbados. I could hop a flight out of the country and leave the murders and the horror behind me. Take up a new identity and start a new life in a foreign land.

I punch up the number of the Fort Myers international airport using my in-dash cell phone. After the call is answered, I'm quickly routed to an airline ticket representative.

"I need a flight to South America," I tell the person on the other end. "What's the quickest flight out?"

"We have a flight leaving for Rio de Janeiro in forty-five minutes."

"Any seats available?"

"As a matter of fact, there are."

"Reserve me one." I give my name and credit card number and hang up.

The drive to the airport is without incident and I lose sight of the shadow-thing in the process. By the time I pull into the parking lot before the airport terminal, the sun is sinking into a beautiful rose-colored horizon. I grab the cash and the passport from the glove box and climb out. Locking up the car, I leave the Mercedes until the smell of Mary's body in the trunk brings the attention of others. By that time, I'll be in Brazil and living another life. As I run toward the terminal building, I scan the darkening sky for some sign of the shadow. I see none.

Once in the terminal, I catch my breath and calm my nerves. My shirt is wet from the humidity and the stress. The mundane process of acquiring my tickets and going though security and customs makes me forget about the nightmare behind me. Soon I'm boarding an airliner along with a stream of other passengers, mostly Hispanics, and tourists bound for a vacation in wonderful Rio.

Eventually, I settle into my seat beside a frail, elderly woman, and pray she doesn't want to talk the whole trip. Just like clockwork, the old woman taps me on the arm.

"Excuse me," she speaks softly.

"Yes?"

"I'm sorry to bother you, but I have a weak bladder." A smile splits the wrinkles on her face. "Would you be so kind as to take the window seat?"

Reluctantly, I trade my seat with hers. To avoid her conversing through the flight, I lean my head back and pretend to take a nap. The lull of the jet taxiing down the runway and taking flight, coupled with the intense stress of the day, puts me under. I fall into a deep sleep.

"Would you look at that?" A voice wakes me. I'm disorientated and not sure of my surroundings. A strange, elderly woman is leaning over me. Looking about the cabin of the jetliner, I remember I'm on a flight to Rio. People are gazing out the windows on my side of the cabin.

"Look at what?" I ask in a distant voice.

"The lights of Miami."

I turn my head and look out the window. The sprawling lights of the city of Miami are spread out like a glowing spider web across the dark landscape. The aircraft has banked for a better view by the passengers and I see the long, silver wing, flashing with amber lights, stretching into the dark. The night sky is alit with brilliant stars and I'm still a bit confused about what I'm doing here on this flight. Then I see it. A black form darker then ebon, keeping pace with the wing of the aircraft, and blocking out stars as it passes before them. The nightmare comes back to me. The murders, the curse the gypsy witch placed upon me, the shadow-thing in the parlor and following my car.

The horror is still chasing me!

I slam down the window cover.

"Hey," the old woman says in a surprised voice. "I wanted to look out at Miami."

"I'm sorry," I say as I run my hands through my hair. "I have a fear of flying. I'll get sick if I look out the window."

"I just want to take a look for a moment," the woman reaches over and raises the window shade.

The shadow-thing is there. Black, ropy tendrils are gripped to the silver of the wing. The billowing mass of darkness slides toward the window glass and I see a face emerge from the obsidian black. Dead-white eyes and an open mouth press against the glass. Screaming in terror, I shut the window panel down.

“What's wrong?" the elderly woman at my side asks in a surprised voice.

"Didn't you see that thing on the wing?"

"What thing on the wing?"

"A witch is flying outside the aircraft!"

Passengers are now looking at me with eyes wide with curiosity. A slim stewardess comes over to my seat.

"Is there something wrong?" she asks in a calm voice.

"He says there is a witch flying outside," the elderly woman speaks up and points at me.

"Something is outside on the wing," I say, realizing how crazy I must sound.

"Sir, I assure you nothing is outside," the flight attendant replies.

Sweat breaks out on my brow. I look up into the eyes of the flight attendant. "Listen to me. I'm not crazy. Before I left on this flight, a gypsy witch put a curse on me. It's following this plane and has attached itself to the wing."

One of the passengers laughs and I hear someone say. "This guy thinks he's in a *Twilight Zone* episode."

Another voice says, "No, it's the Wicked Witch of the West outside the plane."

More laughter.

"I'm not crazy. The thing is out there. The whole aircraft could be in danger."

"Sir, I'm going to ask you to remain calm. You're scaring the other passengers," the stewardess says.

"Okay, okay," I reply shaking my head. "I'll relax. I had a bad dream. I'm sorry."

"Can I change to another seat?" the old woman at my side asks.

"Yes, of course." The stewardess leads the woman away to another seat in the plane.

I shut my eyes again but sense the eyes of others upon me. I don't care. The cursed thing is following me. I concentrate on the whine of the jet engines and think about sunny Rio waiting on the other side of the flight. Am I doomed to be chased by this curse forever? Minutes pass and I feel my breathing slow down again but a pounding ache is still centered behind my closed eyes. In time, a familiar scent tickles my nostrils—the sickly-sweet smell of Madame Zara I first encountered in the fortune teller parlor. I open my eyes. Ropy black tendrils are snaking out from under the closed window panel and twisting up toward me. I scream and leap into the aisle knocking down a stewardess carrying a drink.

"It's in the cabin! The thing is coming in!"

"What thing?" somebody asks loudly.

"Don't you see it?" I point to the mass of writhing black tendrils pouring into the cabin. "It's there! It's coming after me!"

People are panicking and shifting in their seats. A large man in a suit rushes down the aisle toward me.

"I'm the air marshal!" he shouts. Something that looks like a pistol fills his hand. "Clear the way!"

"Save me! The curse is going to get me!" I scream at the man.

I hear a popping noise and a thousand volts of electricity seems to pass through my body. Shaking violently, I fall down upon the aisle carpet. Somebody in the distance screams and I pass out.

My head is pounding and I open my eyes. The bright light makes the pain worse. I try to raise my hand to my forehead but I'm unable to. I look down and there is a pair of handcuffs on each wrist and fastened to the arm of a metal chair. The pain in my head is so bad I can barely focus on my surroundings. I'm in a small room complete with stainless steel cabinets. A man in a business suit sits across from me and for a brief second I wonder who he is. Then my ears pick up the tell-tale whine of the jet engines and I remember every detail of my nightmare.

"Can you hear me, Mr. Hensley?"

"Yes." My voice is hoarse.

"I had to taser you. You probably feel like hell right now."

"Am I still on the airliner?" I raise my wrists until the handcuffs clink against the metal of the chair.

"Yes. We had to put you in the galley." The man shows a smile. "I'm Mr. Johnson, the air marshal aboard this flight."

"Why am I in handcuffs?"

"I think we both know the answer to that." Mr. Johnson reaches over to a coffee machine and pours a cup. "You gave everyone quite a scare. You're the reason the flight has been diverted back to Miami."

"You can't take me back there." I shake my head. "The curse will get me."

"What curse?"

"You have to protect me from it. Lock me away somewhere so it won't get to me."

"This curse placed upon you?"

"Please …" I tilt my head upon my chest. "Please, believe me."

"You can tell your story to the Feds. They are waiting for you when we arrive at Dade International."

The Feds are waiting in Miami. I tell them everything about the murders and the curse Madame Zara placed upon me. I don't care anymore. Days pass, filled with psychological evaluations and interviews by lawyers and doctors. I'm diagnosed unable to stand trial by reason of mental defect. Words like paranoid schizophrenic and criminally insane are tossed about to describe my condition. I take medications that make me lose touch with time and reality. I wake to find myself in some new mental ward. During the sporadic times I have a grip reality, I scream at the orderlies about the curse of the shadow-thing. More isolation and medicine follows.

Something causes me to open my eyes. I'm wrapped up tight in a white straitjacket and crouching in the corner of a room. The walls and one door are all padded. The lights are low and the constant wailing of the other guests of the mental ward has quieted. I cannot hear their echoes coming down the hall. It must be late in the night and the sleep meds have taken hold.

What has brought me back to the nightmare of my reality?

I glance about the padded room and focus on a spot on the wall darker than the rest. My heart pounds as I watch the spot grow even darker. The scent of something sickly-sweet fills the room. I scream loudly and rush forward to slam my body against the door. No one comes to my aid, for my screams are commonplace to the orderlies of this ward. A low cackling laughter begins to fill the air behind me. I respond with my own insane laughter as I turn to face the horror of the shadow-thing behind me.

The curse is there as a shifting mass of obsidian darkness and tendrils. A face emerges from the horror and the dead-white eyes of Madame Zara stare back at me.

"Blood for blood," the thing hisses.

"Blood for blood," I repeat and laugh maniacally as the tendrils of the nightmare reach out to embrace me.

PEST CONTROL

Rob Creegan snuffed out a cigarette and shifted the phone to his good ear. He wasn't sure he had heard the speaker on the other end correctly. "You said you hired other exterminators and they wouldn't do the job?"

"Yes," the man's whiney voice said in the receiver. "They refused. Some even quit in the middle of spraying and wouldn't finish."

"The infestation is that bad?"

"I won't lie to you. Roaches have swarmed the house. It's a nightmare."

Rob thought for a second. *How bad can it be?* In his sixteen years as a professional exterminator, he'd climbed under dilapidated houses and in the dankest corners of basements to spray everything from rats, and spiders to termites. Roaches were hard to kill, but he preferred them to other types of infestations.

"My fee is two hundred and fifty dollars."

"I'll pay a thousand dollars," the voice interjected.

Rob sat up in his office chair. Since he'd gone solo with his extermination company six months ago, things had been off to a slow start. He could use the extra cash to help with some of the overhead. The fact that his ex-wife had been hounding him about his daughter' needing braces didn't help either.

"You got yourself an exterminator."

"Oh, thank God."

"Just give me the address and I can meet you there in less than an hour."

Forty-five minutes later, Rob had an idea why the other exterminators had refused to do the job. Parking his work truck at the curb in front of the address, he stared through the windshield in disbelief at the house. The place looked like something out of a bad horror movie. Sitting atop a hill and Victorian in architecture, the home was a brooding clapboard structure with a peaked gabled roof and black wrought-iron bars over all the windows. A gothic fence, also in black wrought iron, surrounded the property. Even in the light of the afternoon sun, the place looked creepy and intimidating.

Still, a thousand dollars is damn good pay, Rob thought as he climbed out of his work truck and slammed shut the door.

A thin man stood waiting at the front gate set in the fence.

"Are you the one I spoke to on the phone?" Rob asked.

"I'm Mr. Foster, the property owner." After seeing the house, Rob wouldn't be surprised if the owner looked like Bela Lugosi. Instead, the man reminded him of Mr. Rogers clean down to his pastel blue knitted sweater.

"I'm Rob Creegan." Normally, he would have offered a handshake, but the little man had the nervous habit of wringing his hands together like an old, wet rag. Rob decided to forego any hand shaking.

"I hope you're a good exterminator and worth the money I'm offering." Mr. Foster studied him with his inset, beady eyes.

"If it's an exterminator you need, I'm the best."

"I hope so."

"Are you sure you don't need a ghost buster instead?" Rob chuckled and turned his attention back to the house.

Mr. Foster didn't laugh. "Why do you say that?"

"Well, the place looks ... well, it looks like it could be haunted."

"It's not," the landlord snapped back.

"I was just making a joke." *One Mr. Foster doesn't think was funny,* Rob thought. "I didn't mean anything by it."

"I'm sorry, but talk like that makes it hard for me to sell the old place."

Rob nodded and understood. He wouldn't want to spend a night in the creepy old house, let alone buy it. Reaching into the bed of the truck, he pulled out his spray tank and breathing mask. Under the watchful glare of the landlord, Rob strapped on his equipment in preparation to spray the property. For a second, he caught an image of himself in the reflection of the truck passenger window. He did look like a ghost buster with his gray jumpsuit, spray tank on his back, and breathing mask perched upon his head.

"Who you gonna call?" Rob muttered with a chuckle. "Pest Busters."

"What was that?" Mr. Foster asked as he fished a set of keys out of a trouser pocket.

"Nothing." He hefted the tank on his back and said, "Tell me about the house. It looks like it has an interesting history."

"Built about a hundred years ago. My Uncle Louie bought it sometime after World War II and lived in it all these years. He died a month ago and the ownership passed into my hands."

"Uncle Louie?"

"Yes." Foster unlocked the gate. Rusted hinges groaned as he swung it open. "He was a bit of an eccentric. Part magician and part con man, he amassed a small fortune over the years and spent it on many of the oddities scattered throughout the house."

Rob's attention perked up. "Oddities?"

"Yes, things like trinkets, books, and curios from all over the world. That's why there are bars over the windows. My uncle was a very paranoid man and lived in fear someone would come and steal his collection. Now that he has passed on, I plan to catalogue everything and sell it at an auction."

"But can't do anything until the roaches are gone?"

"That's correct."

Foster led the way up the walk to the porch of the house. Rob followed and looked about the front lawn. Dead leaves littered the wilted grass as if it was late fall. *Strange,* he thought, *since it's the middle of summer.*

"How long have the roaches been a problem?"

"For years. They seem to live in the woodwork. Since my uncle died, they've taken over the house, I'm afraid."

As they drew nearer, the peaks of the gabled roof blocked the sun and the shadow of the house stretched out to them like a dark hand. A chill ran up Rob's spine as he stepped into the shade. *The place is definitely giving me the creeps. I can't imagine what the interior is going to be like.*

Mr. Foster continued, "Uncle Louie was an accomplished stage magician. He spent all his wealth chasing ghosts and black magic. In his later years, however, he slipped from eccentricity into complete madness."

"Madness?"

Foster stepped onto the porch. "My uncle came down with cancer in his last years and refused any medical attention. The disease ate a hole through his leg and the pain drove him out of his mind. He would lie on the couch in his roach-infested house and scream in agony for hours at a time. The family tried to offer assistance, but he became belligerent and wouldn't even come to the door. He died alone. It was a week before we found him. The horrid roaches had made a nest in his body by then."

"You're kidding."

"I wish I was." Producing the house key, Foster put it in the lock of the front door. "I hope you don't scare easily, Mr. Creegan."

Rob shook his head. "I've had spiders and rats crawling on me. Roaches don't even compare."

"Good thing." Foster turned the key and opened the door a couple of inches. Instantly, a long, brown roach ran out onto the porch and Rob stomped it beneath his work boot.

"First kill of the day," he joked.

The landlord opened the door the rest of the way and stepped back. Dozens of roaches swarmed out of the house and across the planks of the porch. Surprised, Rob grabbed up the wand connected to the spray tank and released a stream of insecticide across the base of the door frame. The mass of cockroaches died instantly.

Rob peered into the dim interior and heard the sound of skittering movement coming from inside the house.

"Is the electricity on?"

"Yes, there's a light switch on the wall just inside the door."

Rob reached in with one hand and felt along the wall. Roaches crawled across his skin until he found the switch and flicked it. Pulling his hand back, he shook the bugs off and stomped them into the porch boards. Under the illumination of a hanging light fixture, a dingy foyer waited just inside the house. A twisting staircase ran up the wall to the left. A closed door to the right opened to the rest of the first floor. Scurrying roaches ran everywhere over the walls, carpet, and ceiling.

"Jesus," he gasped.

"I told you the infestation was bad."

"You weren't exaggerating. Is the water on in the house?"

"Only the electricity is on. The gas and water have been off for over a month. Why do you ask?"

"Roaches need open water to breed and survive. For an infestation this bad, there has to be a water source."

"There is an old well in the basement. I don't know if it's sealed up or not. What is that white bug?" Foster pointed. "Is that an albino roach?"

Rob glanced over to where the landlord gestured. A large, white roach clung to the frame of a hanging picture and stood still with its antennae twitching.

"It's not an albino," Rob replied. "It's a roach that just shed its husk and exposure to light hasn't changed its pigment yet."

"Gross." Foster said and stepped back further onto the porch. "It's just sitting there looking at us."

"Not for long." Rob sprayed a stream of poison onto the insect. A barely audible shriek came from the creature. The white roach fell to the carpet of the foyer but did not die. Instead, the bug fled and became a pale blip moving amidst the mass of the brown and black roaches. Unlike the other insects running helter-skelter, the white roach ran directly under a door connected to the foyer.

"It's still alive," Foster said.

"That should've killed it. It's a tough little son of a bitch."

"It made some sort of crying sound when you sprayed it. Do roaches do that?"

"I've heard of very large roaches from the Amazon making hissing and clicking noises. I never knew one of this species to make any sound, however."

"Weird."

More than weird, Rob thought. *The infestation is the worst I've ever seen. The house doesn't need an exterminator, it needs a bulldozer.* "Besides a source of water, something else has to be feeding the roaches. Trash, rotted food, or sewage in huge abundance is needed to maintain an infestation of this magnitude."

"In his sickness, Uncle Louie collected lots of things, including trash. I'm afraid he didn't clean any of it up. The bottom floors are filled with garbage, some of it knee-deep in places."

"I see." Rob shut the front door and began walking back to his truck.

"You're not quitting, are you?" Foster followed after him.

"No. I've got two cases of industrial strength bug bombs in the back of my truck."

"You're going to bomb the house?"

"Yes. It will kill off a good portion of the infestation before I spray. I'll cut down the numbers of roaches with the bombs and then come back tomorrow and spray the house."

Returning to his truck, Rob swung open the metal tool box mounted in the bed. He took out two boxes and opened the lids. Packed inside each were twelve canisters like grenades ready for battle.

"Is that stuff strong?" Foster asked.

"The most powerful bug bombs you can buy. Only those with a professional pest control license can purchase these." Rob grabbed up an empty knapsack and began loading it with bombs. "They should do a number on the little bastards."

"So what do I do?"

"I'm going to spray the foyer and clear it of roaches. You stay outside and wait for me. Once I get the foyer cleared, you can come in." He hefted the pack of bombs on one shoulder.

Foster nodded.

They returned to the front porch. Rob slid the breath mask over his mouth as he stepped into the foyer and sprayed insecticide along the walls and baseboards of the room. Roaches died by the hundreds and their bodies fell like rain upon his head and shoulders. Afterwards, Rob stepped outside, pulled down his mask, and tapped out a cigarette.

"Do you mind if I smoke?" He didn't wait to see if Foster minded or not. He lit up anyway.

“Go ahead" the landlord replied. While he was spraying, Foster had left and returned with a broom, dustpan and large plastic trash barrel. "Is the foyer cleared?"

Rob nodded and took a long pull on the smoke. "You can start cleaning it up."

Hesitantly, the landlord began sweeping the bodies of dead roaches into the dustpan. Rob watched as he smoked down the cigarette.

"What's upstairs?" he asked.

"The bedrooms." Mr. Foster dumped out the dustpan. The dead bugs made a sound like loose dirt when hitting the bottom of the trash barrel. "There are four of them. My uncle slept in only one, though. The rest are filled with his junk."

Rob stepped on the cigarette butt and slid the spray tank off his back. "I'm going to bug bomb the bedrooms first. I can set the bombs and then close the doors. That will keep the fumes safely upstairs and force the roaches down to this floor."

"Okay, I'll keep sweeping up this mess."

Slinging the knapsack over one shoulder, Rob climbed the creaking wooden stairs to the upper floor. With every step, his boots crunched on the bodies of roaches. As he neared the top of the staircase, he had a mental image of Norman Bates appearing in his mother's dress with a pair of scissors in his hand. A chill threatened to turn the skin on his arms into gooseflesh, but he fought it back. *Don't let your imagination get away from you, Robbie. Just get this dirty job done.*

He found the doors to four bedrooms just off the second floor landing. Pushing open the first, he discovered a room filled with stacks of cardboard boxes. Yellowed theater posters plastered the walls. Most announced the upcoming performances of famous magicians, using such expletives as: Thrills! Incredible! Never before Seen! Amazing! He didn't recognize any of the stage magicians' names, except one. A playbill advertised a show by Houdini dated in 1920. Wondering how much the poster would bring on eBay, he slid on his breath mask and set the bug bomb. As the mist sprayed upward to fill the room with a lethal fog, he closed the door behind him.

The next room was even more inexplicable. Glass display cases occupied the center of the room. Nailed to the four walls were handmade demonic masks painted in lurid colors. Their evil faces, grimaces showing rubber tongues and carved teeth, leered at him as he entered. Crossing to the first display case, he wiped away dust to peer inside. Arranged on a bed of black velvet were various items and artifacts: rings, daggers, crystals, etc. Some of the things he recognized, others he could not fathom. *It looks like Uncle Louie's been shopping at Lucifer's garage sale.*

Rob set down a bug bomb and froze before he pulled the pin. Hairs bristled on the back of his neck. *Someone or something is watching me!* He turned to look and his gaze centered on a monstrous-looking devil mask painted in blood red. A spot of white showed in the dark of one eyehole. Slowly, he approached to see a white roach nestled in the left eye of the mask. He attempted to grab the pale insect, but it darted back before he got his fingers around it. Taking the mask off its nail, he discovered a small hole in the wall where the roach had disappeared.

This is getting too weird. Rob bent down and pulled the pin on the bug bomb. *The quicker I'm out of this nut house, the better.* He left as the poison fog started to spread throughout the room.

Out in the hall, Rob glanced at the other two doors on the second floor. One was a normal bedroom door, but the other was painted black with an ornate brass knob. In disbelief, he watched a white cockroach crawl across the door's surface and disappear into a keyhole.

Could it be the same damned roach? Rob shook his head. *It didn't seem likely.*

He decided to open the black door. The room beyond proved to be a library with high bookshelves stuffed with various volumes and tomes. A carpet the color of dried blood stretched across the floor. Roaches ran everywhere and over everything. He scanned over the books in the nearest shelf and realized the titles dealt with witchcraft, Satanism, and demon worship. A sense of dread settled into his stomach. *This house needs an exorcist instead of an exterminator!*

He placed another bug bomb on the floor and pulled the pin. White gas sprayed from the canister as he headed toward the door. Without warning, something heavy came crashing down on his back and neck. Dazed by the blow, Rob found himself sprawled face-first on the floor and covered in a pile of books. He tried to regain his feet but the weight of a fallen bookshelf pinned him to the carpet. He turned his head and saw the bug bomb still spewing poisonous fog into the air.

Oh God, I've got to get out! I'll die if I stay in here!

Struggling against the weight on his back, Rob attempted to crawl out from under the bookshelf as the air in the room turned cloudy. Behind his breathing mask, he tasted the insecticide fumes. In desperation, he pushed away books to give himself more room to escape from under the crushing press of the shelf. Adrenalin, driven by fear, flooded through his muscles and he forced the shelf off of him. As he staggered to his feet, Rob caught sight of a white roach a few feet away. The bug's antennae twitched and shivered.

The bastard is just sitting there watching!

He fled the room and slammed the door shut behind him. Coughing and gasping for fresh air, he dropped the knapsack of bug bombs and ripped off the breathing mask. Nausea threatened to make him retch, and his throat burned as if it was on fire. A shooting pain knifed through his neck and down his back. *Did the roaches push the bookcase over on him? How is that possible?*

"Foster!" he shouted in a hoarse voice. "A thousand dollars isn't worth this! You hear me? A damn bookcase nearly broke my back! I'm going home! You're going to get a bill from my chiropractor."

"I can't open the front door!" the landlord yelled back from the floor below.

"What?" Rob still felt dizzy and disorientated. He wasn't sure what Foster meant.

"The front door slammed shut and locked. I can't get it open! We can't get out!"

"Who shut the door?"

"I don't know! Something slammed it shut."

"Bust out a window or something."

"There are bars on all the windows!" He detected a growing panic in the man's voice. "We're trapped!"

"I'll be down in a second." Rob shook his head to clear the dizziness. Out of the corner of his eye, he caught something white on the carpet of the hallway. Forcing his eyes to focus, he realized what the object was. A white roach waited in the middle of the hall.

"What are you looking at, you ugly turd?" he yelled.

A barely audible crying noise sounded from the insect. A second later, a sea of brown and black roaches poured out from under the last bedroom door and raced down the carpet toward him.

"Oh shit!" He grabbed up the knapsack and stumbled to the staircase.

At the bottom stair, Foster stood looking up with fear in his eyes. "What's wrong?"

"Run!" Rob shouted as he half-staggered, half-fell down the stairs. "Run now!"

Foster looked past him, and his eyes went wide with horror at the sight of the seething flood of roaches pouring down the staircase. "Dear God!"

The landlord darted into the other room connected to the foyer.

Rob reached the bottom step and grabbed up the spray tank he'd placed there earlier. Spinning around, he shot a stream of insecticide onto the oncoming wave of roaches. The mass of insects died in droves under the poisonous attack. He sprayed until the tank ran dry exterminating the onslaught. He looked up the top of the staircase. A white roach sat watching from the railing.

"Yeah, I killed them. No more roach army, you shithead!" Rob shouted and threw the empty spray tank toward the strange bug. The white insect scurried away before the hurled tank crushed it.

Reaching into his coveralls, Rob pulled out a pack of cigarettes. He lit one up hoping to remove the taste of insecticide from his throat. He drew heavily on the smoke and let it fill his lungs. His neck and back hurt like hell. Turning his attention to the front door, he tried the knob but found it locked. Someone or something, had sabotaged the deadbolt making the door unable to be unlocked from this side. He pulled aside the curtain of a nearby window to see that thick iron bars blocked any escape. Across the yard, his truck waited parked by the curb.

Damn, I left my cell in the front seat. No way to call for help.

He finished the smoke and smashed the butt into the floor. There had to be another way out of this hell house; a backdoor or a window without bars on it. Maybe the landlord knew a way out.

"Foster," he shouted in a hoarse voice.

No answer.

"Foster," he repeated. *Where the hell had he gone?*

To his right, a door hung partially open. The landlord had fled in that direction. Taking the knapsack with him, Rob entered the next room to find a large living area in dim light. He found a light switch against one wall and flicked it on, illuminating a set of dusty chandeliers. The place was a mess. Heaps of trash and debris littered the floor. Roaches ran rampant through the fetid garbage. A putrid, rotted smell hung in the air. Wading through the filth, Rob pushed his way through to another door on the other end.

"Foster," he called out again. The only noise in response came from the shifting of the cockroaches moving through the sea of trash.

Maybe the guy found another way out and was standing in the backyard waiting for him.

A dining room adjoined the living room. Mounds of rotted food and dirty dishes covered the table and months of refuse littered the floor. Rob pushed his way through the bug-infested trash looking for signs of Foster passing this way through the house. A door hung half open at the other end of the room.

"Foster, are you in there?" he asked. No answer.

He reached the door and shoved against it. Something on the other side kept it from opening further. Sliding through the narrow gap, he entered a rubbish-filled utility room. Just inside the door, Foster lay face down on a pile of trash.

"Are you okay?" Rob knelt beside the landlord who remained perfectly still.

No sign of Foster breathing, he noticed. With a deep dread settling in his gut, he put a finger against the man's neck and felt for a pulse. None. *Oh God, did he have a heart attack?*

Preparing to give CPR, he turned the body over. Instead, he froze in complete shock. Foster's open mouth and nostrils were clogged full of brown roaches blocking his airways. His dead eyes stared back at him in wide, abject terror. *Suffocated by roaches!!* Crying out in revulsion, Rob crawled back away from the corpse until his back hit against the wall. The foul taste of bile filled his mouth as his stomach threatened to heave. He fought back the vomit and closed his eyes to catch his breath. *I've got to find a way out of this house. Get to the phone and call 911.*

From somewhere in the room came a barely audible crying sound. Rob snapped opened his eyes. Across from him, the white roach sat on the face of another painted black door, similar to the one he'd encountered upstairs. Something tickled his legs and Rob looked down. From the mounds of trash on the floor, a mass of roaches raced up his body. Leaping to his feet, Rob attempted to sweep them off his coveralls, but a sea of insects kept pouring from the trash to take the place of the ones he brushed away. Hundreds of roaches crawled up the outside of his overalls and raced toward his mouth and nostrils. In mere seconds, he the filthy bugs covered him. Insects tried to enter his mouth and nose.

"Oh no you don't, you son-of-a-bitch!" Rob screamed aloud and slung off the knapsack filled with bug bombs. "You're not going to kill me like Foster."

Throwing the bag across the room, he struck the door above the white roach. The wailing stopped as it scurried into the keyhole.

"You're not getting away from me!" Rob yelled. Intense rage sent him in a charge through the trash. Reaching the black door, he planted his heel against the wood and broke it open. "I'm coming to get you!"

Swatting away roaches from his eyes, he grabbed up the knapsack from the trashy floor. He ate or spat out the insects trying to invade his mouth and entered the room beyond the black door. A narrow, wooden staircase led down into dim darkness. In the half-light at the bottom, the white roach fled across the stone floor into the shadows. Driven by intense anger, Rob rushed down the steps. His foot tripped over a strand of wire stretched across the stair. Tumbling head-over-heels, he fell the rest of the way down the staircase and landed on his back against the hard floor. The tumbling fall and impact killed most of the roaches swarming his body.

Rob shook his head and tried to clear his senses. His right elbow and knee ached in agony from the fall. Focusing on the room, he discovered it to be a small basement. Sitting up, he took in the rest of his surroundings.

Along one wall, shelves lined with empty glass jars stood ready for canning. The jars were the least unusual aspect of the basement. The rest of the room was a scene out of hell. Painted on the walls were horned shapes with blood-red eyes. A circle of strange ancient symbols had been etched in stunning detail upon the stone floor. In one dark corner, a metal plate half-covered the opening to an old well and the air stank of stagnant water.

The well room, Rob realized and reached out to grab his knapsack of bombs. *Where did the albino bastard go?*

Scanning the dark corners, he caught a glimpse of a pale blip in the shadows. More anger rose within as he snatched a canning jar from a nearby shelf. Glass container in hand, he threw himself forward as the white roach attempted to flee. In one deft move, he swept the insect into the jar and screwed on the lid.

"Now I've got you," he said. "Let's see what the hell you are."

He twisted the jar around and peered through the glass. Something was very different about this roach. Rob focused his sight to see the insect better. A scream caught in his throat and he nearly dropped the jar in shock. The white roach stared back at him with the tiny face of a human. Eyes, nose, and mouth were all manlike. In the place of the creature's two forelegs were human arms and hands. The thing blinked at him with beady eyes full of intelligence.

"It can't be," Rob gasped.

The creature opened its human mouth and let out a silent scream from inside the jar.

A loud wail sounded behind him. He stuffed the jar in the pocket of his coveralls and turned around. From under the lid of the well, a wave of thousands of white roaches poured from the stagnant hole in the floor. They entered the circle of cryptic symbols and began to form into a shape. Seeing something beyond his ability to comprehend, Rob stepped back, stunned by what he was witnessing. The roaches massed together and a shape rose from the center of the circle. Completely created out of the undulating mass of living insects, a human form now stood facing Rob.

"I have returned home," a distorted voice boomed from within the body of the being. "Not even the depths of Hell could keep me. I've done what Houdini could not. I've conquered death itself."

"Uncle Louie?" Rob asked in disbelief. On instinct, he reached into the knapsack with one hand and began pulling the pins on the bug bombs.

The impossible face of shifting white bugs gazed upon him.

"You speak my name." An arm formed out of insects pointed toward him. "Who are you? Why are you in my house?

"I'm the pest exterminator." Rob threw open the knapsack and spilled out the twenty hissing canisters of insecticide upon the floor at the feet of the unholy abomination. "Consider yourself exterminated."

Something like a laugh from a fevered nightmare escaped from the horror. "Your poison has no effect on me." The being stepped forward out of the circle on legs created out of white roaches. "You will soon serve as a nest to my roaches."

"Oh shit!" Rob replied.

In terror, he turned and charged up the steps. At the top he looked back. The bug-created Uncle Louie climbed the staircase behind him. Beyond the horrible creature, the white poison fog of the bug bombs filled the air of the basement. Coughing on the insecticide, Rob pushed his way out the black door and slammed it shut behind him. He threw his weight against the wood as the bug-infested form pounded against the door on the other side.

"You will not escape me," the inhuman voice hissed through the door. "My roaches will feed upon your flesh."

The crying wail from the mouths of a thousand white roaches blasted through the house. Rob put his hands over his ears to shut out the noise. The sound stopped and a few seconds of intense silence followed. He turned his attention to his surroundings. Something was moving through the trash toward him. The skittering of countless insect legs began to grow louder in the room. Behind the door, the Uncle Louie thing laughed in a garbled voice.

"Exterminator indeed," the thing spoke. "You will be the one exterminated."

The trash on the floor moved aside as a tidal wave of brown roaches swarmed toward him. In mere seconds, the insects raced up his body. Rob looked down to see the white fog of the insecticide creeping from under the door. The basement was filled with the gas.

Swatting away the roaches crawling on his face, Rob said. "Do you know what the danger is in using bug bombs in an enclosed space, Uncle Louie?" He reached into his coverall pocked and produced a Bic lighter. "Let me demonstrate." He flicked the lighter and touched the flame to the white fumes escaping from under the door.

The insecticide ignited and the basement exploded. The door Rob leaned against blew apart from the blast into a storm of splintered wood. The concussion sent him sprawling to the floor. Up from the basement, a boiling flash fire erupted and engulfed the demonic form of Uncle Louie in the doorway. The piercing scream of thousands of white roaches followed as their bodies burst from the heat of the searing flame.

Rob lay still, trying to catch his breath. The house caught fire like an old tinderbox. Flames spread along the ceiling and fed on the trash on the floor. The smoke and the smell of the insecticide sickened him and he fought to breathe.

It is time to live or die, Robbie.

He sat up and peered through the thickening pall. The blast had knocked a hole in the wall and sunlight shone through from the other side. Standing on shaky legs, Rob staggered toward the opening. Fire licked at his feet and caught onto the bottom of his coveralls. He squeezed his way through the hole and crawled out into the clear air of the backyard. Behind him, flames devoured the back of the house and moved toward the rest of the structure. Fire crackled and roared as the hundred-year-old home began to collapse in on itself from the spreading inferno.

Rob stared up at the sky and watched the cloud of black smoke rise from the destruction of the home. For a second, the dark cloud took the form of a devilish face before it dissipated into the afternoon sky.

He lay back in the grass of the yard and began laughing like a madman.

* * * *

Homicide Detective Saunders raised the crime tape just high enough for him to slip under. The smell of smoke from the house fire still hovered thick in the air. He looked around the collection of emergency response vehicles to find Jim Beeker, his partner, on the other side of the wrought iron fence. The rookie detective stood talking to the assistant fire chief. Catching sight of Saunders, the young man ambled over to his side.

"What do we have?" Saunders asked.

Beeker pulled up a notepad and flipped it back a couple of pages. "House fire caused by a possible insecticide explosion,"

"Insecticide explosion?" He turned his attention to the pile of smoldering rubble which was once somebody's home. "You mean insecticide caused this?"

"That's what the assistant fire chief says."

"I hope I remember that the next time Doris wants me to bug bomb." Saunders watched as more firemen opened another hose and sprayed a stream of water onto the smoking ruin of the house. "So why did I cancel a dinner date with my wife?"

"We might have a possible homicide."

"Possible?"

Beeker referred to his notes. "One body found in the house. Partially burned but the fire wasn't the cause of death. Roaches killed him."

"Roaches?"

"The man's mouth and throat were filled with them."

"Can they do that? Kill a man?"

"I don't know, sir. It seems very unlikely. We'll know more once the ME gets here."

"Do we know who the dead man is?"

"Not yet. His wallet and identification were burned in the fire."

Saunders nodded toward an ambulance where paramedics were attending to someone on a stretcher. "Okay, what else do we have? Who are the EMTs working on?"

"One survivor," Beeker replied. "A pest exterminator. Suffers from exposure to insecticide and smoke."

"He was in the house fire?"

"Apparently."

"Okay, partner, you continue talking to the fire chief, and I'll go ask our survivor a few questions."

Beeker smiled. "Good luck with questioning him. I think he's delirious from all the bug spray he inhaled. Talks crazy stuff about roaches from hell and someone named Uncle Louie."

Saunders let out a short sigh. "Why do I always get the crazy ones?"

Crossing to the curb, Detective Saunders approached the back of the ambulance. A man in gray coveralls lay strapped to a gurney as EMTs attached an oxygen mask to his face. One paramedic turned and nearly ran into the detective standing off to the side.

"Is he okay?" He showed him his badge.

"He inhaled a powerful dose of insecticide. He's suffered various bumps and bruises, as well. We got him stabilized, but he is still in respiratory distress. We're going to take him to the hospital for observation."

"Can I talk to him for a bit?"

"Make it quick. We're about to load him into the wagon."

Saunders stepped up to the side of the gurney. In the flashing emergency lights of the ambulance, the man looked gray and pallid. The name patch on his coverall front said Creegan.

"Mr. Creegan, I'm Detective Saunders. I'd like to ask you a few questions, is that all right?"

The man's glassy eyes turned to look at him. He gave a weak nod.

"You were spraying the house when the fire started?"

The man nodded yes again.

"We found the body of one man in the ruin of the house. Do you know who he is?"

Creegan's shaking hand reached up and pulled down the oxygen mask. "It's Foster, the landlord," he said in a hoarse voice.

"Is there anybody else we need to be looking for in the ashes?"

"No."

"Can you tell me what happened?"

The man's face became confused. His eyes appeared as if they were looking at something far away. "The house was filled with roaches … the worse I've ever seen … but there were something worse than cockroaches … something evil," he replied in a halting voice. "Something from Hell … demon roaches."

"Demon roaches?" Detective Saunders repeated in a tone of voice that did little to hide his skepticism.

Creegan reached out and gripped his forearm tightly. "You must believe me … Uncle Louie summoned them … he came back from death … from the grave."

"Uncle Louie?" He pulled his arm free from the man's grip. "Perhaps, Mr. Creegan, we can talk better once you have recovered from the insecticide poisoning and cleared your mind."

Nodding to the paramedics, Detective Saunders watched them start to load the man into the ambulance.

"You've got to believe me," Creegan reached into the pocket of his coveralls and removed a glass jar. "I got proof … look at its face …"

He took the jar from the shaky hands of the man. The gurney was lifted and rolled into the back of the ambulance.

Creegan raised his head before the paramedics closed the doors, "Look at the roach ... look closely at its face ... the face of the devil." His eyes were wide and fixed on the detective's. "Look and you'll know."

The ambulance doors swung closed, shutting off Mr. Creegan's frantic voice. Detective Saunders focused his attention to the jar in his hand. Something pale white rested on the glass bottom. He turned the jar to get a better look at whatever it was. A white roach, he realized. Studying the insect closer, he saw something very odd about its appearance. He brought the glass closer for a better look. The roach's face—a human face—twitched, and tiny eyes opened to stare back at Saunders. The insect's mouth opened to let out a tiny scream as human-like hands pressed against the inside of the jar.

"Dear God!" Saunders cried out in shock. The glass jar slipped from his grip, fell to the pavement, and shattered. Stunned by disbelief, he watched the white roach run along the pavement of the road while making a crying sound. The fleeing insect ran a few feet before a black shoe suddenly stepped down upon it. Detective Saunders looked up to see his partner standing there.

"If you want to look at roaches you should go to the house fire. There are like a million dead ones in there."

"What?" Saunders asked, shaking his head as he tried to come to grips with the impossible thing he had just seen.

"The house was a roach motel." Beeker raised his shoe to see the bug smashed into a gooey mess against the bottom of his sole. "Yuk. An albino roach." He scraped the bottom of the shoe against the curb. "That's gross."

LIVE BAIT

"Dude, are you sure they didn't film Deliverance around here?" Todd Cooty asked as he shut the truck door of the Toyota pickup behind him. Outside, the air cooked in the Oklahoma heat and vibrated with the constant hum of locusts.

"You have to get off the main road to find the best fishing spots," Drew Mitchell, his college roommate, replied, exiting the driver's side. "I'm just glad we found this bait shop along the way. I got to use the crapper really bad and we can get you a rod and reel while we're here."

The pickup was parked on a patch of gravel in front of a whitewashed building, a conversion from a roadside filling station that had seen better days. Two outdated gas pumps waited like old soldiers standing guard in the middle of the parking lot. A large hand painted sign, strung with the bones of catfish heads on fishing line, announced the name of the place as:

Broscoe's Bait Shop. Beer. Bait. Gas. Taxidermy

"Tell me again why I agreed to go on this lame fishing trip." Todd dropped his Styrofoam cup of watered-down Pepsi into a trash can brimming with garbage and the stink of rotting fish. A cloud of flies buzzed into the air.

"Because you're a virgin when it comes to the fine art of fishing," Drew said. "I still can't believe you never went fishing in your life. For that matter, I can't believe you never been laid, either."

Todd looked away and fought the embarrassment reddening his face. For Drew Mitchell, who was good-looking and popular, getting laid was easy. For Todd, with his rail-thin body and big nose, finding sex for the first time turned out to be a tortured exercise of fumbling and rejection. Life left him twenty years old and still very much a virgin.

"Oh, I get this whole fishing thing, now," Todd said. "It's for guys who can't get any on summer break from college. We're two city boys on an impromptu fishing trip; you know how gay that sounds? It's Brokeback Mountain gay."

Drew chuckled. "I can't help you with getting laid but I can take you out and teach you how to get your pole wet."

"There you go talking about sex again."

Drew laughed and walked toward the entrance to the shop.

In the shadow beneath the front door awning, Todd noticed a man sitting off to one side. *Funny, I didn't see him there when we pulled up,* he told himself. He wore stained overalls with an equally dirty white T-shirt underneath. Jutting out from the sleeves were meaty arms ending in raw-looking hands with scabbed knuckles. Scraggly facial hair, which no razor had touched for days, framed his face. Atop his head perched a greasy ball cap with the words: *Fish Fear Me.* Real fishing hooks pierced the brim in several places. As they approached the shop door, the stranger squinted at them with bloodshot eyes.

"Afternoon, y'all," the man said and picked up a white Dixie cup in which he spat brown tobacco juice.

"Afternoon," Todd said in unison with Drew.

"You boys goin' fishin'?" Reaching into a white plastic bucket at his feet, the man pulled out a large catfish, which he placed on the top of a wooden barrel. He then took a filet knife and split the fish's underbelly in one smooth motion. Todd and Drew watched transfixed, but said nothing. Noticing there was no response to his question, the man looked again at them both. "I asked, was you two boys goin' fishin'?"

'We thought we would try our luck at Grover's Lake," Drew said.

Reaching into the fish's open belly, the man's calloused hands removed a glob of organs. His gaze fixed on Todd. "You look a little ill there, boy. You ever see a man gut a fish before?"

"This is my first fishing trip."

The man smiled. Half of his teeth were missing and the remaining ones were stained brown.

"First time fishin'?" He picked up his cup and spat. "Boy, you're in for a real treat. I've been fishin' since I've been chewin' tobacco and that I've been, doing since I was seven." He stood and wiped a hand on the thigh of his overalls. "The name's Broscoe. I own this here little bait shop."

Todd shook the offered hand which felt rough as sandpaper. "Todd. And this is Drew."

Broscoe reached across and shook Drew's hand. "Glad to meet you."

"Sir, do you have a restroom I can use?" Drew asked.

"On the east side of the building. Make sure you shake the handle.

Damn thang don't always flush right."

Drew nodded and disappeared around the corner of the building.

Broscoe went back to filleting the fish. "So what's been keeping you so busy that you never went fishin'?"

"College." Todd smiled. "I guess you would say I'm a city boy."

"There are things you won't learn in college." Broscoe chopped down with the knife and severed the head of the fish. "Like gutting a catfish." He tossed the fish head to the ground and nodded toward the door of the shop. "But don't let old Broscoe keep you standin' out here in the sun, boy. Go on inside. My wife will fix you up."

"I'll do that," Todd said before opening the door.

A small overhead cowbell jangled as he entered. Sitting at the register counter, a busty red-haired woman looked up from reading a Reader's Digest. In one hand she held a pink fly-swatter at the ready.

"Welcome," she said with a smile crying out for much-needed dental work. She swatted a big, black fly landing on her open magazine. "I'm Louise, is there anything I can help you with?" Turning the Digest over, she shook the dead fly out onto the floor.

"Just dropping in to pick up a few things. My friend will be along in a bit."

Louise nodded and returned to her magazine.

Todd walked around the store. The odor of fish and mustiness permeated the air. Above his head, the walls were covered in mounted catfish and bass, their bodies frozen in time with wide open mouths. Rods and reels, fishing hooks, lures, tackle boxes, and gear Todd didn't recognize filled the shelves. Against one wall, a large refrigerated cooler hummed. Remembering the watered-down Pepsi he'd thrown away, Todd looked through the sliding glass doors at the stacks of cold pop and beer six-packs. As usual, Drew had all the money. Todd would have to wait until he returned from using the restroom before getting something to drink.

On the wall next to the cooler unit, he noticed a series of yellowed newspaper clippings in picture frames. One clipping caught his eye with a headline reading: *Is it a Man or Fish? The Legend of Catfish Joe.* An artist's rendition of a half-man and half-fish accompanied the article. The drawing reminded him of the Creature of the Black Lagoon rendered with a catfish head. Intrigued, Todd read the story along with the picture. The clipping told about a legend handed down from the Indians of a fish man who lived in the backwaters of Grover Lake. People swore to have seen the creature lurking in the lake for years.

"Oh, that's the legend of Catfish Joe you're reading there."

Involved in the article, Todd jumped at the sound of a woman's voice. He glanced to the side. Louise stood beside him with the pink flyswatter in her hands.

"Catfish Joe?"

"Haven't you ever heard of our local legend? Well, that lake in Scotland has got the Loch Ness monster and there's a lake up north that's got the legend of Blue Champ, or whatever, well down here in these part, we got old Catfish Joe."

"What is he? A big fish?"

"Oh, no. I suspect he's more man than fish. Got a body like a man but a head like a catfish. Huge claws and teeth to boot. He's a mean one, too. Some of the ranchers around here claim Catfish Joe drags cattle into the water and strips them to bone just like those man-eatin' fish do on the Discovery channel. You see that one news story on the wall there?" She pointed with her pink flyswatter to a yellowed news clipping. "That's about them two boaters on the lake who drowned last year and were never found. I suspect that was Joe's doin'."

Todd looked at the woman. Her eyes showed a hint of madness. *Delusional and crazy*, Todd thought to himself. *She believes every word she is saying. The end result of generations of inbreeding*. The cowbell at the front door jangled and he glanced over, hoping to see Drew returning from using the john. Instead it was Broscoe coming in from the outside.

"You mean people have actually seen this thing?" Todd asked and added, "Have you seen it?" He expected her to go into some fantastical account about the fish monster.

"I never seen it but my husband has, haven't you dear?"

Broscoe joined them and spat into his cup.

"Ol' Joe? Yeah, I've seen the ugly bastard. About three years ago. I was laying a trot line early one morning when something grabbed the line and nearly pulled me out the damned boat. I thought I had hooked a tree stump but when I looked over the side, there was old Joe, bigger than life and uglier than sin. He was looking up at me with eyes as black as death and a smell worse than rotted fish. I fired up the outboard and got the hell out of there." Broscoe spat again into the cup and wiped a long string of drool from his straggly chin. "Every few years, a couple of big city reporters with tape recorders and video cameras come down here to write a story on the legend. I tell them that Catfish Joe is real and they look at me with that smart-ass smirk they save for talkin' to stupid rednecks."

"Where would a creature like that come from?" Todd asked as he returned his gaze to the artist's drawing.

"Let me tell you, boy, that there are things of this Earth that science doesn't comprehend. I suspect Joe comes from a race of creatures that were here before we climbed out of the trees."

"The fossil record doesn't support that." Todd shook his head.

"Is that what that college of yours teaches?" Broscoe leaned in close with an insane glint deep in his eyes. "There are all kinds of weird unknown things in the world. Just because you don't believe doesn't mean that they aren't true. Science wants to turn a blind eye, but they are there. Hidden in the dark and secret places where no one goes or wants to go. Joe's one of those and I'm going to catch him. There ain't no fish I can't catch. I just got to have the proper bait.

The cowbell at the door rang and Drew entered the shop. Todd let out a sigh of relief.

"Hey, dude, did you find a pole yet?" Drew asked from across the store.

"I really didn't look, yet," Todd replied as Broscoe and Louise returned to stand behind the cashier counter.

Drew walked across to where he waited. "What are you doing here in the corner?"

"Man, check this shit out," Todd pointed to the news clippings. "People have seen a fish monster living in the lake."

Drew shook his head. "It's bullshit, dude. All these local lakes got some legends related to them people swear are real. You hear all kinds of stuff—lost Indian treasure, Bigfoot, ghosts of outlaws, flying saucers; the list goes on and on."

"Broscoe claims he saw this fish thing named Catfish Joe. He's weird, too. There is something in his eyes I don't like. The guy is whacked."

"He's just shitting you since you're a newbie and from the city." Drew picked up a black fishing rod. "This is a nice standard Zebco, a great starter pole for you, man. You can't go wrong with this."

"Works for me," Todd said and added, "Hey, don't I need like a tackle box or something?"

Drew smiled and picked a green plastic box off the shelf. "There you got a rod and tackle; you're so ready to go fishing."

They crossed the shop and put the gear on the counter next to the cash register.

"My friend needs some nice lures to help catch a catfish with," Drew said.

"Lures!" Broscoe spat brown juice into his cup. "You don't fish with lures to catch catfish. The best bait is live bait. When you push that hook through that worm and feel it wiggling on the line. When you cast it in the water and you know that bait is alive right before the fish strikes. That's real fishing."

"Oh, hush, you old fart!" Louise began ringing up the items on the register. "Let these boys fish the way they want."

"I suppose we could get some worms or minnows," Drew replied.

"Now you're talkin', son," Broscoe said and shouted. "Jessie Mae, come on up front, girl!"

A back door opened, revealing another room. A teenaged girl stepped out and was so gorgeous Todd fought to keep his mouth from hanging open in shock. With skin-tight cutoff shorts, a plaid shirt tied up to reveal a long stretch of taut, tanned stomach, and unbuttoned enough to expose a lot of freckled cleavage, she was the epitome of a country beauty. Braided blonde pigtails enhanced her fresh, natural beauty. She looked more like a Playboy model prepared for a photo shoot then a real girl. Todd locked eyes with Drew and knew he was thinking the same thing.

"This here is my daughter, Jessie Mae," Broscoe announced.

"Hi," she smiled at them both. "What you need, Daddy? I was back there filling the minnow tanks."

"Daughter, dear, why don't you go and fetch a container of your finest night crawlers for these two boys."

"Sure." Jessie smiled coyly at them both before walking out of the room. Todd's heart raced as the girl turned to show the finest butt he'd ever seen stuffed into denim.

"Where you boys plannin' to go fishin' at?" Broscoe's voice broke the spell of watching his daughter walking away.

Drew cleared his throat. "I figure we will probably go throw our lines off the dam and see what we can catch near the spillway."

"Why son, you ain't goin' to catch nothin' down by the dam. That's where all those city fishers go. That spot is all fished out." Broscoe spat into his cup and wiped his chin. "Why don't you let ol' Broscoe tell you where you can catch a big one?"

"Let these fellas fish the way they want, you old coot." Louise said.

"Hush, woman! I'm goin' to help these boys catch a big'un!" Broscoe turned to Drew. "You do want to catch a big'un?"

"Sure."

"Then you boys need to go to my secret fishin' hole."

"Secret fishing hole?" Todd asked and glanced at Drew.

"Yeah. Grover Lake is one of the largest in the state. There are secret places where no white man has probably ever seen. I know such a spot. It's way back off the road and nobody fishes there. That's where I caught all these fine trophies stuffed and mounted on the wall around you."

"Sounds good to me," Drew said. "Do you have a map so we can find it?"

"Ain't got no map," Broscoe scratched his whiskered chin. "I tell you what. You two boys look like fine upstandin' youths. I reckon I can let Jessie Mae go with you and show you the secret fishin' hole."

"I think we better take a rain check on …" Todd said.

"Sure, we would love to have your daughter show us her secret fishing hole," Drew interrupted.

Todd shot him an angry look.

"That's the spirit." Broscoe slapped Drew on the shoulder. "You won't be regretting this when you pull a nine pound cat out of that lake."

"How much do I owe for the rod and tackle box?" Drew opened his wallet. "I also need a six-pack of Budweiser with that."

"Now you boys ain't plannin' to be drinkin' and drivin' with my daughter in the truck, are you?" Broscoe spat in his cup and looked serious at them both. "I hope not, 'cause I'm trustin' that you boys will be gentlemen and treat my Jessie Mae with respect. No foolin' around, okay? She's only sixteen years old."

"Did I say Budweiser?" Drew stammered. "I meant six-pack of Pepsi."

Louise rang the total on the register and Drew paid as Todd went over and grabbed the six-pack out of the cooler.

"Now you boys go on out to your truck and I'll send Jessie out there shortly." Broscoe opened the door to the shop to let them out.

"Thanks for all your help and great service," Drew said before they exited the store and back out in the bright sunshine and heat of the day.

"Dude, we can't take that guy's daughter with us," Todd said as they walked toward the truck.

"Are you kidding me?" Drew threw the fishing gear into the truck bed. "Little Miss Daisy Duke is a certified country hottie. Did you see the legs on that chick? Jessica Simpson's got nothing on her."

"Drew, she's jail-bait and her father is a half-drunk redneck who thinks there is a fish-man living in the lake. He scares the shit out of me."

"That is why you never been laid, Todd," Drew replied while patting him on he shoulder. "You're always too scared. You got to learn to jump at the opportunity whenever it arises. Now be quiet because here she comes."

Todd turned to see Jessie Mae crossing the parking lot toward them. In her hands she held a white Styrofoam container. "Daddy said that I should show you his secret fishin' hole."

"Just hop right in and we'll get on the road," Drew said.

"Daddy also told me that I should never ride with strangers." Jessie glanced at them both with deep blue eyes.

Drew opened the truck door. "I'm Drew Mitchell and this is Todd Cooty. There, we aren't strangers anymore."

"I guess not." Jessie slid into the center of the front seat and put the bait container between her long brown legs. Drew climbed in behind the wheel as Todd sat next to the passenger door.

"Now, how do we get to this secret fishing hole?" Drew asked starting the truck.

"Just turn south on this highway, then I'll tell you where to turn off. It's not easy to see from the road so you might miss it."

"Let's party!" Drew stepped on the gas and sprayed gravel behind the truck as it pulled out of the parking lot.

* * * *

Todd concentrated on looking out the front windshield as the truck drove down a back road sweltering in the Oklahoma sun. The awkwardness and anxiety he got from being in close contact with a pretty female returned in spades as he rode next to Jessie. The sexual tension of such a beauty sitting close to him overwhelmed his senses. His knees began to shake as glanced out of the corner of his eye to catch a glimpse of her brown legs and the open area of her shirt exposing her freckled cleavage.

Jessie Mae burst into laughter.

"What's so funny?" Todd asked, shocked by the outburst.

"It's this cup of worms between my legs. I can feel those night crawlers squirming inside the cup. It just kind of tickles."

"We can stop and put them in the back of the truck with the rest of the gear," Todd offered.

"Oh, that's all right. It feels kind 'a good."

"I can't believe you're only sixteen years old," Drew said.

"Yeah, everybody says I look older than I am."

"What kind of name is Jessie Mae? Your last name isn't Clampett, is it?" Todd asked with a chuckle.

"Nope." She shook her pigtails. "My last name is Farmer."

"You're kidding, right?" Drew asked.

"My name is Jessie Mae Farmer and my daddy is Broscoe Farmer."

Drew and Todd burst into laughter.

"What's so funny?"

"It's the way you talk," Todd said. "It's so country."

Jessie hung her head down and looked at her hands. "I ain't no city girl like you and your friend are used to. You two probably think I'm just a dumb redneck hick."

"No, the way you talk is really cute," Todd said and added, "It fits you."

"Thank you, Todd. You're cute, too." She smiled and slid her hand into his. "I'm so glad that my Daddy let me go with you two. I was getting tired of cleaning smelly minnow tanks and sweeping up around the bait shop."

Todd looked down in disbelief. *She's holding my hand!* Swallowing hard, he squeezed her fingers gently to see if it was real. She responded by leaning in closer and putting her head on his shoulder. Heart pounding with excitement and knees shaking, Todd settled back in his seat.

This can't be happening. This girl is coming on to me.

"Are we getting close?" Drew looked over and caught Todd holding hands with Jessie. His eyebrows shot up in an arch as if he didn't believe what he was seeing, either.

"You're on the right road. Just a few more miles and I'll tell you where to turn," she answered.

Todd reached out and put an arm around her shoulder and drew her close to him. The scent of her was intoxicating as she snuggled closer against his bony chest.

What are you doing? Todd asked himself. *This girl is only sixteen!*

"Tell me, Jessie," Todd spoke in order to take his mind off the closeness of her body. "Back at the bait shop, was that stuff about Catfish Joe for real?"

"It's for real, all right. I've never seen him but Daddy swears by it. He's going to catch him one day, too." She shot up straight in the seat. "Oh, stop the truck!"

Drew slammed on the brakes. "What happened?"

"You missed the turnoff."

Looking back over his shoulder, Drew said, "I didn't see any place leading off the road."

"You see that hole in the fence?" Jessie pointed to a break in a fence on the other side of a roadside ditch. "That's the place."

"That's a road?" Drew asked. "I don't even see a trail through the trees."

"There's one beyond that fence and it leads back to the lake."

"Dude, do you think your truck will make it through there?" Todd asked as he studied the fence opening.

Drew slammed the truck into gear. "There's only one way to find out. It's time to see what this truck will do off road. Hang on; this is going to be a bumpy ride."

The truck gunned down the ditch and up the other side before it drove over the downed fence and into the wooded area beyond. Drew let out a loud whoop and fought the wheel as the truck bounced and bucked over the rough ground through the trees. The violent motion kept throwing Jessie over onto Todd's lap.

"What's that hard thing that keeps hitting me in the hip?" she asked as she tried to keep from bouncing around in the seat.

"It's not what you think." Todd said with a smile. "It's my cell phone."

"I'm glad you brought the cell, Todd," Drew said as the truck dipped and jumped. "We might need it to call someone to pull us out of here if we get stuck."

The three of them laughed and giggled as the truck bounced on its suspension along the trail. Finally, the pickup slid to a halt. Todd looked out the front window to see they were parked on the edge of a cove of brown lake water.

"We made it," Drew announced. "Daddy Broscoe's secret fishing hole at last."

Climbing out of the truck, they stretched. The air around the shaded cove carried the stench of dead fish.

"It smells bad, like something died here," Drew said.

"This cove is kind of off the main lake so it don't get drained out properly. Some dead fish end up in here. It's still a good place to fish, if you can stand the smell." Jessie reached out and took Todd's hand again.

He put his arm around her shoulder as Drew went to the back of the truck and pulled out the fishing gear.

Handing over the Zebco and tackle box, Drew whispered. "It's time to start fishing, lover-boy. I don't see you complaining about bringing little miss jail-bait now."

Todd ignored Drew and turned to Jessie. "What am I supposed to do with this?" he asked fiddling with the rod and reel in his hands.

"You mean to tell me you ain't never gone fishin' before?" Jessie's eyes met his in disbelief.

"Never."

Drew burst into laughter. "That's not all he hasn't done before."

"Shut up, dude." Todd's ears began to burn.

"You're a true city boy, aren't you?" Jessie took the rod and reel from his hands. "First thing we will do is attach a bobber to it." Opening the tackle box, she removed a red and white bobber and expertly fastened it to the fishing line. "The second thing you do is open that container of worms and pull you out a big juicy night crawler."

"Gross," Todd said as he removed the lid from the container. He reached into the wriggling mass and removed a slimy worm. "Okay, I got one."

"Now you slide that hook through the worm's body and then push the point out the other side."

"Like this?" Todd tried to stick the hook through the worm. Instead, the slimy worm slipped through his fingers and fell to the ground.

"No. Let me show you," Jessie grabbed his hand. "You've got to thread the hook through it. Feel it wiggling as the hook goes through its body,"

"I couldn't ask for a prettier girl to show me how to hold my worm," he said as he leaned in close to her.

"There, all done," Jessie said. "That wasn't so bad, was it?"

"It wasn't for me, but the worm might have a different opinion."

"Silly, let's go down to the water and I'll teach you how to cast in your line."

They both walked down to the water's edge where Drew had already started fishing.

"I have to warn you, the smell of the dead fish is stronger by the water," Drew called out.

"Any bites yet?" Todd asked.

Drew shook his head. "Not yet. You know what's strange?"

"What?" Todd looked out over the lake water in the cove

"Can you hear how quiet it is here? Where are the sounds of birds, locusts, and frogs? It's dead still. Weird."

Todd listened to the air around him. Drew was right. The cove was very quiet and lacked the ambient background noise one would expect at a lake in the country.

Jessie pulled on his hand. "I got an idea. Up in the trees a ways, I got my own private hole to fish at. Todd, baby, would you like me to show it to you?"

"Is that all right with you, Drew?"

"You two go on up there. I'll stay here and watch the truck. Just be within shouting distance in case I need you for something." Drew recast his fishing line into the muddy water.

Jessie pulled harder on his hand. "Come on, let's go. Daylight's a-burnin' and I want to see you catch a big fish today."

Todd followed her up a small hill and deeper into the woods. Through the trees to the left stretched the brown of the lake but he noticed she wasn't leading him toward the water. Reaching the trunk of a wide tree, she leaned up against it and faced him with a sultry look in her blue eyes. Todd swallowed hard.

"I don't see any lake here," he said trying to keep the nervousness out of his voice. "I think you brought me up here for something else besides fishing, Miss Jessie Mae Farmer."

She smiled coyly, "I figure since you ain't never went fishin' before you ain't never kissed a country girl before, either." Her hands slowly unbuttoned the front of her plaid shirt. "It looks like you get two firsts today."

With heart pounding in his ears, Todd dropped the pole to the ground. Everything was happening so fast. His head was dizzy with desire for this girl. He no longer cared if she was sixteen. He reached out and placed his hands on her slim hips and bent in for a kiss. *This is it,* he told himself, *the moment I've been waiting for.*

The barrel of a shotgun against his neck stopped him.

"It looks like to me, boy, you got sinful designs on my daughter," Broscoe's voice growled in his ear as he cocked the shotgun.

In shock, Todd pulled his hands back from the girl. "I didn't do anything. I didn't even touch her," he sputtered with a squeaky voice as he fought to hold his bladder.

Jessie quickly buttoned her shirt. "Daddy, it's about time you got here. I just about had to kiss this queer."

"Jessie?" Todd asked in surprise. "What the hell?"

"Hell is right, boy, and you're standin' in the middle of it," Broscoe used the barrel of the shotgun to shove him up against the tree.

"He's got a cell phone." Jessie reached into his pants pocket and removed the phone.

"Throw it in the lake," Broscoe said and spat onto the ground.

Trying to come to grips with everything happening, Todd watched in dismay as Jessie threw the phone through the trees. It landed in the lake water with a heart-breaking plop. He realized he had been set up all along.

Fucking idiot, he told himself. *A girl like Jessie would never fall for you.*

"What's the meaning of this?" Todd asked. Tears wanted to form in his eyes, but he fought them back. "You said you wanted to help us catch some fish. We trusted you."

"Oh, you're gonna catch a big fish, all right. Just like I said." Broscoe turned to Jessie Mae. "Girl, go get your mama and tell her to bring the truck up."

"Sure, Daddy." Jessie took off running through the trees back toward the road.

Broscoe spat onto the ground. "What did you think you were gonna git off my daughter?"

"Nothing,"

"She would never put out to a piss-ant like you. I'll tell you a secret." Broscoe's face leaned in close enough for Todd to smell the stench of his tobacco. "Daddy is the only one that gits to dip into that honey pot."

"You're sick," Todd snapped back.

Broscoe chuckled. "Now you're goin' to do what I say or I'll blow your piss-ant brains all over these woods." He shoved hard with the barrel of the shotgun. "Start walkin' back to your friend."

Holding his hands over his head, Todd walked out of the woods and back down the hill toward where Drew sat at the bank fishing. Broscoe shoved the barrel of the shotgun in his back to keep him moving. Hearing someone coming up behind him, Drew turned and a look of confusion flashed across his face.

"What the fuck?" Drew asked as he stood.

"Your little piss-ant friend tried to rape my daughter." Broscoe shoved Todd hard with the shotgun and he fell onto his knees into the dirt of the bank.

"Todd, what happened?"

"I didn't rape his daughter."

"Where's Jessie?" Drew asked.

"Save your breath, Drew," Todd replied. "She's in on this. We were set up from the beginning."

"Set up for what?"

A rusted old pickup truck pulled slowly down the bank and parked beside Drew's newer Toyota. A steel cable winch was mounted on the front grill above a license plate reading: *I'd Rather Be Fishing.* Out of the cab came Louise and Jessie Mae. They walked down the bank and stood beside Broscoe holding the shotgun.

"Did anybody see you pull in the truck?" Broscoe asked.

Louise shook her head. "No one."

Broscoe handed the shotgun over to Jessie. "Baby-doll, hold the gun on these two while I go get some gear out of my truck."

"Sure, Daddy." Jessie took the shotgun and aimed it at Todd and Drew sitting on the bank with their hands up.

"Jessie, I can't believe you're involved with this," Drew said. "We've done nothing wrong to you or your family. It's not fair to treat us like this."

"It's like Daddy always says. Life just ain't fair."

Broscoe came back and threw an inflated inner tube on the ground in front of Todd. "That's right, baby-doll, life ain't always fair. Sometimes it's the shits, too, as you boys are goin' to find out."

"If you kill us, the police will come looking. Drew's father is an attorney," Todd said.

"I'm friends with the local sheriff. I just tell him I came upon you two raping my daughter and had to shoot you both." Broscoe replied and put an arm around Jessie's shoulder. "You'll back me up on that story, won't you, baby?"

Jessie nodded. "I'll tell the sheriff how these two city boys were raping me in the woods when daddy found them."

"That's my girl," Broscoe said. "Besides I ain't goin' to kill you if you do what I say."

"What do you want from us?" Drew asked.

Broscoe threw a life vest on top of the inner tube. Attached to the front were large iron hooks. "You boys are goin' to help me catch old Catfish Joe."

"You really believe that a half-man, half-fish lives in the lake?"

"I sure do and so will you after today. This is Joe's resting spot. He's nearby, too, 'cause I can smell him." Broscoe pulled a large wooden handle of a tree-axe out of the cab of his truck. "Now one of you boys is goin' to float out in that there inner tube to see if Joe takes the bait. I don't give a rat's ass who, but one of you is going to do it."

"And if we do as you say?" Todd asked.

"Listen, you boys can both survive this. If Joe don't take the bait then I'm nothing but a crazy son of a bitch and you two can go home. If you don't tell the police of our fishin' venture, I won't tell them about you all trying to rape Jessie." Broscoe pointed at the inner tube with the axe handle. "Now one of you strip down to your undies, put on that vest and inner tube, and get your ass out in the water or I'm going to start knockin' in your heads with this stick here."

Todd let out a sigh and turned to his friend. "We've got no choice, Drew. Who's going out in the water?"

"I'll do it. It was me that got us in this mess. I should have listened to you back at the shop when you said not to take Jessie with us."

"I would do it," Todd replied, "but I don't know how to swim."

"I was on the high school swim team, remember?" Drew started taking off his shirt. "Listen, I'll float around out there for an hour or so. Nothing will happen and we can go home. We will never go fishing again, Dude. Agreed?"

"Agreed."

Drew finished stripping down to his white briefs. His body was lean and muscular in the sunlight.

"Now, what do I do?" Drew asked.

Broscoe spit a stream of tobacco juice. "Put that vest on real tight."

Drew picked up the vest and examined the large iron hooks connected by steel cable sewn throughout the front.

"Jessie, dear, can you help him with the vest?" Broscoe asked as he took the shotgun from his daughter. "Nobody can bait a hook better than you, darlin'"

"Sure, Daddy." Jessie crossed over to Drew and began strapping the vest around his chest with a series of Velcro straps. "All done."

Returning by her father's side, she took back the shotgun. Drew stepped into the inner tube and raised it up around his waist.

"If Catfish Joe doesn't make an appearance, we get to go home?"

"That's right." Broscoe scratched his chin. "You look like you're in pretty good shape, boy. You know how to swim?"

"I was Captain of the high school swim team."

"That's what's a troublin' me. You look fit enough that you could swim across this whole damn lake. What's to stop you from slippin' out of that vest and swimmin' away?" He swung the axe handle like a bat against Drew's shin. There was the sickening crack of bones breaking as Drew fell to the ground. Broscoe swung the axe handle again and shattered the other leg. "That should keep you close and not swimmin' off."

"Fuck!" Drew screamed in pain. Todd looked at Drew's legs. Both were broken with pieces of jagged bone jutting out the shins.

"Why the hell did you do that?" Todd screamed at Broscoe.

"Shut the fuck up, piss-ant, or you're next!" Broscoe pulled a length of cable from the winch on the front of his truck. He clipped the hook to a ring on the vest.

"Ma, you get in the cab of the truck and operate the winch."

Louise climbed into the truck and started the engine. The winch began whining as it let out more steel cable. Using the axe handle, Broscoe pushed the inner tube carrying a groaning Drew out into the brown lake water. "Keep runnin' the cable out, Ma. As far as she goes."

Todd watched in anger and frustration as his friend floated further out in the cove. The whining of the winch stopped about a hundred feet out. He glanced at Jessie holding the shotgun. She paid more attention to Drew on the inner tube than to him. He had no doubt Broscoe was going to kill them both. He could see it in the crazed look in the man's eyes. A strategy began to form in his mind. He barely knew how to dog paddle but if he reached Drew, he could unhook him from the cable and use the tube to float them both out into the lake. A passing boater might find them. It was better than staying here and getting killed by this insane family of inbreds.

"How long do we wait?" Jessie asked her father.

"Fishin' is a patient man's sport," Broscoe answered and shouted to Louise in the truck. "You just be ready with that winch, Ma, if Joe takes the bait."

Time crawled as Todd waited for his chance to act. He watched Drew floating in the water. In a state of pain and shock from his broken legs, his friend clung to the inner tube with his head lilting to the side. The lake cove was quiet and still. Brown water lapped in a rhythm against the sand of the bank. All eyes were on the bait floating on the end of winch line.

Suddenly, Drew shot up. "Hey, there's something out here! There's a fish or something swimming by me! Reel me back in!" He shouted across the distance toward the bank.

Broscoe turned to Louise in the truck. "Get ready to hit the winch!"

Realizing this was his one chance, Todd shoved Jessie aside and knocked the shotgun out of the way. In absolute fear, he ran into the lake.

From behind, he heard Broscoe shout, "Don't shoot! You'll scare off Joe!"

Todd dived into the warm water and attempted to swim the best he could. Luckily, his hands found the winch cable attached to Drew in the tube and he used it to pull himself along. Each time his head broke above the waves he heard Drew's voice shouting frantically ahead. After he thought he'd swallowed half the water in the lake, Todd reached the black inner tube. He grabbed onto it with one hand to hold himself up. In the center of the tube, Drew floated with his head leaned to one side. His face looked pale and bloodless.

"Hey, buddy," he said in a low voice as he opened his eyes and saw Todd holding onto the side of the inner tube.

"I'm going to get us out of here, Drew," Todd sputtered above the waves. "Once I unhook the cable, we are going to float away into the lake." He grabbed the winch hook snapped to the ring of the vest.

"Don't bother." Drew's voice was barely a whisper. "You know that fish-man thing?"

"Catfish Joe?" Todd replied as he fumbled with the winch-hook.

Drew nodded weakly. "It's eating me."

The water around the tube grew warmer. In horror, Todd looked down to see a fountain of red blood spreading out from Drew's body. Something big brushed against his legs underwater. The next instant the surface exploded upward in a geyser of lake water. A hulking man-like creature with greenish-gray scales loomed in the air over Drew in the inner tube. Todd caught a glimpse of black inhuman eyes set deep in a large fish head. A huge mouth opened revealing a maw of sharp teeth. Two scaly arms snagged onto Drew's shoulders. With a loud hiss, the monster bit down on Drew's head and dived back into the water. Drew's body snapped violently back and then forward again. He no longer had a head. Blood pumped out of his severed neck stump in a crimson fountain.

Todd screamed. He pushed himself away from the bloody nightmare and desperately kicked to stay above the surface. In the direction of the bank, he heard Broscoe's shout, "Hit the winch!"

A loud hissing accompanied with tremendous splashing shook the water in the direction of the inner tube. Todd felt something big brush past his legs as he dog paddled his way toward the bank. Every time his head managed to break above the waves he heard Broscoe's shouting above the splashing and the whine of the winch motor.

"We got him, Ma! He's runnin' the line! Keep it tight!"

"Look at that ugly bastard fight! We hooked him good!"

"He's wearing himself out! Bring him on in, Ma!"

Finally, the dirty bottom of the lake bumped beneath his feet. Dazed and exhausted, Todd staggered forward and fell onto the muddy bank to catch his breath. Next to him, he heard a sucking kind of noise and turned his head to see the source of the sound. Catfish Joe was sprawled out onto the bank beside him. A steel cable ran from a hook in its mouth to the winch on the front of Broscoe's truck. In the sunlight, the creature was a man-sized mass of scales and fins with humanlike arms ending in webbed hands. Gills moved on the side of its neck, gasping for air. Broscoe, holding the wooden axe handle, walked around the monster, admiring his catch.

"I told you, baby-doll, there wasn't a fish I couldn't catch." Broscoe said to his daughter, who stood off to the side holding the shotgun aimed at the creature.

"What are we goin' to do with it now, Daddy?" Jessie asked.

"You'll see," Broscoe swung the axe handle with all his might against the head of Catfish Joe.

There was a sickening crunch sound and the creature fell still.

"What about him?" Jessie pointed to where he lay on the bank.

Too exhausted to do anything, Todd watched as Broscoe walked over to stand above him.

Spitting a stream of tobacco juice onto the ground, he raised the axe handle over his head. "Well, piss-ant, you believe me now about Catfish Joe?"

"Please, don't," Todd pleaded.

The axe handle came down and Todd's world became darkness.

* * * *

The roadside sign read:

Broscoe's Bait Shop. Beer. Bait. Gas. Taxidermy

The Home of Catfish Joe

"Can we stop, Daddy?" Little Tommy Walker asked from his child safety seat in the back of the SUV.

"What do you say, dear?" Nora Walker asked her husband behind the wheel.

"I promised Tommy I'd take him fishing," Fred Walker replied. "I guess it's about time he went into a real bait shop."

"I just wonder what a Catfish Joe is," Nora said.

"I have no idea."

The gravel popped under the tires of the SUV as the vehicle pulled up in front of the little shop. Stepping out in the hot Oklahoma sun, the Walker family unloaded from the SUV and made their way to the door of the shop. From somewhere in the shade, a man in overalls stepped forward and greeted them.

"Howdy, folks," he smiled showing brown, rotted teeth. "The name is Broscoe."

"Hello, I'm Fred and this is my wife Nora."

Broscoe tipped the brim of his greasy ball cap. "Nice to meet you, ma'am."

"This here is little Tommy," Fred pushed his son forward to shake hands with the dirty man in overalls.

Tommy shook Broscoe's hand, "My daddy is taking me fishing for the first time."

Broscoe smiled, "I was about your age when my daddy took me. Maybe you'll catch a big'un."

"Mister, is this your store?"

"Sure is," Broscoe reached out and opened the front door. "Go on inside, Tommy. I got something in there you ain't never goin' to see anyplace else."

Broscoe followed the Walker family inside. "Let me introduce you to everyone. That's my wife, Louise."

"Howdy," Louise said putting down her pink flyswatter.

"Over there stocking the pop is my daughter, Jessie Mae."

Jessie stood up and wiped her hands on her tight cut-off jeans. "Nice to meet you, folks.

"And over there sweepin' the floor is Jessie's cousin, Todd-boy."

Nora Walker stepped back in repulsion as Todd-boy stopped sweeping and looked at her. One side of his skull was misshapen. He began walking toward her in a slow stagger.

"Ud gollu awa frug yourm," the retarded young man mumbled through the drool on his lips.

Broscoe stopped his approach and placed the broom back in his hands. "Now Todd-boy, go on back to sweepin' the floor. Don't want you scarin' away this fine family." He turned to Nora and said. "Poor boy hasn't been the same since the farmin' accident."

Little Tommy, wide-eyed, pointed. "Dad, look at all the fish on the walls."

"Caught all those and stuffed them myself," Broscoe said. "But my prize catch is in the back room, Tommy, would you like to see it?"

"Can I Daddy?"

"I don't see why not."

Broscoe bent down and picked the boy up. "I'll bring your son right back."

Holding little Tommy in his arms, Broscoe stepped into the backroom of the shop where vats filled with minnows gave the room a strong smell of fish. A floor-to-ceiling glass case stood in one corner with something large and dark inside. Reaching out, Broscoe flipped up a light switch. Red and blue bulbs popped on, illuminating the interior of the glass case in a garish light.

Tommy reeled back in fear. "Is that a monster?"

Broscoe chuckled, "No. That there is Catfish Joe. I caught him and stuffed him myself. Usually I charge a fella five dollars to see old Joe but since it's your first time goin' fishin' I let you see him for free, Tommy."

"He looks like a monster to me." Tommy turned his head away. "Please let me go back to my daddy, now."

"Sure."

Broscoe turned out the light and left the room. When he put Tommy down, the boy ran to his father's arms.

"What did you see, little sport?" Fred asked as he picked up his son.

"It was a monster, Daddy." Tommy buried his face into his father's shoulder and trembled in fear.

"Let's go," Nora said.

"Well, I guess we better get back on the road," Fred announced to everyone in the store and followed his wife out of the shop. "It was nice meeting you."

Once back at the SUV, Nora asked, "What scared Tommy? The boy is shivering."

"I don't know," Fred answered while strapping Tommy into the child seat. "Something Broscoe showed him in the backroom."

"It was a big monster, Daddy. Can we go home now? I don't want to go fishing anymore." Tears formed in the little boy's eyes.

"A monster? Why would they have that in the back room?" Nora slid into the passenger seat and shut the door.

"Probably something made out of papier-mâché and wire," Fred commented as he climbed behind the wheel. "Some of these roadside places have carnival-like attractions to milk the yokels of money."

"Oh, look dear," Nora pointed. "The whole family is coming out to wave good-bye. Even the retarded cousin is trying to wave to us. Isn't that cute?"

Fred looked out through the windshield. Broscoe and his family stood in front of the store waving. An uneasy feeling tingled deep in his gut. He wanted to get as far away from the little bait shop as he could. He put the SUV in reverse and backed out across the gravel, kicking up a cloud of dust.

Broscoe stepped forward and smiled a tobacco-stained grin.

"Ya'll come back, hear?"

Complete the trilogy of terror

with

Undead Flesh

and

Ebon Moon.

Both available on Amazon.

What would you do if the zombie apocalypse happened tomorrow?

Meet Jack Garret. Wishing to reconnect with his family, he takes them on a much-needed vacation to the Grand Canyon. While driving through Oklahoma, a massive earthquake strikes and shatters the landscape. However, this is no natural phenomena, for in its wake, the sun turns dark and the dead crawl from their graves. Uncertain what has happened, Jack leads his family on a desperate journey through a devastated countryside to find an escape from the nightmare. On the way, he will face hordes of zombies, brutal rednecks, crazed religious fanatics, and the darkest fear in his heart.

SAVAGE TERROR WAITS UNDER A DARKENING MOON.

Seeking to escape her psychopathic husband, Jessica Lobato flees Chicago with her five-year-old daughter Megan. Reaching the small town of Hope Springs, Oklahoma, they rent a trailer house out in the country and think they are finally safe. However, this small town has a very dark secret; one that emerges when the moon is full. A pack of werewolves hides amongst the populace and secretly kills selected people to satisfy their hunger. Megan is the next chosen by the pack to be devoured during the upcoming full eclipse of the moon. Jessica is about to learn there are worse things to fear in the night than a murderous husband. Ebon Moon is a tense, bestial tale of lycanthrope horror the way a werewolf novel should be.

A WORD FROM THE AUTHOR

I hope you enjoyed 13 Nightmares. Please feel free to write a review and post it. Or you can email it to me. I'd love to hear from you. If you liked this novel, don't hesitate to check out my other books. I'm sure you'll enjoy them too. You can find me at the following online locations.

Email: dragonmac007@yahoo.com

Website: dennismcdonaldauthor.com

Blog: hauntedfunhouse @ blogger

Twitter: Nightmarewriter

All the best,

Dennis McDonald